WHO MURDERED THE LIBRARIAN?

While I was in the bathroom, I put my thoughts about Vicky's murder into order. Porter was the obvious prime suspect. That couldn't be disputed. He'd gotten to the library before any other potential witnesses, so he had the opportunity. If he truly had dangerous plants in his greenhouse, he had the means. And if he was obsessed with Vicky, as some people believed, he had the motive.

As Dad liked to say, "if" was the biggest two-letter word in the English language. So, if Porter wasn't the murderer, who was? Ozzy? It seemed like a stretch to me, but, to him, maybe five thousand dollars was an amount worthy of committing murder.

My third suspect, Gary Napier, had motive in spades. A few minutes of research at the county assessor's office would confirm Gary's claim about the home's ownership status. If his name was on the deed, that left him in line to receive all the proceeds from the sale of the house.

As I rinsed off the shampoo, I ruminated over Gary's means and opportunity. Just because he claimed he came to town after the call with Matt didn't make it true. What if he was having money problems and saw the house as his way out of debt? Until I established his whereabouts the day of Vicky's murder, I couldn't rule him out.

Matt might not have been willing to completely rule out Brent, but I was. I knew Brent as well as I knew anyone outside my immediate family and Sloane. He said he didn't do it. I believed him one hundred percent. It was simply a matter of time until Matt confirmed his indisputable innocence.

That left me with three credible suspects.

Books by J.C. Kenney

A LITERAL MESS
A GENUINE FIX
A MYSTERIOUS MIX UP

Published by Kensington Publishing Corporation

A Mysterious Mix Up

J.C. Kenney

LYRICAL UNDERGROUND
Kensington Publishing Corp.
www.kensingtonbooks.com

LYRICAL UNDERGROUND BOOKS are published by
Kensington Publishing Corp.
119 West 40th Street
New York, NY 10018

First Electronic Edition: January 2020
ISBN-13: 978-1-5161-0858-9 (ebook)
ISBN-10: 1-5161-0858-2 (ebook)

First Print Edition: January 2020
ISBN-13: 978-1-5161-0861-9
ISBN-10: 1-5161-0861-2

Printed in the United States of America

To my father, Jack Cangany. A child of the Great Depression, he went on to fight in the Pacific during World War II, earn his college degree, marry the love of his life, and raise eight kids. He was an example of the Greatest Generation at its finest. Thanks for everything, Dad.

Acknowledgments

As always, major thanks go to my agent, Dawn, who's done so much to help me find my place in the writing world. Thanks also go to my editor, John, for his continued belief in The Allie Cobb Mysteries. Without the support of my wife and sons, I wouldn't be on this journey, so thank you, Nancy, Seamus, and Aidan. Last, but not least, thank you, reader friends for welcoming Allie, Ursi, Sloane, and the rest of the gang from Rushing Creek into your lives and your hearts. I am eternally grateful.

Chapter One

If all the world is truly a stage and we're the players, I was relieved beyond belief to have my time in the spotlight behind me. I'd been in my old stomping ground of New York City for a national book conference. That meant three days of getting up at five, followed by meetings with editors, authors, and other folks in the book business. That was combined with educational breakout sessions and interspersed with meals and social activities, so my head never hit the pillow until midnight.

The nonstop schedule included my appearance on two panels. The first was a discussion of women-owned businesses. The second talked about the pros and cons of being your own boss. Those appearances had been as terrifying as they were exhilarating. It was still hard to imagine that little Allie Cobb had become someone whose words came with a sense of authority in the wonderful world of publishing, but it was true and oh so empowering.

The conference had been a thrilling time, full of seeing old friends and making new ones, but when two days of travel were added, the trip had left my inkwell of energy dry.

I was ready to be back home again in Indiana.

My exhaustion gave way to anticipation as my rideshare driver pointed out a sign indicating we were entering Brown County. In twenty minutes, I'd be safe and sound in my apartment, snuggling with my feline fur baby, Ursula, or Ursi for short.

Ursi wasn't the only one I'd be snuggling with, though. A very special house sitter and his faithful canine sidekick were waiting for me, too. The thought made me smile as I checked my hair in the sunshade mirror. I wanted to look good for the house sitter, also known as Brent Richardson, my boyfriend.

It was dark when the car rolled to a stop in front of my building, the sun having set during the hour-long drive from Indianapolis International Airport. A chilly April breeze knifed through my Cobb Literary Agency fleece as I waited on the sidewalk for the driver to unload my luggage.

I shivered.

Not from the cold, though. It was in anticipation of seeing three of my favorite people in the world. Okay, technically, only Brent was a person. The others were my tortoiseshell kitty, Ursi, and Brent's golden retriever, Sammy. I loved them both like they were my own children, so they might as well have been human.

As the driver pulled away, I hoisted my bag over my shoulder, grabbed my suitcase, and turned toward the door of my building. To my great pleasure, my very own welcoming committee was waiting for me.

Grinning from ear to ear, Brent opened the door. With his right hand, he was holding Sammy on a leash. With his left, he had Ursi on her leash.

"Welcome home, babe!" He gave me a kiss on the lips that made my knees weak.

I wanted it to last forever, but Sammy nosed himself between us, begging to be petted. Meanwhile, Ursi almost knocked me over by bumping her head against my shin, demanding attention.

"Hello, young lady." I picked up my cat and kissed her on the head. "And to you, too, Sammy." I scratched the dog's ear as Brent took my luggage.

"All right, kids. Let's let Allie get upstairs so she can relax." He struggled up the steps with my bag, suitcase, and Sammy in tow.

I chuckled as Ursi and I followed them to my second-floor apartment. It was good to be home.

Once we were all safely inside the apartment, Brent removed the animals' harnesses. Sammy went to his bed in the corner of the living room while Ursi sauntered to the kitchen for a drink of water. Evidently, their welcome home efforts were complete.

Brent, on the other hand, was scurrying around like every inch of his six-five frame was on fire. First, he dashed to the couch and fluffed the cushions. Then he went to the bedroom to drop off my luggage. Next, he took my computer bag and delivered it to my office. Only when I was comfortable, with my feet propped up on the coffee table, did he take a seat.

"To what do I owe such regal treatment?" I glanced around the apartment.

It was spotless. The cleanliness called to mind a time when Luke and Rachel, my older brother and sister, had friends over while our parents took me to Chicago for the weekend to celebrate my birthday. Nobody got hurt and nothing got broken, but my siblings' efforts to eliminate any evidence of the festivities resulted in the first floor of our house being cleaned until it shined like polished silver.

It had taken Mom and Dad all of about ten seconds after they opened the front door to figure out something was amiss. Mom finally called them out on their misdeed when she found a beer can in the refrigerator's vegetable crisper.

Neither Mom nor Dad drank beer.

The interrogation lasted five minutes. The lecture about making good choices lasted half an hour. The smile on my face at seeing my older sibs get in trouble lasted a week.

At the moment, I could totally imagine how my mom felt all those years ago.

"This place looks awfully nice. Did you have a party with a bunch of young ladies and have to clean up?"

Brent laughed. "I figured you'd appreciate coming home to a clean apartment." He went to the fridge and returned with a bottle of white wine and two glasses. "Tell me about your trip."

"Wow. Where to start." I took a drink to gather my thoughts. As it danced over my taste buds, the refreshing, semisweet wine had a touch of apple and pear to it. Riesling, my favorite. Brent had all his bases covered tonight.

He knew I'd been stressing about my two panels, so I started with those. "The room was full, and we got tons of great questions from the audience. After the Be Your Own Boss session, I had two women thank me and say the session was the motivator they needed to strike out on their own."

"That's awesome." Brent gave me a fist bump. "Gotta be pretty cool to have people tell you things like that. Then again, you're living proof of no guts, no glory, am I right?"

"Guess so." It had been a little over two years since I'd said goodbye to New York City and my job with a well-respected literary agency and returned to my home town of Rushing Creek, Indiana, to assume the reins of my deceased father's literary agency. I still missed my dad. I always would.

I took another sip of wine and massaged the back of my neck to release some tension that had taken up residence there during the trip home. Despite my weariness from the long day of travel, I had a great life. And I wouldn't trade it for anything.

"It's amazing people think of me as an expert on anything. But it's a good way to be amazed. If I can help someone, even in a small way, find a job they enjoy, the effort's totally worth it."

"That's my girl." Brent wrapped me up in his long arms.

His body heat warmed me and made me feel safe as I told him about the rest of the trip. A lot of my report included meetings with editors, taking pitches from authors, and visiting with colleagues. It would bore most people to death. Not Brent. He gave me his full attention while I spoke.

"How about you? I hope cleaning out Ursi's litter box every day wasn't too much of a hassle." I snuggled into him, the stubble of his beard tickling my cheek.

"Nah. It's actually easier than having to scoop Sammy's poo when we're out for a walk." He pointed at a stack of papers on the coffee table. "By the way, I got through the resumes for your intern. I scheduled interviews with four."

"Sweet." I glanced through the pages Brent handed me. Business continued to be good for the Cobb Literary Agency. So good, in fact, I'd begun to think about getting help. With thirty authors now signed, handling all aspects of agency business, from reading query letters to calculating royalty statements, was becoming a challenge. I wasn't ready for another agent, but an intern sounded good. I wanted someone in town who loved to read a wide variety of genres, was well versed in grammar, and was willing to work ten to fifteen hours a week. If I could find that person, I'd be set.

If only.

"Or maybe not so sweet." I tossed the documents on the coffee table. "Not the strongest group of candidates, huh?"

Brent shrugged. "Wanting someone local is limiting your candidate pool. There are a lot of smart, talented people in the area. Just not a lot who meet the qualifications you want."

I didn't want to ruin the good welcome home vibes, so I kissed Brent's cheek. "You're right. I set the parameters. I have to live with the results. It's not like I need someone tomorrow, right?"

Ursi jumped on my lap and gave me a long, penetrating look. Her unblinking, golden eyes were hypnotic. Evidently satisfied she'd sufficiently punished me for going out of town by ignoring me, she was now ready to have me shower her with undivided attention. I complied by scratching her between the ears.

"Indeed." He took a small sip of wine. "I've got news. Vicky Napier's retiring. She's going to make an official announcement to the library board later this week."

The wineglass came to a stop inches from my lips as I tried to make sense of Brent's words. When they wouldn't compute, I returned the glass to the table. Sensing trouble, Ursi leapt from my lap and dashed to the bedroom.

"Are you sure? Mrs. Napier's too young to retire." When Brent wouldn't maintain eye contact, desperation set in. "She can't retire. When I was a kid, she promised me she'd be the librarian forever. It was a pinkie promise." I grabbed a throw pillow and held it against me in an attempt to ease the sudden aching in my midsection. Mrs. Napier was one of my heroes. Growing up, Luke revered ballplayers. Rachel admired celebrity chefs. As a nerdy bookworm, I looked up to Vicky Napier.

She was the one I turned to for refuge from the challenges of youth. She was the one who, along with my parents, empowered me to believe in myself and follow my dream of becoming a literary agent.

To me, the thought of the Rushing Creek Library without Vicky Napier at the helm was like trying to pass off Buffy the Vampire Slayer without Sarah Michelle Gellar as Buffy. It simply made no sense.

"She admitted it's sudden, but I guess she decided now was the right time."

"She's in her mid-sixties at most. Did she say if she has plans?"

Brent swallowed and adjusted his collar, apparently sensing I wasn't going to like his answer. "She's moving to Florida as soon as her house sells. She wants to be near her sister."

"Wow. I guess it's too late for me to try to talk her out of it." I scratched my head. "Well, she's given this town a lot over the years. She deserves to enjoy retirement."

I got to my feet. Instead of being sad at seeing Mrs. Napier go, I'd be happy for all the time I got to spend with her.

With a spring in my step, I headed for the kitchen. "I know just the thing. I'm going to bake her a batch of cookies. She always loved oatmeal raisin. Then I'll go with you to the library tomorrow and give them to her."

"I'll help you." Brent's footfalls echoed off the hardwood floors. As a large man who wasn't light on his feet, stealth wasn't a part of his repertoire. "Besides, there's something else."

The excitement in his voice brought my search for cooking raisins to a halt. As I faced him, his wide eyes made quite a pairing with the voice.

"By the look of you, it must be good news, so don't keep me in suspense."

He ran his thumb and second finger around his lips. He always did that when he was excited and needed to force himself to slow down.

"Vicky said she was going to recommend I take her place. I'm sorry I didn't tell you earlier, but she made me swear I wouldn't speak a word of this until she talks to the board."

"No way." I left the package of raisins on the counter and threw my arms around him. "Congratulations. That's better than when Westley and Buttercup rode off into the sunset in *The Princess Bride*."

I gave him a long kiss. "This calls for another glass of wine while you help me bake. What do you say to that, Mr. Richardson, Rushing Creek Librarian to Be?"

"Allow me to pour, and then I am at your service."

"I like the sound of that."

I poked him in the belly with a mixing spoon and winked. It had been a long, tiring day of travel, but the good news made me feel as if I'd just woken from a long night's sleep on the most comfortable down-filled mattress ever created.

With the festive vibe in full swing, I cued up Brent's favorite musician, jazz saxophonist Kamasi Washington, and got to work on the cookies. And the wine. It was a celebration, after all.

It was past midnight, and way past my regular bedtime, when I put the last of the three-dozen cookies we'd take to Mrs. Napier into a plastic container. She'd insist on sharing them with her staff, so my guess was they'd be gone in two days.

As I slipped into bed and snuggled up against Brent, with Ursi purring at my feet and Sammy snoring in his doggy bed under my bedroom window, I smiled. We had our own little family, and maybe, in the not too distant future, we'd be able to make this arrangement permanent.

First things first, though. I had an old friend and hero to congratulate. I drifted off to sleep rehearsing what I was going to say to Mrs. Napier when I handed her the cookies. She was a special woman, and I couldn't wait to tell her what she meant to me.

Chapter Two

"Will you relax?" Brent pulled on a purple polo I'd given him for his birthday. "I'll be ready to go in a minute. Besides, it's not like I have to punch a clock or anything. I'm volunteering. We'll get there when we get there."

I forced my foot to stop tapping. I'd been ready to leave for fifteen minutes. Waiting on someone was something I wasn't accustomed to. "I know, but I want to get there before the library opens. I was hoping on having a few minutes alone with Mrs. Napier."

He tied his shoes, tan chukka boots he'd polished while I'd been gone, and slapped his hands against his thighs. "Let me put Sammy in his crate and we're outta here."

The dog seemed unsympathetic to my eagerness to get going and kept dashing behind furniture pieces until Brent corralled him in the bathroom. Ursi wasn't any help as she observed the entire affair from her favorite spot, a seat cushion atop an end table placed under a living room window.

Despite my eagerness to get going, I couldn't help laughing at the sequence. It was right out of a Looney Tunes cartoon. "Does he fuss that much all the time?"

While Ursi didn't love it when I put in her carrier, she tolerated it and never fought me. Then again, I always showered her with praise and kitty treats while I maneuvered her into the carrier. She was no dummy. When the potential for snacks was involved, my kitty's behavior was exemplary.

"No." Brent sucked in a few deep breaths. The great golden retriever chase had left him winded. "He probably thinks since you're here, we should be going for a walk. He'll be fine."

I went to the crate and tossed a doggie biscuit to the poor canine, who'd looked at me with the saddest eyes. "We'll be back soon and I promise to let you out as soon as we come through the door. Then we'll go for a walk. How about that?"

Sammy gave me a *woof* and started gnawing on his biscuit. With his tail now flipping back and forth like a fuzzy metronome, the insult of being crated while Ursi had the run of the apartment was evidently forgotten.

"Feel free to call me Madame Dog Whisperer from now on." I gave Brent a wink, grabbed the container of cookies, and headed for the door.

I got into his truck and immediately started bouncing up and down in the passenger seat like a kid on the way to see Santa Claus. Once I'd come to grips with Mrs. Napier's decision, I'd become truly happy for her. And eager to give her my best wishes.

Sure, it was a surprise, but the woman had dedicated her life to Rushing Creek. She deserved to enjoy retirement while she was still healthy and active.

The truck's engine rumbled to life. It reminded me of her connection to Brent and her recommendation to have Brent succeed her. I smiled at the thought. If I was going to lose my favorite librarian, getting my favorite guy to replace her wasn't a bad deal.

As we headed north on Washington Boulevard, the main thoroughfare through Rushing Creek, my phone buzzed. It was an e-mail from one of my authors, asking for my thoughts on a new story idea. While I was reading the e-mail, the truck slowed, and we turned into a parking spot in front of the general store.

A peek at the clock confirmed the library opened in fifteen minutes. Before I could protest, Brent put his hand on my arm.

"I'm going to get a card. That's all. I promise I'll be fast." Leaving the engine running, he was out of the truck and entering the store in the blink of an eye. With his long, lanky frame, he could cover a lot of ground in a short amount of time when motivated.

I was still typing out my reply when he opened the door and handed the card to me. "Told you. Dash, that kid from *The Incredibles*, has nothing on me."

"You're such a dork." I took a pen from my purse and chuckled as I looked at the funny farm animals on the front of the card.

"True, but I'm your dork." In seconds we were back on our way. We'd arrive at the library before it opened, as promised.

One of the great things about Rushing Creek was that you could get from one end of town to the other in ten minutes if you were traveling by car. That was why a mere five minutes later, we pulled into the parking lot of the Rushing Creek Public Library.

Two vehicles were already there. I recognized Mrs. Napier's silver SUV, but the red pickup next to the SUV wasn't familiar. As Brent signed the card, I asked him about the truck.

"It's Porter Rasmussen's. The guy who cleans the restrooms and takes out the trash."

"Gotcha." With the minor mystery solved, I got out of the truck, eager to see Mrs. Napier.

When I lived in New York, many of my colleagues were convinced I must know everyone in my hometown on a first-name basis. I understood the logic. After all, when one came from a community of 3,216, how hard could it be to get to know everyone in town?

My colleagues were partially correct. Outgoing folks like my mom and Angela Miller, Rushing Creek's mayor, not only knew everybody, they knew what was going on in the lives of their fellow citizens.

That wasn't the case with me. Growing up, I had a small circle of friends and when I left Rushing Creek, it was more than a decade before I came back for good.

Every May, my dad used to take Luke, Rachel, and me to the garden center to pick out flowers to give Mom for Mother's Day. Porter Rasmussen had owned Rushing Creek Hardware and Garden Center. Sometime after I headed off to college, Porter sold the business to a chain of hardware stores and retired. From what I'd heard, he'd spent his years in retirement with the local garden club and helping at the library.

"That's some serious dedication to the library. If I was retired, I'd try to find a more fun way to help out." As we neared the entrance, I glanced at the container. *Should have asked Brent to get a bow I could stick to the lid. I'll make her some more before she leaves town.*

"Porter's got an ulterior motive." Ever the gentleman, Brent opened the door to the library with his key fob and stepped aside. "He brings Vicky flowers every week. He's got a crush on her."

Thunderstruck, I stopped just inside the threshold as memories of recent visits to the library filled my mind. At least a dozen times, I'd asked Mrs. Napier where she got the flowers she displayed on the checkout counter. She always gave me the same answer.

A secret admirer.

I shook my head. "All this time and I never knew. I am such a dunce."

"You're not a dunce." Brent dropped his messenger bag behind the checkout counter. "Vicky liked to keep it on the down low. She doesn't exactly have the feelings for Porter he has for her."

"Speaking of which, where is she?"

He creased his eyebrows and frowned. Normally, Vicky was at the checkout station no later than five minutes before opening time. Above us, the fluorescent lights gave off a low hum. Other than that, all was silent.

We went to her office. Nobody was there. The restrooms were empty, too.

"Maybe they went to get coffee?" Brent's voice wavered as we headed for the stacks.

"Not a chance." I broke out in goose bumps as we crossed from the nonfiction section to the children's area. His concern wasn't lost on me. Something was off. My pace quickened as my anxiety increased.

"Vicky? Porter? What's up with the hide and seek?" Brent's voice echoed off the cinderblock walls. When nobody answered, he pointed toward the staff break room.

We raced to the door. Brent pushed it open without breaking stride. I plowed into him when he stopped cold two steps into the room.

"Oh, my God."

With his huge frame frozen in place, I had to squeeze past him to see what the problem was.

"Oh, no. No." The cookie container slipped from my hand and a wave of vertigo plowed through me as I processed the scene before me.

Mrs. Napier lay on the floor as if she'd collapsed. A pool of vomit was congealing around her head. The remains of a teacup, shattered into a million pieces, was inches from her hand.

Porter Rasmussen was on one knee, hovering above her. He looked at me, eyes wide and mouth agape. Sweat glistened on his paper-white forehead.

"I, I…" He blinked but said no more.

With his green pallor and slack jaw, Brent was going to be no help, so I went to the stricken woman's side. I placed my fingers on her neck, praying I'd find a pulse. Adrenaline dumped into my system when I found one.

But it was weaker than a newborn kitten's.

"Call nine-one-one." I tossed my phone at Brent then cleared Mrs. Napier's airway.

My phone clattered to the floor. I yelled at Brent, which got him moving for a moment, at least. I blew out a long breath and began chest compressions as he relayed the situation to the operator.

"She's unconscious…I don't know what happened…Allie Cobb's giving her CPR…Hold on, I'll ask." Brent tapped me on the shoulder, breaking my rhythm as I labored to keep my hero alive. "Does she have a pulse?"

I pressed my fingers on the carotid artery and held my breath. After counting to twenty and getting nothing, I went to Mrs. Napier's wrist. Still no pulse. In a move of utter desperation, I put my head to her chest. A tear ran down my cheek and landed on her paisley patterned blouse. Nothing.

With a tidal wave of tears building, I sat back on my haunches and wiped my cheeks with my sleeves.

"Allie?" Brent placed his hand on my shoulder, as gently as a leaf landing on the ground after it fell from a tree.

The words were there, but it took three attempts before I could get them out.

"I think she's gone."

Chapter Three

I was still by Mrs. Napier's side when two paramedics in navy blue uniforms burst into the room. They were as graceful as ballet dancers as they eased me out of the way and got to work on Mrs. Napier. My hopes for a miracle were dashed when they stopped work mere minutes after their arrival.

My mentor, my friend, my hero, Vicky Napier, was dead.

Tears filled my eyes as the paramedics put in a call for the coroner. And for the police.

Brent took me in his strong arms when the police arrived, followed shortly by the coroner. The Rushing Creek Chief of Police, Matt Roberson, who also happened to be my ex-brother-in-law, guided Porter, Brent, and me out of the break room and sat us down at a round table near the nonfiction wing.

"Can I get any of you something to drink? Water? Coffee?" The gesture was a kind one. It let us know Matt didn't consider us potential suspects in a murder scene.

Not yet, at least.

He was relaying our orders over his collar microphone when Officer Jeanette Wilkerson joined us.

"The scene's been secured, Chief. If you don't object, I'll get started on evidence collection right away." Jeanette turned her attention from her boss to me. "I'm sorry for your loss, Allie. I know how much Vicky meant to you. And to you, as well, Mr. Rasmussen. Brent." She nodded to us and strode toward the break room.

"Evidence collection? Isn't that a bit much, Chief?" Porter's tone was defiant, but he wouldn't make eye contact with Matt. Instead, he kept alternating between smoothing the sleeves of his oxford shirt and running his hand over his bald head.

"Standard procedure when the coroner's involved." Matt pulled one of his standard small notebooks from his shirt pocket then popped a piece of gum in his mouth. "Can each of you tell me what you saw when you arrived on the scene?"

I didn't buy Matt's standard procedure comment for a second. Maybe it was true. The way Matt was standing at attention while he chomped on the gum he used when stressed out made me think something else was going on, though.

Given the trying circumstances, I didn't want to let Porter gain an upper hand. Before the older man could open his mouth, I jumped in and recited everything I could recall from the moment Brent and I entered the library.

After scribbling in his notebook, Matt eyed Brent and me without saying a word. It was a classic Chief Matt Roberson interrogation technique. He wanted to use the silence to make us squirm. We had nothing to hide, so I engaged Matt in a stare down.

Our battle of wills came to an end when a Latino police officer with closely cropped brown hair strode up and distributed our drinks. I'd met Officer Gabriel Sandoval the previous autumn when a high school classmate of mine had been murdered. Gabe was a nice enough guy and gave me a little smile as he dropped a couple of sugar packets on the table in front of me.

The grandson of Guatemalan immigrants who came to Indiana as migrant farm workers, Gabe was fiercely proud of his Latino heritage. He'd once confided in me that being one of a handful of brown-skinned children in a community dominated by white-skinned people was a challenge growing up. Because of his appearance, he'd often felt like an outsider.

Being an outsider was something I identified with. Growing up, I'd never hung out with the cool kids. When Gabriel confided in me, it created a bond between us. I trusted him. And gave him a heartfelt thank you for the coffee and sugar.

When the interruption was over, Matt flipped to a new page in his notebook with a grumble and looked at Brent. "Anything you'd like to add?"

"No." Brent took off his glasses and rubbed them with a cloth. "Vicky was fine last night. Well, maybe a little on edge..." He shook his head. "I can't believe it."

"Last night?" Matt kept his tone neutral, but his right eyebrow shot up. "What about last night?"

"I was here at closing time. We left the library together. She was telling me about her plans to get her house on the market as soon as possible. She seemed antsy."

"When was this?"

"Regular closing time is eight, so about eight fifteen. I got home and had taken Sammy for a walk by the time Allie got home—"

"Which was a little after nine," I said.

Matt gave me a stony look, but if I could help Brent by butting in, I'd do it in a heartbeat.

"What do you mean by antsy?"

Brent glanced at the white ceiling tiles above us and blew out a long breath. "Like something was on her mind, bothering her. I figured she was worried about getting her asking price for the house."

"Had she hired a realtor?"

"I don't know."

"Did she say why she was selling the house?"

Brent and I exchanged a glance.

He nodded. "She told me she was retiring and planned on moving to Florida. She has a sister there."

"Did she mention anything else that was bothering her?" Matt's stare held Brent with the focus of a surgeon performing heart surgery.

"Not that I can remember. Sorry. I was wanting to get back to the apartment in time to give Allie a nice welcome home."

"Uh-huh. Did the two of you spend the night together?" The corner of Matt's mouth curved up as Brent's cheeks turned ruby red.

"Nice try, Chief. Yes, in fact, we did. We never left each other's sight." I leaned back and crossed my arms, resentful of the implication, even if it was in jest.

Matt cleared his throat and shifted from one foot to the other. "Mr. Rasmussen, what time did you get here this morning?"

"I clocked in at eight forty. You can verify it." The older man began breathing like he'd just finished a trail run with my bestie, Sloane. With trembling fingers, he took a drink of his coffee, spilling a few drops on his faded blue jeans.

"We'll do that. Now, can you tell me when you got here?" Matt's tone was neutral, but he was gripping the pencil so tight, his knuckles were white. The tension among us increased as each second ticked by.

"I don't know. A few minutes before that. Vicky's car was already in the lot. I always say good morning to her before I gather the trash. When she wasn't in her office, I went looking for her. And..." He slurped another drink. This time, he managed to get it all in his mouth.

I couldn't help wondering why he chose that moment for a break. Was it a delay tactic to give him time to concoct more to his story? Maybe Matt could tell if it was, but I couldn't.

"And?" The question had an edge to it. It was as if the chief was triple-dog-daring Porter to lie to him.

I'd been on the wrong side of the table for a Matt Roberson interview. It was an unnerving experience. The man was a master of the short, open-ended question.

"First, I checked the store room, then the stacks. Sometimes she's out on the floor shelving returned books when I arrive. When she wasn't there, I went to the break room. I opened the door, and there she was, on the floor."

"What did you do next?"

"It's all such a blur. The next thing I remember is being by her when Allie and Brent showed up." He wrapped his bony fingers around the coffee cup and shivered.

"Okay." Matt got to his feet and called Jeanette over.

They exchanged a few words in quiet tones.

Jeanette shook her head twice and nodded once, but that was all I could glean from the conversation. After a few more words from Matt, she returned to the break room without as much as a glance in my direction.

Some friend. When I needed reassurance things would be okay, she was all business. I tried to tell myself she was focused on doing her job. She had work to do. That commitment to her work made her a great cop. That it wasn't personal.

It was a sign something serious was going on, though. Something more serious than a woman having a fatal heart attack or stroke.

Matt returned to the table, crossed his arms, and gave us a long stare that would have made an Old West gunslinger proud.

"Here's what we're going to do. Mr. Rasmussen, Brent, I'm going to need you two to come to the station so we can take formal statements." He signaled to Officer Sandoval. "Gabe, please take Mr. Richardson. I'll take Mr. Rasmussen."

"Wait." I shot to my feet. "What—"

"Allie, you're free to go. I've got your number if I need to reach you."

"Not so fast." I dashed around the table and planted myself right in front of Matt, fists on my hips and elbows out wide to create as much of an intimidating figure as possible. Being five one and tipping the scale at one hundred ten pounds wasn't going to threaten Matt, but I gave myself an A for effort when he took a half step back.

He put one hand up. "Now, Allie—"

"Don't 'Now, Allie' me. Are you arresting Brent?" I willed my knees to stay steady. Now wasn't the time to show Brent fear by having them knocking.

"No. I'm not." He turned toward Porter. "I'm not arresting you, either. The sooner we get going, the sooner we'll finish."

Porter closed his eyes and let out a long sigh. After a few seconds, he opened them and motioned Gabe to lead the way.

I turned to Brent and opened my mouth, but nothing came out.

"It's okay, Allie. I get it." He handed me the truck keys. "I may have been the last person to see Vicky alive. Am I right?" When Matt nodded, he smiled. "I don't know if I can tell you anything helpful, Chief, but I'm more than happy to tell you everything I can."

"In that case, shall we?" Matt tipped his Rushing Creek Police Department baseball cap to me and escorted Brent toward the door.

They were almost there when I finally regained my voice.

"Don't worry, Brent. If someone killed Mrs. Napier, I'll figure out who did it. They won't get away with it. I promise."

The library door swung open and closed again, cutting me off from my beau.

Too angry at the situation, the death of Mrs. Napier plus the questioning of Brent, to waste time on despair, I marched to the break room. The door had been propped open, but a sign was hanging from a yellow, horizontal pole that had been inserted between the left and right sections of the doorframe. The words, spelled out in bold, red lettering, stopped me in my tracks.

Crime Scene—Do Not Enter.

If that wasn't bad enough, the coroner was bent over Mrs. Napier, conducting an examination. It broke my heart that they hadn't even covered her with a sheet. I didn't care that police procedure dictated leaving the body as undisturbed as possible during the initial investigation. It seemed cold, uncaring. Mrs. Napier deserved better.

Then it hit me like a kickboxing shot to the abdomen. The Rushing Creek PD was really treating Mrs. Napier's death like a murder. Not wanting to screw up the crime scene, I toed the imaginary line the sign created and leaned forward.

Jeanette, sporting blue, plastic gloves, was going through a cabinet by the refrigerator. As she dictated something to an officer who was helping her, she turned in my direction.

I waved, hoping she would take a break from her evidence collection to fill me in.

After a short conversation with her assistant, she removed the gloves and dropped them in a clear, plastic trash bag by the door.

"Hey." She put a hand on my shoulder. "How are you holding up?"

"Been better." I pointed at the sign above my head. "Is that really necessary?"

"Afraid so. Cause of death is undetermined, so we need to proceed with caution." She removed her shoe covers and guided me to a chair at a nearby table. "I know you want answers. Right now, we don't have any, but we'll get them. I need you to trust me. Let Matt, me, and the rest of our team do our jobs. Can you do that?"

"I can, but do I have to?" I forced a chuckle. Since I'd returned to Rushing Creek from New York, I'd gotten a reputation as an amateur homicide detective. Though I'd earned it fair and square, it was a reputation I wish I'd never obtained.

Jeanette pursed her lips, so I gave her a friendly tap on the shoulder with my fist. "I'll be a good girl and stay out of your way. Promise."

My friend gave me a long, quiet look. The pledge didn't seem to have convinced her one bit. "I need to get back to work. Go home. Take Ursi and Sammy for a walk. I'm sure Brent will catch up with you in no time."

If the request had come from any other cop, I would have ignored it and tried to weasel my way into the crime scene. But it didn't come from any other cop. Jeanette was my friend. She'd earned my trust and now was the time to show it. I owed her that.

"You're right." I jangled Brent's keys in my hand. "I'll talk to you later. Text me if I can help with anything."

Jeanette gave me a hug, and I made my way out of the building. Every step was a challenge, like a slog through wet cement. The Rushing Creek Library had been a source of joy and adventure all my life. It had served as a portal to far flung parts of the globe and beyond, millions, even billions of miles away from small-town Indiana. In high school, it even provided me with a place to make money, as I spent untold hours providing tutoring and editing services to fellow students.

Now it was home to a crime scene. The victim was the library's patron saint, Vicky Napier. As I turned the key and the truck's massive engine rumbled to life, I shook my head in a vain attempt to make the madness go away.

Vicky had given her life to Rushing Creek. She'd spent her entire career at the library. I'd never heard an unkind word said about her.

And yet, someone had murdered her.

Why?

I pounded on the steering wheel as I piloted Brent's behemoth south on Washington Boulevard, known to locals simply as the Boulevard. Instead of getting any answers, all I got from my burst of anger was a stinging palm and a raised eyebrow look of alarm from Maybelle Schuman, Rushing Creek's chief gossip. I shuddered to think what awful rumors she'd manufacture about Vicky.

I parked the truck in a spot a block away from my building that had angle parking so I didn't have to parallel park. Since I didn't own a car, when it came to parking, I'd rather walk a few blocks than deal with the stress of maneuvering Brent's massive machine between two other valuable machines.

As I climbed the stairs to my second-floor apartment, my bike came into view. I smiled. A bike wasn't complicated. I could change the tires and do most of the maintenance myself. As small as Rushing Creek was, I could get from one end of town to the other on my two-wheeler in fifteen minutes. Between the basket on the front and the saddle bags that hung over the rear tire, it could handle virtually all errands, from groceries to simple hardware items.

As I ran my hand over the black, vinyl seat, a bit of the tension building up inside me dropped away. Life had gotten complicated and, right now, I needed as many uncomplicated things as possible.

Once inside the apartment, I scooped up Ursi, let Sammy out of his crate, and dropped onto the couch for a snuggle with the fur babies. My kitty started purring while the golden retriever settled his head on my leg and closed his eyes. After a few minutes of pet therapy, I gave each of them a treat.

"Okay, guys. Enough self-pity. Life goes on and so must I." I grabbed the Brent-approved resumes and took them to my office.

In New York, I'd have gotten a hundred or more resumes for a literary agent intern position. All of them would have met my requirements of a bachelor's degree in either English or creative writing and one to three years of writing experience.

Rushing Creek wasn't New York, by any means. In many cases, that difference was a good thing. I was happy in my little, southern Indiana town. Life was good here, the present circumstances being an exception. As I studied the resumes, disappointment filled me. None of the candidates had the necessary college degrees, and I had to stretch so far I could reach from one end of my office to the other to find the relevant experience.

That was okay. Three candidates were from the Rushing Creek area, which was something I wanted. My hometown had given me much since I'd returned from New York. The least I could do was repay it by giving someone local an opportunity to work in my field.

When I was finished putting the interviews on my calendar, I attacked my inbox. I'd been able to keep up with the most critical e-mails while out of town, but that still left a few hundred I needed to get through.

I'd just e-mailed an editor about a thriller manuscript I'd submitted a few weeks back when a rattling at the front door got me out of my seat as fast as a hobbit who'd been called for second breakfast.

"Hey, you." I hit Brent at a full sprint, knocking the air from his lungs when I reached him. With him trapped against the door, I hugged him as tight as I could.

I didn't let go until Sammy wedged his way between us and Ursi was pawing at my leg, with her claws out. Despite my desire to hold on to Brent forever, I gave in to the fur babies and led him to the couch. Once he was seated, I got him a glass of cold water and some pain reliever. I knew all too well how taxing a police interview could be, both physically and mentally.

He took my offerings without comment and downed the pills and water in one long pull. "Thanks. That was an…experience. Don't want to go through that again."

"Matt can't possibly think you had anything to do with this, does he? You and Vicky were friends, for God's sake." I wrapped my arms around myself as a chill came over me.

"I don't think so, but he's trying to cover all his bases. He said I had a motive. That with her gone, I could take her place."

I barked out a laugh. "That's absurd. I assume you told him about your recommendation."

"I did." When he looked at the empty glass, I got him a refill. "He said unless some corroborating evidence surfaces, all he can do is take my word for it. And he's not ready to do that. At least not yet."

"We'll see about that. Let me get my notebook and we can start a suspect list." I turned toward my office. Before I'd gone two steps, Brent grabbed me by the wrist.

"No, Allie. Please. You promised your private eye days were over." He took off his glasses and rubbed his eyes. They were red-rimmed. "I can't handle the thought of you putting your life in danger again."

And there it was. The elephant in the room. Yes, I'd investigated two murders recently committed in Rushing Creek. And yes, I'd managed to catch the killer both times. But, yes, I'd also ended up in the hospital both times. And I'd promised Brent my sleuthing days were over.

I couldn't stand idly by and leave the investigation to the Rushing Creek Police, though. Vicky meant too much to me. I had to do something. Allie the Investigator was going to have to make her return.

Chapter Four

I was drinking coffee the next morning while I processed author royalty payments the agency had received covering the first quarter of the year. While my ever-growing client list thrilled me, it also meant I had to maintain a much more disciplined schedule. Thus, I'd started getting up at seven sharp during the work week. That way I had a few hours where I could work without distraction.

A knock on the front door brought my calculations to a halt. A quick check at the bottom corner of the computer screen indicated it was a little after eight. Way too early for a surprise visit from Sloane. My bestie usually texted before stopping by, and besides, she never got up before nine unless it was a race day. It was one of the perks of her life as a professional trail runner.

Given the events of the last twenty-four hours, I held my breath as I approached the door. Brent and I had spent the previous evening talking with my mom, my brother, and my sister, so I was certain it wasn't any of them. After taking a moment to build up my courage, I opened it.

Matt greeted me with a tip of his Rushing Creek Police Department baseball cap. "I've got news. Mind if I come in?"

Unable to speak due to the million potential reasons for his visit running through my mind at once, I waved him in. Ursi padded up to him and rubbed her head against his pants leg. I chose to take that as a good sign.

"Is Brent here? The news is for him, too." He bent down to scratch Ursi behind the ears.

"Yeah. I'll get him." I motioned toward the kitchen. "Help yourself to some coffee."

Brent was in the bedroom. Still fast asleep, he had one arm draped over a snoring Sammy. The rest of him was covered from head to toe by the comforter. Unable to doze off, he'd tossed and turned until I gave him some cold medicine to knock him out. Given all he'd been through, I hated waking him up, but I didn't want to leave Matt waiting. Maybe he had good news.

A girl could always hope.

"Time to get up, sleepyheads." I shook Brent's shoulder with one hand while I scratched Sammy behind the ears. The dog snorted and burrowed under the covers while Brent opened his eyes and rewarded me with a smile.

He yawned and stretched his long arms. "Hi. To what do I owe this pleasant wake up?"

"We've got a visitor. Matt Roberson. Says he has news." I tossed his robe at him. "Get dressed."

Five minutes later, the three of us were seated around my kitchen table, coffee cups in hand, while the fur babies gobbled up their breakfasts in the corner of the kitchen.

"So, this news of yours. What is it?" I sipped my coffee, keeping my hands tightly wrapped around the cup so they wouldn't tremble.

"I'll dispense with the pleasantries." Matt opened his notebook. "We got the preliminary autopsy result on Vicky Napier. The report indicates foul play, likely poisoning."

The world swam before my eyes and a buzzing filled my ears. I had to grab the table to keep my balance.

"Allie!" Brent grabbed my wrist. His complexion had taken on an ashen tone and his grip was shaky. "Are you okay?"

"Yeah." I shook my head to clear out the fuzziness from the shock of Matt's statement. "No. I mean why would anyone want to kill her? She—"

"She meant a lot to you." Matt took a long drink of his coffee. There were dark circles under his eyes and a day's worth of stubble on his chin. If he'd gotten any sleep, it hadn't been much. "She meant a lot to this town."

"Is there any more you can tell us?" Steam rose from the ceramic carafe as Brent filled Matt's coffee cup. "I hope you know we want to help in any way we can."

"I do have some good news for you, Brent. The coroner marked the time of death at about eight thirty, almost a half hour before you arrived at the library."

"That means he's in the clear, right?" I sat upright in my chair as the welcome news brought clarity back to my brain. With my senses returned to full alert, I gave Brent's hand a gentle squeeze.

Brent's jaw unclenched, and some color returned to his face. "Not completely, I'm afraid. We still have more work to do. As of now, Brent, you're still the last person to see her alive." Matt studied his notebook for a moment. "I've got Officer Sandoval canvassing Mrs. Napier's street, checking to see if anyone saw her between the time you parted ways with her and the time of death."

I slouched back into my chair and mumbled a curse word under my breath. "What am I supposed to do now?" Brent got up and paced from the dining table to the front door and back again.

"You're free to go about your business. Don't leave town without checking with me first, though." When Brent nodded, Matt got to his feet. "I need to get back to the station. I'll be in touch."

Despite his protest that it wasn't necessary, I offered to walk Matt to my building's entrance. When we were in the hall, I pulled the door closed behind me.

"You don't seriously think Brent had anything to do with this, do you?" I blocked the stairwell. Matt wasn't going to escape without answering a few of *my* questions.

"Do I think he murdered Vicky? No. Do I know he didn't do it? Same answer." He put his hands up to head off my response. "I'm sorry, Allie, but he had motive and opportunity."

"They were colleagues. He was spending his vacation helping her out, for God's sake. What possible motive would he have?"

"With her gone, he's a prime candidate for her position. No more traveling the state doing his genealogy installation projects. And no more long-distance relationship with you."

"How dare you?" Anger welled up as I struggled to refrain from slapping Matt across the face. "You should be ashamed of yourself for making an accusation like that."

"I'm sorry." He leaned against the wall and let out a long sigh, the kind filled with weariness and frustration. "I know you care about Brent, but I have to be guided by facts, not emotions. Until I get more facts that clear him, I have to consider him a suspect."

I bit back a spiteful retort and counted to ten in my head. Not all that long ago, I had been in Brent's shoes. Being accused of murder had been one of the worst experiences of my life, but Matt had been unwaveringly fair, thorough, and guided by the search for truth. Despite my unhappiness with the current situation, his track record spoke for itself.

"I'm sorry, too. I was being unfair. If there's any way I can help, please let me know."

Matt surprised me by putting his arm around me. "I can't imagine how tough this is for you. You're strong, though. And trust me, we'll find the killer. The real one."

I returned to the apartment to find Brent hovering over the stove. The tantalizing aroma of eggs, bacon, and toast made my mouth water. I was a decent cook and proud of my skills in the kitchen. Brent, on the other hand, was a maestro with a spatula. The meal didn't matter. When he cooked, it was a production. And a delight to my taste buds.

"Since I'm halfway off the hook, I thought we'd have a little celebratory breakfast." He sliced a few mushrooms and dropped them onto the eggs. After a minute or two, he flipped one half of the eggs onto the other and sprinkled the omelet with cheese. After adding the bacon and toast, he handed me the plate with a bow.

I spread blueberry jam on my toast while Brent scrambled some eggs for himself. When he joined me at the table, he smiled. "Bon appetite."

"You're in a good mood for just being rousted from bed to talk to a police officer." I chewed on a forkful of eggs and practically melted in ecstasy. There was no way someone who cooked this heavenly could commit something as heinous as murder.

Not that I had any doubts about Brent's innocence, regardless of Matt's equivocation.

"Better to be half-exonerated than not at all. To be honest, for a while, I thought I was going to need a lawyer." He shoveled his scrambled eggs into his mouth like a man who hadn't eaten in a week. Then again, due to the stress from yesterday's events, until now his stomach had been too upset for him to eat anything since he'd returned from the police station.

Since I'd eaten some yogurt with fruit before he got up, I slid my half-uneaten plate toward him. He took it without comment and, like a magician, made it disappear in seconds.

After breakfast, I filled our coffee cups and we got comfortable on the couch. Sammy jumped into an opening between us. Ursi, not to be outdone, settled herself on the arm of the couch and bumped my elbow to let me know it was time for head scratches.

"I can't stop thinking that if I hadn't been so slow getting dressed or if I hadn't insisted on stopping to get a card, we might have gotten to the library soon enough to save her. Know what I mean?" Brent scratched Sammy's ear as the pooch lay his head on his thigh.

It didn't take Jane Marple to deduce Brent's question wasn't rhetorical. The shock of Vicky's murder had worn off. The denial phase was in the past. We were going to have to come to terms with the sudden, violent loss of one of the most important people in our lives.

What I wasn't going to allow was to have Brent slip into a deep well of self-recrimination. Asking ourselves "what if" would accomplish nothing. And it sure wouldn't help catch Vicky's killer.

Then I had a brain blast. "Let's go for a walk. The fresh air will do us good and I'm sure Ursi could use some exercise."

Brent looked out the window. April in Indiana meant the crocuses were blooming, the grass was growing, and the tree buds were popping. It also meant lots of rain.

Today, we had gray skies, but no precipitation. That would work.

A bit later, we were on our way. We had no destination in mind, so we let Sammy and Ursi take the lead. It was enough to simply be out of the apartment and out of doors. Despite the cloudy skies, the breeze from the south provided a touch of warmth. It was a welcome sign that sunny skies and balmy temperatures weren't far off.

I had to give the fur babies credit for the direction they were taking us. I was a little concerned we'd end up on the Boulevard. While walking along the Boulevard wasn't in and of itself a bad thing, spending time on the most heavily trafficked street in town would likely mean lots of sideways glances made in Brent's direction. Neither of us wanted that.

Instead, Ursi, with tail as erect as a flagpole, took charge and led us across the Boulevard and down the street. She didn't stop until we were in front of Big Al's Diner, my favorite restaurant in the world. Rachel owned the Rushing Creek Public House, which I adored, but Big Al's would always be number one in my heart.

When Sammy got up on his front paws to get a look inside the diner, the door opened.

"If it isn't one of my favorite foursomes of all time." Al Hammond, the owner of Big Al's stood in the doorway. A mountain of a man, he took up the entire entryway, but his intimidating size, shaggy hair, and massive beard couldn't hide the fact he had the heart of a kitten.

He scooped up Ursi with one hand and gave her a nose boop while he scratched Sammy underneath the pooch's chin, laughing all the while. His shoulders slumped when he put Ursi down and turned his attention to Brent and me.

"I'm so sorry." He took me in a giant bear hug. "I know how much Vicky meant to you, Allie."

When he released me, he wrapped an arm around Brent and gave him friendly pats on the back. "You too, young man."

We chatted about Vicky for a few moments before Al was summoned back to work. Before he let us go, he dashed into the diner and returned with two steaming, to-go cups of coffee. "The world's a little colder today. Thought you might enjoy these on the rest of your walk."

We thanked him and promised to return soon, without Sammy and Ursi, to try Al's latest lunch specialty, a turkey burger topped with homemade salsa and guacamole on a pretzel bun. My stomach rumbled just thinking about it.

Resuming our stroll, we headed north and soon arrived at an unsettling destination.

The Rushing Creek Public Library.

The building was dark. A hand-lettered sign taped to the inside of the glass entrance door said it was closed until Saturday. Floral arrangements and a few stuffed animals had been left at the foot of the door.

A shiver went through me that even the hot coffee couldn't overcome. While Ursi sniffed the flowers, I peered inside. A vision formed before my eyes. Vicky was opening the door, apologizing for making me wait even though opening time wasn't for another five minutes, just like she did during the summers when I was growing up. After a minute, I looked away. It was not to be.

Not now. Not ever again.

"I still can't believe she's gone." Brent pressed his forehead against the glass. "If only I'd seen something. Or noticed something. She didn't deserve to die like that. I can't help feeling like it's my fault."

"Don't say that. Don't even think it. Someone else murdered her, not you. This isn't your fault." I turned us around and pointed at a park bench across the street. We hadn't discussed Vicky's murder beyond our mutual disbelief.

It was time to change that.

A minute later, we were seated on the bench, with Ursi curled up on my lap and Sammy seated at Brent's feet. We had the park to ourselves. I was thankful for the chance to speak freely.

"Tell me about the night before last. When you and Vicky were closing."

Brent rubbed his hands together in a slow deliberate motion. It was a habit of his when he was formulating what he wanted to say about something. "It had been a busy day. I'd spent a couple of days deciding which books should go into the book sale. Since it was the library's first sale, Vicky wanted final approval on everything. She was preoccupied, though. I couldn't get her to focus. On top of that, whenever I closed with her, she always talked about getting a cup of tea and then heading to bed with something new to read. That night, she didn't. It was like something was bothering her."

"Maybe it was her retirement announcement. That was going to be a big change for her."

"Maybe." He removed his glasses and rubbed the bridge of his nose. He had a pained look, and his eyes were filled with guilt. "When I asked what brought about the decision to retire, all she'd say was this day would eventually come."

Our conversation was cut short when a woman with a floral arrangement in her hands approached us. Her wavy black hair and stocky build were unmistakable. It was Frederica Hampton, the owner of Marinara's Pizza Place. Frederica, or Freddie as she was commonly known, was also the president of the library board and one of Vicky's oldest friends.

Brent shot to his feet and offered his seat to Freddie. I had to suppress a chuckle at the deference he was showing the woman. Then again, her opinion would carry great weight when the decision was made to name Vicky's replacement.

Vicky's replacement. God, I hated thinking about it, especially given the circumstances.

"Ms. Hampton. Please join us. We were just reminiscing about Vicky."

"Thank you, Brent." She shook my hand as she sat. "Good to see you, Allie. How's your mother?"

We chatted for a few moments about pleasant things before I offered my condolences.

"Thank you." She looked at the flowers and wiped a tear from her cheek. "I don't know what I'm going to do. Rushing Creek simply won't be the same without her."

"I have to leave town Sunday, but I'll do all I can to help you and the rest of the library's staff until then." Brent looked at the library for a moment, then shook his head. The sadness radiating off him was palpable.

"I appreciate it. I'm sure the rest of the board members do, too. I heard about your trip to the police station yesterday. I hope it wasn't too traumatic."

Brent shrugged. "No. It was stressful, but Chief Roberson was just doing his job. He actually stopped by earlier today to let me know I'm pretty much in the clear, so that's good, I guess."

"That's definitely good. I couldn't see you as the murderer, anyway."

"You knew Vicky as well as anyone." I nudged Ursi away from the flowers. "Do you have any idea who would want to harm her?"

Freddie raised an eyebrow. "Are you putting on your private eye hat again?"

I'd made a promise to Brent. But Vicky was my hero. If I could help catch her killer, I would.

"This isn't about me. It's about Vicky and getting justice for her." I flexed my right hand. On some days, especially cold, damp ones, the knuckles still ached from being broken in the act of catching a killer the previous September.

"Agreed." With her free hand, Freddie scratched Sammy behind his ears. "This time around, arresting the murderer should be a snap."

"Why do you say that?" Instantly, I was on high alert, ready for any information that would clear Brent and solve the murder in the process.

Freddie straightened her spine and cleared her throat. "I know who killed her."

Chapter Five

"What?" Brent and I uttered the question at the same time, our shocked response upsetting Ursi so much she jumped from my lap.

My blood turned to ice as I processed Freddie's claim. A hand squeezed my shoulder. It was Brent. He was leaning on me for support, with his eyes closed and his hand literally over his heart.

I took a deep breath. Composure was needed. When I was calmed down a bit, I asked the million-dollar question. "Who?"

"Isn't it obvious?" She stared at me for a few seconds then at Brent. When neither of us responded, she tugged on the collar of her jacket. "It was Porter. Had to be."

"How do you know? Did Chief Roberson talk to you?" My hand had locked itself around Freddie's wrist. If this woman knew who killed my hero, I needed details.

Freddie lowered her gaze until it fell on my hand around her wrist. I released her with an apology.

"Don't worry about it." She grimaced as she rubbed her wrist.

Evidently, I'd squeezed a little too hard. Okay, a lot too hard, but this was critical information.

"The chief talked to me yesterday afternoon, after he released you"— she nodded in Brent's direction—"and Porter. Since I'm the library board president, he thought it was important to bring me up to speed on the whole sordid affair."

"And he told you who did it?" I kept my tone neutral, but, on the inside, I was trembling with impatience.

"Not exactly." Freddie stared at Ursi, who was sniffing her black leather shoes. "But it doesn't take a genius to know who did it. It was that horrible man Porter."

I blinked a couple of times as I absorbed the information. Of course, Porter would be a prime suspect. But the murderer? Surely, Matt could have shared that with us. Then again, maybe not, if he had a reason to keep information close to the vest.

"If you'll excuse me, ladies. I need to take Sammy someplace where he can use the restroom." Brent squeezed my shoulder and led Sammy toward the other end of the park.

My guess was he needed to be alone for a minute. I couldn't blame him. He and Vicky had become good friends in the year and a half they'd known each other. It was a relationship vastly different than the one I'd had with her. Their relationship had been one of equals, business colleagues. So much of ours had been a relationship between an adult and a child that, even in recent years, it was still more like that of a mentor and mentee.

Freddie's brow crinkled as Brent and Sammy took their leave. "I'm sorry if I've upset him. I thought you'd like to know."

"It's been a trying couple of days. I'm sure it's nothing personal. What did Chief Roberson say to you?"

"He told me what happened, about you and Brent finding Porter hovering over Vicky's body. Then he said he'd questioned both Brent and Porter." She leaned close to me and spoke just above a whisper. "I'd bet my restaurant Porter's the culprit."

Now things were making sense. Matt hadn't made a collar. Freddie was simply guessing.

I despised gossip. In Rushing Creek, rumors moved faster than the luxury car the great Jay Gatsby himself drove. I needed information, though. Even if it lacked a solid basis in fact. While I had Freddie's attention, it couldn't hurt to find out what she really knew, or thought she really knew.

"Why do you say that? I thought Porter was a decent guy."

"That's what he'd have everyone think, but underneath that friendly façade, he could be scary. People think he had a harmless crush on Vicky, but that wasn't the case."

The last part caught my attention. I was among those who figured Porter's feelings for Vicky weren't much more than platonic. I asked for details.

"He'd become obsessive. He kept bringing her flowers, even though she'd asked him to stop over a year ago. Sometimes, she'd hang out at my house and vent that she didn't feel safe when he was around."

"If she was feeling threatened, why didn't she go to the police?"

Freddie ran her fingers over the flower petals. "You know this town, Allie. She was afraid that if she made an official complaint, word would get out. She didn't want to deal with the gossip. I don't think she ever fully recovered from the nasty rumors about her divorce."

I racked my brain to dredge up memories of Vicky's divorce. She and her husband had split up twenty years ago, so my recollections were fuzzy, like an out-of-focus photograph. I'd deal with that issue later, though. "But if he had a crush on her, why would he kill her? It doesn't make sense."

"He wasn't thinking clearly. Did Brent tell you she was planning on retiring and moving to Florida?" When I nodded, she took a deep breath, as if trying to build up the courage to share her thoughts aloud.

"I think he couldn't bear the thought of living without her. He must have overheard her telling Brent and..."

I wrapped my arms around myself, unable to find the words to catch up with the mixed emotions swirling within me. When I finally found the words, they were less than insightful, but it was the best I could do. "So, one of those 'if I can't have you, then nobody can have you' situations, huh?"

Freddie shivered, and I didn't think it was due to the chilly April temperatures. "When you put it that way, it seems awfully cold, but yes."

"Wow." My limited articulation abilities obviously hadn't improved. Then my brain finally kicked in. "Okay, I get the why, but what about the how? When Chief Roberson stopped by this morning, he said the preliminary autopsy report indicated poisoning was the cause of death."

Freddie half-smiled. "That's easy, unfortunately. You know Porter used to own the hardware store, yes?" She reached down and scratched Ursi between the ears. "When he retired, he got really involved with the garden club. Those flowers he brought Vicky? He grew those himself. Wouldn't surprise me to find out he slipped her some plant-derived poison."

"Yikes. Forgive me for saying, but that's kind of harsh, isn't it?" I grimaced. The thought of someone right here in little Rushing Creek, Indiana, growing something he knew was poisonous was more disturbing than anything out of a Poe story.

And I'd seen with my own eyes some awful things in my hometown.

Freddie clenched her jaw and gave me a long stare. After a silence that seemed to go on for hours, her shoulders sagged. A tear escaped and ran down her cheek. She wiped it away as she sniffed. "Vicky was more than my library colleague. She was my neighbor. She was my friend. I guess my emotions are still too raw to keep my mouth shut, but I want justice for her. I hope you can understand that."

"Of course. We all want justice for her. The thought of Porter killing someone..." I gathered Ursi and held her close. "He seems like such a nice guy."

"Yes, well, looks can be deceiving." She got to her feet. "I'll just add these flowers to the memorial and then I need to get to work. Come see me at the restaurant. We can reminisce about Vicky over some breadsticks."

"I'd like that."

While Freddie was placing the flowers next to the others, Brent rejoined me. "Sorry. When Ms. Hampton started talking about Porter, I had a flashback to yesterday morning. I didn't want to have a breakdown in front of her."

By virtue of Freddie's position on the library board, she'd been Vicky's boss. And would be the boss of Rushing Creek's next librarian. It was understandable Brent would want to have his act together in her presence.

"No worries. She knows you and Vicky were friends." I gave him a quick summary of Freddie's suspicions. When I finished, a weariness came over me. "I think we need something to lift our spirits. How about a hot chocolate?"

"Best idea I've heard all day."

Creekside Chocolates was another one of my favorite places on Earth. First, the sweets and chocolate-related drinks were absolutely to die for. Second, and more importantly, the store was owned by my friend Diane Stapleton. She was a kind soul who was always ready with a smile to pick me up or a piece of wisdom to help me navigate my way through life's challenges.

A native of Chicago's south side, the African-American woman had moved to Rushing Creek a few years ago. She brought an outsider's perspective to local issues I valued as much as an astronaut valued oxygen. Diane was a good friend, and I often found myself on the threshold of her store, in both good times and bad.

An electronic ding-dong accompanied a whoosh of warm air as I pushed open the door. Diane looked up from a tablet she used to track inventory and other shop-related tasks and waved.

"Hey, guys." She placed the tablet on a counter and took me in a warm hug. "I'm so sorry about Vicky. She was a real sweetheart."

"I didn't know you knew each other." Despite my unceasing efforts to get Diane to read more books, her reading time was spent on trade periodicals, e-zines, and graphic novels like *The Watchmen*, which she purchased at Renee's Gently Used Books. Thus, she wasn't much of a library person.

"She came in to get treats for her part-timers. She always got a chai for herself. And left a very generous tip."

Since we had our fur babies with us, Diane told us to take a seat at a table on the sidewalk while she made our drinks. We didn't talk while we waited. Instead, I held Ursi as she napped on my lap while Brent rubbed Sammy's belly and told him in whispered tones that he was a good boy. It was a relief to take a few minutes and let my mind drift. Between the book conference and the craziness since I'd gotten home, my metaphorical inkwell still needed to be refilled.

My moment of quiet came to an end when Diane placed a cup of hot chocolate with whipped cream on top in front of me. It was a cure for every ailment I might be suffering from. Peppermint sprinkles gave the topping a festive look and a sweet complement to the glorious confection.

After handing Brent a hot chocolate with cinnamon sprinkled on the top, Diane put a hand on my shoulder and took a seat next to me. "How are you holding up?"

"I don't know." I massaged the back of my neck. "We paid the library a visit. When we were there, Freddie Hampton came by." I told her about my conversation with the library board president.

"Wow." Diana wiped her hand across her brow. "That's insane."

"I know, right? I'm trying to process it all." I took a drink. "Without much success."

"Then let's do this." Diane put one arm around me and the other around Brent. "Come to my place for dinner tonight. We can talk about it if you want. And if you don't, we won't."

It took us all of two seconds to take her up on the offer. To me, not having to make dinner was as appealing as Rhett Butler was to Scarlett O'Hara.

Despite my desire to forget about the world and hang out at Creekside Chocolates until the end of time, I had to prep for my first intern interview. The walk home would help me set the news of the morning aside and focus on the interview.

Holding interviews in my apartment seemed unwise from a personal safety aspect, so I met my candidate in Renee's Gently Used Books, which was conveniently located on the first floor of my building, directly below my apartment. The store's owner, Renee Gomez, was also the owner of my building and had happily agreed to let me hold my interviews in the store. As a lover of books, I couldn't ask for a better landlord than someone who shared my passion for the printed word. And didn't mind letting me use her workspace for my job.

Renee, who had jazzed up her usual ensemble of head-to-toe black with a small scarlet brooch in the shape of a bird, was putting price tags on a stack of paperbacks when I arrived.

"Hey, Allie, your interview's already here." She pointed toward an area at the back of the store where four plush chairs and a couple of end tables had been organized into a reading nook. Customers were encouraged to sit and read or simply get comfortable and chat with a cup of the Jamaican blend Renee always had brewing.

I accepted the coffee Renee offered with a smile. I adored my hot chocolate, but coffee was the oil that kept my inner gears turning. For me, life without coffee was simply impossible to consider.

When I reached the reading nook, I introduced myself to the candidate, a woman with short, salt-and-pepper hair and large, round glasses. Her name was Talullah, but she insisted I call her Tally as we exchanged greetings.

A sinking feeling in my gut grew as I took the seat catty-corner from her. Something undefinable felt wrong about the situation. On the other hand, Tally and I were both here and I needed help, so I got started.

"On your resume, you indicated you did copy editing work for the *Brown County Beacon*. Tell me about that." The *Beacon* was the local weekly newspaper. While the world of news media was a different animal from the world of fiction publishing, I was confident many of her claimed editing skills could be useful.

"Well." She rubbed her hands on her jeans as she looked toward the front of the store. "It was twenty years ago, and I worked in the classified ads section for about six months."

I glanced at Tally's resume. She'd fudged the length of time she'd worked for the *Beacon*. Strike one. It also said nothing about classified ads. Strike two.

I took a deep breath as the knot in my stomach tightened and soldiered on. "Can you give me details of what you did in the classified ads section?"

"A little bit of everything. I answered the phone, wrote down what the customer wanted the ad to say, entered the information into the computer, and wrote up the bill."

There wasn't much actual editing in her answer. If I tried to stretch it like a piece of bubble gum, I could make myself accept writing down ad copy as editing. I didn't want to stretch that far.

I asked a few more questions, gently drilling down to the truth of the matter. It took almost twenty minutes, but I finally got Tally to admit she had zero editing experience. Her work at the *Beacon* had been a temp job while the office assistant was out on pregnancy leave. Once the truth was out in the open, I ended the interview as quickly as I could without being rude.

I wasn't looking for someone to hang out with. I was looking for someone smart, capable, and trustworthy. The intern was an important position. It was pivotal to the growth of the Cobb Literary Agency.

Tally's cheeks were pink as we said goodbye. I sensed she knew she'd been caught lying and was happy to finish the interview without me getting angry. Once she was out of the store, I dropped back into the seat with a groan.

"Not who you're looking for, huh?" Renee topped off my coffee and took Tally's seat.

"No. It's not just that, though." I rubbed my temples. A headache was chugging down the tracks and had me in its sights. "It's everything else, too. God, I want to run a way to a tropical island and live out the rest of my days in a grass hut."

"I know." She gave my hand a reassuring squeeze. "You'll get through this. We'll get through this, together. Just like we did last fall, right?" When I nodded, she stood. "I just got in some classic editions of Nancy Drew and Trixie Belden. Care to take a look?"

The invitation was like offering sugar water to a hummingbird. I adored collecting first editions and early printings of books. So much so that the bookshelves I'd built when I moved in upstairs were almost full. I'd been toying with asking Renee for permission to have floor-to-ceiling bookshelves installed. That was for another time, though. Exhaustion was enveloping me like a low-hanging cloud.

"Maybe next time. I need a nap." I gave Renee a hug, headed upstairs, and went straight to bed, stopping only long enough to remind Brent to take Sammy outside for a potty break before we headed to Diane's.

A few minutes later, or so it seemed, Brent was nudging my arm to wake me up.

"Five more minutes." I covered my head with a pillow.

"Sorry. We're due at Diane's in an hour, and I need to get back to my mac and cheese."

That got me moving. Brent's mac and cheese was a gift from the gods. I'd pestered him at least a dozen times to get him to reveal the recipe. I'd been rebuffed every time. He didn't make it often, so that meant tonight would have a special culinary treat, along with the great company.

Just what I needed to lift my spirits.

Brent and I arrived at Diane's home a little after seven. Nestled in a tree-filled neighborhood on the north side of town, the house was a single-story ranch with a two-car, attached garage. Solar-powered lights lined the concrete driveway, which gave the brick-sided structure a warm, welcoming vibe.

Diane greeted us with hugs and clapped her hands in delight when Brent gave her the mac and cheese. "I've heard tales about this delicacy. Can't wait to try it." Brent grinned from ear to ear at the compliment.

Since it was only the three of us, Brent and I settled in around the dining room table while Diane turned on an Alicia Keys record. The only thing that divided the kitchen from the dining room was an island with a stove-top insert, so we chatted while she tossed a salad in a glass bowl.

As the weather got warmer, Rushing Creek would see increased tourist traffic. Diane was looking to hire another high school student to help with the anticipated uptick in business.

"Any suggestions, Brent? I was hoping the part-time kids at the library might know somebody." Diane placed the salad, along with homemade vinaigrette dressing, on the table.

"The library's opening tomorrow. I'll ask around." Using stainless steel tongs, Brent scooped some salad onto my plate, then Diane's, and finally his. "This looks amazing. Mind if I dig in?"

The conversation stayed on pleasant topics through the salad and into the main course, a barbecue brisket with three sauce options. Brent's creamy mac and cheese accompanied the tender beef and the spicy sauces so well, I polished off two helpings of both without a second thought.

We moved to the living room for a dessert of melt-in-your-mouth apple pie à la mode and flavored coffee. Decaffeinated, given the hour. As Brent collected the plates, I let out a long breath and patted my stomach.

"That dinner was totally amazeballs. Is there anything you can't cook?" I'd visited Diane for dinner several times, and every meal she'd prepared had been worthy of a five-star review.

She shrugged. "I've never been able to pull off a baked Alaska."

The response made me laugh so hard I snorted. "God help us. How do you live with yourself?"

"Somehow, I manage." She chuckled. "I'm sure I sleep better than whoever poisoned Vicky."

Brent rejoined us. "Speaking of which, the two of you know this town better than me. What's your take on Freddie's explanation?"

I recited the conversation, taking my time to make sure I didn't leave anything out. When I was finished, I looked at Diane. She was smart and had a knack for looking at things through a clear lens.

"It fits the scenario. I've seen Porter's greenhouse. He's supplied the shop floral arrangements for some of the bigger tourist weekends. He invited me to check it out before I bought anything to prove he's legit." Her gaze moved from me to the low pile carpet. "Or was legit, I guess." "I always thought he was a little too clingy," Brent said. "I mean, flowers every week for years on end? Maybe I should change 'clingy' to something more sinister."

"I don't know." Something at the back of my brain was bothering me, like a mosquito bite on your back that was just out of reach. "It seems too cut and dried. The Porter that Mom talked about when she came by last night doesn't sound like a killer. And she's about as good a judge of character as anyone in town."

The room became as silent as a crypt in the middle of a cemetery as two sets of eyes stared at me.

After a while, Diane cracked her knuckles, the sound reverberating off the walls like a shotgun blast. She got to her feet and began pacing. "What are you saying, Allie? You don't think he did it?"

"I don't know." I massaged my jaw. The right words were hard to come by because I truly didn't know what to think. "When it comes down to it, I want as thorough of an investigation as possible. No stone unturned, no interview overlooked. If Porter did it, fine, he needs to go to jail. But what if he didn't?"

Brent let out a long sigh as his head dropped until his chin touched his chest. "You're really going to investigate this, aren't you? Despite everything that's happened to you in the past."

My mouth had become desert dry. I took a drink to give me time to think, but I'd made my decision. Matt Roberson as a good cop and a good man, but Vicky was my hero. I wanted her death avenged.

"Yeah." I looked from Brent to Diane, not for support, but for acceptance of my decision. "I'm gonna catch her killer. If it's the last thing I do."

Chapter Six

"Is there any way I can talk you out of this?" Brent glanced at me from the driver's seat of his truck. His knuckles were white, thanks to the vice-like grip he had on the steering wheel. It was Saturday morning, and we were on our way to the library. He was going to help the remaining staff.

I was going to start my investigation.

"For the last time, no." I crossed my arms and stared straight ahead. "And stop begging. It's beneath you."

On the way home from Diane's house the previous evening, he'd reminded me of my promise to give up murder investigations. Before we turned in for the night, he'd recapped how I'd ended up in the hospital, twice, thanks to my investigations. And when I'd insisted on accompanying him to the library so I could do some poking around, he'd resorted to preying on my emotions.

It wasn't going to work.

In silence, he turned into the library's parking lot and brought the truck to a stop in his usual spot. He put the vehicle in park but didn't shut off the engine. "Let me ask you one final question. What I don't get is why you won't leave this to the police. Don't you trust Matt? And what about Jeanette? She's one of your best friends. Don't you trust her?"

I scratched my ear. This was the question I didn't want to deal with. Did I trust the Rushing Creek Police Department? The answer was yes.

Matt was an effective police chief. While I considered a couple of the older officers dead weight, the younger officers, like Jeanette, Tommy Abbott, and Gabe Sandoval, were talented and dedicated public servants. They could examine evidence, follow clues, and interview witnesses with steady hands and clear eyes.

It wasn't a matter of confidence, or lack thereof, in local law enforcement that made me decide to investigate Vicky's murder. It was a compulsion from within that was driving me to find justice for my childhood hero.

I spread my fingers against the dash and leaned into it while I tried to put my feelings into words. There was no logical reason to take on another murder investigation, especially given how busy I was with the agency. Still.

"Vicky's done"—I swallowed the lump in my throat—"Vicky did so much for me over the years. My gut tells me there's more here than meets the eye. I can't stay on the sidelines. It's the least I can do to repay her for everything she did for me."

Brent frowned. "The least you can do?"

"Well." I rubbed my hands together to ward off the morning chill. "Okay, fine. It's not the least I can do. That would be nothing. You know me. I'm not good at doing nothing."

Brent barked out a laugh, which broke the tension that had built up in the truck's cab. In return, I let out a long breath to release the knot of tension that had grown in my gut.

"Promise me one thing." He opened his door. "If you sense even a whiff of danger, you'll back off and leave it to the cops. Deal?"

"Deal." With a sense of purpose residing in peaceful coexistence with relief at having Brent's support, I leapt from the truck. It was time to get to work.

We had a few minutes before the library was scheduled to open, so Brent gave the staff a pep talk while I took a quick peek in the break room to make sure there wasn't anything left behind that might upset someone. Then I headed out to where everyone was gathered.

Initially, I thought Freddie's suggestion that Brent take a supportive, cheerleading role with the staff was odd since he wasn't a regular employee. His chat with the group proved my concerns were unwarranted.

He'd first come to Rushing Creek twenty months ago to install a genealogy section in the library. The project lasted six weeks. During that time, he got to know the staff. And me, despite some initial concerns he might be a murderer. Since then, as Brent and I grew closer, whenever he came to town, he took time to help around the library, even if it was only for a few hours.

The thing was, in order to make the library's budget go further, Vicky had chosen to work an insane number of hours, usually sixty to seventy per week. That let her rely on part-time help, which kept personnel costs down. The savings was directed to programming and book purchases.

Because of her reliance on part-time staff, Vicky had welcomed Brent's continuing involvement at the library with open arms. In time, he became an unofficial big brother to the high schoolers, and that was why his role was so important now.

The smiles among the tears coming as the young ones joined Brent in a group hug confirmed his involvement at the library had paid off in spades.

"Looks like you guys are going to be okay, huh?" I gave his hand a squeeze as the group broke up.

"Eventually." He squeezed back. "Vicky was like a second mom for these kids. She sent them cards on their birthdays. Got them presents when they graduated from high school. She," his voice caught, and he had to close his eyes for a moment. "She cared about them. And they're going to miss her."

Brent removed his round, wire-rimmed glasses and wiped his eyes with a tissue. The kids weren't the only ones who were going to miss their leader.

I was about to head to Vicky's office to snoop around when Freddie arrived. Dressed in a tan sweater and brown slacks, she had an air of quiet dignity as she went from employee to employee to have a private word with each of them.

It was a kind gesture from the library board president. It showed she cared. Saturdays were the busiest day at her restaurant, yet she was willing to take time out of her busy schedule to support the team here.

Since the library had been closed for a couple of days, the book return bin was overflowing, so I was helping organize the books to check them in when Freddie came alongside me.

"Thanks for being here, Allie." She picked up a handful of books that had spilled onto the floor and handed them to me.

"Happy to help. Mrs. Napier deserves it."

We chatted for a few minutes before Freddie had to get going. When she was gone, I left the books on a cart so they could be put back on the shelves. A gray-haired woman with a name tag that read "Phyllis" accepted the cart with a sad smile and began checking them in with a barcode reader.

Patrons, with wide eyes and tentative steps, were drifting through the doors. They were practically shoulder to shoulder. The library was always busy on Saturdays. It appeared today was going to be no different. Someone had scooped up the flowers left by the entrance and placed them with care on the checkout counter. Another person had come up with some vases and was making a floral arrangement.

A lump formed in my throat as an image of Porter bringing Vicky flowers flashed before my eyes. Sure, obsession drove people to do unspeakable things, but Porter resorting to murder? Well, if I'd learned anything since I'd returned to my hometown, it was that people were capable of anything. With that macabre thought, it was time for me to fade into the background so I could get to work.

Since Vicky's life was taken from her at work, intuition suggested I start my search by reviewing the library's business records for anything fishy. I dreaded the thought of discovering she was doing something underhanded like embezzlement, but I had to maintain a sense of objectivity. If illicit or unethical behavior had led to her demise, I'd deal with it.

With Matt's admonishment to be careful echoing in my ears, I opened Vicky's office door. The room was still. Dust motes floating on air currents produced by the HVAC system were the only things in motion. The click of the door as I closed it startled me. Now that I was inside, alone, it was much too quiet.

Over the years, I'd spent my fair share of time in this room, talking about all things bookish with Vicky. Today was the first time I took a good, hard look at it.

Every inch of the cinderblock walls was covered with posters of books and literature-themed motivational quotes. Five black filing cabinets, each four drawers high, were lined up against the back wall.

A dozen three-ring binders were perched atop the cabinets. Each binder carried a label with the word "Financials" and a year along the spine. I grabbed the binders for the three most recent years and went to Vicky's desk.

The desk bumped against the wall to the left when one entered the room. Two computer monitors and a keyboard were situated in a corner of the desktop by the wall. A laptop lay in a docking port between the monitors and the keyboard.

I dropped my purse in the plush visitor's chair that had been donated by a local furniture maker and stepped around the desk. A cotton throw blanket commemorating Rushing Creek's 150th anniversary was draped over the back of Vicky's seat. I ran my fingers across the soft fabric. The loose weave against my fingertips conjured memories from high school. On cold winter nights, Vicky and I hung out in this room after closing, drinking hot chocolate. She was wrapped up in the blanket complaining she was overdue for a visit to her sister, who lived on Florida's Gulf Coast.

"I'm sorry, Vicky, but I have to do this." I sat and dropped the binders on the desktop.

As I searched for a pen and paper to take notes, I pondered why I could refer to my hero by her first name now she was gone when I couldn't do it when she was among the breathing. When no answer came to mind, I put the question aside. Psychoanalysis could wait for another day.

A couple of mind-numbing hours later, I rubbed my eyes and moved away from the desk. A review of the library's financials for the last five years hadn't turned up anything odd. Two binders that contained board meeting minutes seemed in order, too. With a yawn, I headed for the door in search of caffeine.

The library was buzzing like a beehive. The computer stations were full. A fairy tale was being read to a group of toddlers sitting on neon-colored pillows. A poster memorializing Vicky had been taped to a wall. A line of patrons waiting to sign their good wishes on it snaked through the center of the checkout area. I blinked away a tear. In the worst of times, the good people of Rushing Creek, Indiana, population 3,216, had a knack for demonstrating the best in people.

Once inside the break room, I leaned against the door and massaged my neck muscles. My earlier visit to the break room had been brief. Once I'd determined there were no remnants of the crime scene, I'd made a hasty retreat.

This time, I had no choice but to linger as I brewed a pot of coffee. While the water gurgled, I wandered about the room, peeking inside cabinets and rooting through drawers. There was no method to my madness. If there had been anything important, the police would have already taken it.

My supposition was confirmed when I looked in the fridge for some creamer. There were no liquid containers to be found. No ketchup, no two-liter soda pop bottles, and no creamer. In fact, the only things left were a pizza box from Marinara's, a sandwich in a Ziploc bag, and some fried chicken in a plastic container.

I had a soft spot in my heart, and another one in my belly, for Marinara's. Everything on its menu smelled amazing and tasted even better. Freddie claimed her secret was a notebook of recipes passed down from her Italian grandmother. It didn't matter to me where the recipes came from. All that mattered to me was I'd eaten at Marinara's for twenty years. Every meal had been delicious.

My mouth was watering simply looking at the box, so, after a glance over my shoulder, I gave in to my inner college student and lifted the lid to take a whiff. Inside was a quarter of a Chicago-style deep dish pizza. Utterly mouthwatering.

I closed the fridge before weakness overcame me and I stole a piece. Whoever had bought the pizza was a lucky person. I chuckled when I concluded it was probably one of the kids working today. It would be so like a teen to order a pizza on a Friday night and eat the leftovers the next day. Ah, the simple joys of youth.

Since no creamer was to be found anywhere in the break room, I added an extra packet of sugar to my coffee, poured a cup for Brent, and got back to work.

His eyes went wide when I handed the drink to him. "Employees aren't supposed to have drinks out on the floor. I need to set a good example." He pushed it back toward me.

"You're a volunteer helping out during a tough time. I think Freddie and the rest of the board members will give you a pass." I tossed two sugar packets on the counter in front of him and leaned close. "Speaking of pass, do you happen to know if Vicky kept any files locked down with additional password permissions?"

"No. As far as I know, the credentials I gave you should give you access to the whole system. Why?"

"I didn't find anything helpful when I went through the financial docs, and I guess I was hoping you might know about something I don't."

"Sorry." He scratched his chin. "Check her e-mails. You'll find her log-on credentials in her top left drawer. She could never remember her passwords, so she kept them on a note card. If she was feeling threatened by Porter, maybe she reported it to someone. From what I know, she never deleted anything, so if she did complain, it'll be there."

I gulped. *Never deleted anything.* I'd been planning on tackling the filing cabinets. Brent's suggestion made a lot of sense, though. How long would it take to find them, though?

"I better get to it. Wish me luck." I trudged back to Vicky's office. Sure, I had vitally important work to do, but reviewing e-mail was more soul crushing than studying financial records.

Or maybe not.

After a half hour searching in vain for something incriminating against Porter, I stepped away from the computer. I'd found a couple of threads in which Vicky expressed mild annoyance about Porter to Freddie, but nothing more serious than that. To the board president's credit, she took Vicky's complaints to heart and had offered a variety of suggestions to remedy a situation that had become increasingly uncomfortable.

There was no discussion of getting the authorities involved, though. Not helpful, when what I really wanted was something I could take to Matt.

When I sat back down after getting another cup of java, I came across an e-mail folder with a label that got my full attention—Ozzy Metcalf.

The owner of Ye Olde Woodworker, Ozzy was Rushing Creek's cantankerous old coot. He tended to treat fellow locals with disdain so he could save his limited amount of charm for tourists. Sloane said he wasn't all that bad, but she saw the best in everyone. Maybe I was too hard on the man, but he'd never made the effort to be nice to me.

On the other hand, he was dating my friend Shirley Price. Shirley owned Soaps and Scents, the shop where I got the personal care products that had helped cure me of long-term insomnia problems. Her shop was also located next door to Ozzy's. Believe it or not, it wasn't until a property dispute between them was resolved that their relationship took off. Love could be such a strange thing.

Ozzy didn't have warm feelings for Vicky. Quite the contrary, apparently. Based on the e-mails, the library had hired the man to create some woodcarvings to celebrate its centennial. He completed the artworks but claimed the library paid him five thousand dollars less than the agreed-upon amount.

Vicky refused to back down, insisting the library had a valid contract with him and refused to pay the additional amount. Despite efforts by Freddie and the rest of the board members, the parties were unable to reach a settlement. Ozzy refused to deliver the pieces and even claimed in one e-mail he couldn't sell them to anyone else because of their one-of-a-kind nature.

The e-mail exchanges ended with Vicky informing Ozzy if he didn't stop contacting her demanding payment, she'd go to court to demand he turn over the pieces immediately. If he didn't comply, she'd ask the court for a judgment to recover the money the library paid to him.

It was no secret among Rushing Creek residents that Ozzy was disagreeable and was prone to rash, hot-headed behavior. But was murder an appropriate solution to a five-thousand-dollar legal dispute? No amount of money was worth committing murder. But that was just my opinion.

Was a four-figure dispute worth killing to Ozzy? He was gruff and mean, but a murderer? At this point, I needed to keep an open mind to all possibilities. That meant Ozzy needed to join Porter on my suspect list.

Since Ozzy barely tolerated me in the best of times, approaching with my suspicions would be about as successful as the *Titanic's* maiden voyage. I could approach Shirley, though. It would take delicacy since they were an item, but it was something that had to be done.

Lucky me.

Chapter Seven

One of the hands-down, best things about my life was my role as Aunt Allie to Theresa and Tristan, Rachel's twins. Having just turned seven, they were brown-haired, blue-eyed balls of kinetic energy who kept their mother on her toes twenty-four hours a day.

Their nonstop motors had led Matt to suggest signing them up for the youth soccer league. Matt knew nothing about soccer, but as a father, and a policeman, he knew all too well how much trouble kids with energy to burn could get in. He didn't want his and Rachel's offspring to end up on the wrong end of the law, so having Theresa and Tristan run up and down a massive grass field while under adult supervision was as appealing as an ice-cold lemonade on a hot summer day.

And now here I was, on the sidelines of the soccer pitch to cheer on T and T as they played their first game of the season. After spending so much of the day holed up in Vicky's office, I was more than ready to enjoy an hour in the blessed late afternoon sunshine, shouting encouragement to a bunch of seven- and eight-year-olds as they hustled after a red-and-white soccer ball.

Rachel and I were chatting about the kids' team name, the Aces, and their adorable powder blue uniform shirts when my mom, Luke, and Sloane joined us.

"Good to see the Cobbs out in force on this fine Saturday afternoon." Luke gave Rachel and me hugs. "Where's Matt?"

My sister rolled her eyes. "At the station. He'll be working nonstop until they get this murder case solved."

Mom put an arm around Rachel. "I'm sure he'd be here if he could. You can't deny how far he's come as a father in the last year."

"I know." Rachel kicked at a clump of grass. "It's just hard on the kids when he doesn't show like this. And it's hard on me when I have to tell them work got in their father's way again."

A young man in a black T-shirt and matching shorts blew a whistle and waved both teams to the center of the pitch. The wind was blowing away from us, so I couldn't hear what he was saying, but it seemed popular as the players all cheered when he was finished. A few minutes later, when the starting lineups had taken their positions, he blew his whistle and the action began.

We focused on the game, cheering whenever one of the players, regardless of the team, made solid contact with the ball, until Sloane nudged me. "I heard Porter did it and it's only a matter of time until they make an arrest. Is that true?"

"I don't want to speculate."

Theresa broke away from the pack and kicked the ball at the goal. We held our collective breaths until the ball rolled out of bounds, wide of the mark. I hollered encouraging words to my niece, promising her she'd score next time.

"Come on, girlfriend. You're the Kickboxing Crusader. Where evil lurks, you're there. Right, Luke?" Sloane elbowed her husband in the ribs.

"Uh, yeah, I mean what Sloanie said. You're investigating, right? And swapping intel with Matt?" He rubbed his ribcage.

Sloane's elbows belonged on an FBI list of lethal weapons.

"No, she's not." Mom was watching the game, but we clearly had her attention, too. "In case you've all forgotten, she made a promise last fall to leave that kind of work to the police."

A player on the other team broke from the pack with the ball. He was a small boy, but way faster than anyone on the twins' team. In his yellow jersey, he was like a mini lightning bolt. His ball-handling skills proved he was the best player on the pitch, too. After three more kicks to keep the ball in front of him, he popped the ball past the Aces' goalkeeper with an effortless display of grace and skill.

"No problem, guys. You'll get it back." I clapped so hard my palms stung. The encouragement was important, but it also was a way to steer the conversation away from Mom's comment. What she didn't know wouldn't hurt her. She'd find out what I was up to soon enough.

At halftime, Luke and Mom went to the concession stand to get us popcorn and drinks. When they returned, my dear mother, whom I loved with all my heart, frowned when she handed me a drink.

"I just heard you spent most of the day at the library. In Vicky's office. Tell me you weren't lying to me earlier."

The can of Diet Coke hovered between us, the water droplets running down the can's exterior reflective of Mom's icy feelings toward me.

"Who told you this? I don't see Maybelle around anywhere."

"Don't get smart with me. Not about this." She gave the can a small shake. "I don't want to have to spray this all over you."

That broke the tension. Growing up, I was my father's daughter, thanks to the endless number of our common bookish interests. Because of that, my relationship with my mother had been more on the serious side. Since Dad had passed away, the relationship had morphed, in a good way, with more joking and affection shared between us.

"You got me, Sheriff." I put up my hands in surrender.

After sharing a laugh, I guided her to an area where we could talk without being heard. Once we were alone, I took a deep breath and spilled the beans.

When I was finished, she closed her eyes and shook her head. "Allie, Allie—"

"I know, Mom. It's not that I don't trust Matt. I do. This is something I have to do, though. For her."

"Your dad and I raised you to do three things. Make good choices, think for yourself, and follow your heart." She pulled me into a tight hug. "I'm so proud of you. Try not to end up in the hospital again, okay? My heart can't take that."

"I'll try my best."

We returned to the game in time to see one of the Aces score a goal to tie the score at one. Later, Theresa got another chance at a goal. This time her shot was true, and, after a few nail-biting minutes and an amazing save by the Aces' goalkeeper, the team in blue took the victory.

It was a wonderful way to end a difficult day. There was a new Greek restaurant in town, so Sloane and Luke invited me to join them for dinner so we could check it out. We stopped by the library to get Brent and chose a cozy booth close to a fireplace.

The burning logs in the hearth created a relaxing ambiance and took the edge off the chill from standing outside, cheering on the kids. In the mood to unwind, I ordered a bottle of wine and artichoke dip for an appetizer.

"Are you going to order our entrees, too?" Sloane stuck her tongue out at me.

"I'm transitioning to take-charge mode, my friend. It's what we superheroes do." I crinkled up my nose at her, grateful for our special friendship. Her free-spiritedness was good for my soul. I was a lucky woman.

While we dined, Sloane caught us up on her latest trail-running exploits. She'd finished second in her class at the national championships the previous fall. Our celebration of that feat had been exceeded only by the raucous reception at her and Luke's wedding a few weeks after the race. The fabulous result had her convinced she'd bring home the title of national champion this coming autumn.

I marveled at my bestie's metamorphosis over the last few years. She'd always been her true delightful self when it was just the two of us. For as long as I could remember, though, around others, she turned into an anxiety-ridden, nervous wreck.

The change began when her father, bestselling author and notorious drinker Thornwell Winchester, swore off alcohol in response to my dad's cancer diagnosis. When Thornwell got sober, he started treating Sloane with kindness and respect. They were emotions he'd rarely shown her in all the years she was growing up. He even made efforts to reconcile with his ex-wife, Kathryn. That inspired Sloane to repair her fraught relationship with the woman.

About the same time, Sloane and Luke started spending time together. Their relationship got more serious after first my dad, then her dad, died.

It was as if Sloane had been forced to navigate the depths of Hell and somehow made it through. Though still scarred from those battles, some of which went on for years, she emerged stronger, more confident, and more aware of those around her who truly loved her.

She was still the same old Sloane Winchester I'd known and loved all my life and would know and love the rest of my life. These days, though, she was happy and confident, both with herself and with those around her. It was heartwarming for everyone to get to know the Sloane Winchester I'd known for years.

Even if she did put me in my place a lot more than she used to.

While I was finishing the last of my gyro salad, Sloane leaned in close to me and whispered in my ear, "That guy that just came in, in the blue suit jacket, isn't that Mrs. Napier's ex?"

In as casual a manner as I could manage, I turned my head in the direction Sloane was nodding. I took in a little breath when I recognized the man who was being seated at a table near the entrance. It was, without a doubt, Gary Napier, Vicky's ex-husband.

I'd seen the man a dozen times over the years and only once since I'd moved from New York, but the shoulder-length blond hair that was parted down the middle, cleft chin, and crooked nose were unmistakable.

A knot formed in my stomach as the reason for his presence in town dawned on me. I took a long drink of my white wine while considering the consequences of his appearance.

"You might want to go easy on the vino." Brent took my empty glass and placed it on the table.

"Sorry, guys." I nodded toward Gary. "That's Vicky's ex-husband. Now that she's gone, he shows up. Coincidence? I don't think so."

"He looks vaguely familiar." Brent snapped his fingers. "He was at the library today. He signed the poster."

"Maybe he's in town to pay his respects," Luke said. "Not everything has to be a conspiracy, Allie."

He had a point. He hadn't been as close to Vicky as I'd been, though. The hurtful comments and whispered rumors during and after the divorce proceedings had extracted a toll on the woman Brent never saw.

During one of our late-night conversations, I'd asked Vicky why she and Gary split up. She told me Gary wanted kids. Vicky wanted kids, too. After ten years of trying, they'd had no success getting pregnant, though.

Testing proved the problem wasn't with Vicky. She was relieved, but he got angry and refused to be tested. Instead, he blamed her and demanded a divorce. Rumors spread that the breakup was due to everything from infidelity to financial misdeeds.

While those close to Vicky and Gary knew there was nothing to the rumors, they still stung. Gary left town a week after filing for divorce, which left Vicky to deal with the whisperings alone.

And now he was back.

"There's one way to find out why he's here." I got to my feet. "Order dessert. I'm going to have a chat with Mr. Napier."

I had no idea what I was going to say, but once I'd covered half the distance to his table, Gary looked up and made eye contact with me. It was too late to turn back now.

"Hi, Mr. Napier." I stuck out my hand as I introduced myself. "You probably don't remember me, but I spent a lot of time at the library with your ex-wife when I was growing up. I wanted to offer my condolences. May I join you?" Without waiting for a reply, I took the seat across from him.

"Thank you. It was a shock when Chief Roberson called me." He took a long drink of the beer the waiter had placed in front of him. "I still can't believe it."

"Indeed. It's very upsetting." I made a tiny circle in the white, linen tablecloth with my index finger. "So, at the risk of sounding indelicate, what brings you to town?"

"I get it." He chuckled, then drained his beer. "Ex-husband shows up a few days after the murder."

Keeping interrogation lessons learned from Matt in mind, I kept my mouth shut. Gary wasn't comfortable, and hopefully my silence would make it too tough for him to stay quiet.

"Allie Cobb. I remember Vicky going on about you. She got a kick out of how much you loved the library." He blew out a long breath. "Truth be told, I'm here because of the house. I want to make sure it isn't broken into or vandalized. Despite how things ended, we made some good memories there."

A lump formed in my throat. With Vicky's sister in Florida and her parents deceased, there were no family members nearby to look after her things. I wanted to hate the man, but, with this act of decency, I couldn't.

"That's very kind of you."

"Thanks. There was an oversight in the divorce settlement, so it turns out my name's still on the deed. Hopefully I'll be able to get it sold quickly. It would make a great home for a young family."

Or maybe not so kind of him. More like calculating. Or greedy. I handed him one of my business cards. "If you need help with anything, e-mail me. I'm happy to do whatever I can."

We said our goodbyes and I headed back to my table, thankful I always kept a couple of business cards in a pocket. Hopefully, he'd take me up on the offer. It would be a perfect way to keep tabs on him.

"Get anything good?" Sloane raised her eyebrows in anticipation of a juicy report.

"Maybe." I stabbed my fork into a piece of baklava and slid it into my mouth, pausing just long enough to savor the gooey sweetness. The paper-thin dough melted in my mouth, while the nuts provided a satisfying crunch. It was a bite of sugary paradise and exactly what I needed after the conversation with Gary.

I recounted my conversation as my fabulous dessert disappeared, bite by delectable bite. The more I talked, the situation seemed to grow increasingly shady, but I was trying to keep Luke's admonishment in mind.

"Okay, maybe I was wrong." Luke took a drink of water. "I'd bet that house is easily worth two hundred grand."

"Seriously? In Rushing Creek, Indiana?"

Vicky's house was beautiful, but that amount was jaw-dropping.

"I think that's a conservative number." Sloane wiped her fingers on a cloth napkin. "What are the three key factors in real estate? Location, location, location. That house is in a great, old neighborhood. It's got a good-sized lot and, with only one person living there, I'd bet Allie's apartment lease there hasn't been much wear and tear."

My bestie was in the final stages of selling her father's one-hundred-acre estate. Over the last year or so, she'd taken a deep dive in to the real estate world and had become quite knowledgeable about property values in the area. Her word was golden in my book.

"Okay, let me get this straight." Brent placed his hands on the tablecloth, spreading his long fingers out like a fan. "That guy over there divorced Vicky decades ago. He moved away. She got the house, but nobody got around to taking his name off the deed. Now, a couple of days after she's murdered, he shows up, ready to sell the house for at least two hundred thousand dollars. Does that sum things up?"

"Sounds about right," I said.

"And it sounds like a motive for murder that the Kickboxing Crusader needs to investigate." Sloane extended her fist toward me.

I bumped my knuckles against hers. "Things definitely aren't quite so cut and dried, are they? I've got work to do."

Chapter Eight

The following morning, I snuck out of bed without waking Brent. It was Sunday, which meant Mass, followed by brunch with Mom. It also meant my beau would be leaving town to return to his job today, so I wanted him to be well rested for his trip.

As I led Sammy by his leash down the stairs and out the door to a nearby grassy area, my heart was lighter than it had been in days. The thought of Brent getting a job here in Rushing Creek was more enticing than reading a Jane Austen novel by the window on a rainy day. And not just because I wouldn't feel compelled to take his canine outside and wait around for the pup to do his business while Brent snoozed away.

It meant we might have an actual future together. Brent's current job took him all over the State of Indiana, managing the installation of genealogy departments in public libraries of all sizes. His work was funded by a grant, so there was no shortage of libraries happy to retain his services.

While this was great for library patrons all the way from Angola in northeast Indiana to Evansville in the southwestern part of the state, it left Brent and me with two serious challenges. First, the short-term nature of the installations meant he only spent a few weeks in any city or town before moving to the next. It was a transient lifestyle that suited Brent well since he had no attachments beyond Sammy.

It was a lifestyle that, to me, was as appealing as fresh roadkill. I loved my job, my apartment, and my hometown. More than that, after spending almost a decade on my own in New York City, I appreciated how fortunate I was to have family and friends nearby. I didn't want to give that up for a life that was basically living out of a suitcase.

The second issue was even thornier. With every installation Brent completed, his waiting list grew shorter. When we met, he'd completed work for about one third of the libraries in the state. Now, he was finished with over half of those interested. We'd spent one evening discussing his future and reached an unavoidable conclusion.

At his current pace, Brent would work himself out of a job in about three years.

What would he do then? Take his program to another state? The grant only provided funding for Indiana, so that option was filled with uncertainty. He could apply to work at a library, but with his Ph.D. in library science, finding a position to fit his skillset might not be easy.

Now, here we were. While it was under the worst of circumstances, depending on how the library board chose to proceed, there might be a job opportunity here in Rushing Creek for Brent.

If he did apply, and if he was offered the job, what would he do about his current commitments? I knew the man well enough to know he wouldn't quit without making sure someone was lined up to take over his genealogy installation work. How long would it take to find a replacement his funders would approve? So many questions remained unanswered. Well, nobody said life was easy.

Man, talk about it being the best of times and the worst of times.

As I threw the plastic bag containing Sammy's droppings into the dumpster behind my building, a disturbing thought stopped me short. If my investigation into Gary Napier led Matt into doubting Porter's guilt, would the police chief move Brent into the suspect column again? After all, it wasn't unreasonable for one to consider a steady job a prime motive for murder.

I shook my head. Brent was innocent, beyond a doubt. And if Matt wanted to put him under the microscope again? I'd deal with that possibility when, and if, it came to pass.

Once back inside, I settled down on the couch with my laptop and a cup of coffee. I had an hour before I had to get ready to meet Mom at church, so sixty minutes of peace and quiet would be perfect to start editing a client's manuscript. With Sammy on the seat cushion next to me and Ursi lurking over my shoulder, I got lost in a thrilling world of espionage and money laundering with the Andes Mountains for a backdrop.

A while later, my phone beeped to let me know my editing time was up. With a grumble, I shut down the computer, gave each of my furry friends solid scratches behind the ears, and headed for the shower.

While I was in the bathroom, I put my thoughts about Vicky's murder into order. Porter was the obvious prime suspect. That couldn't be disputed. He'd gotten to the library before any other potential witnesses, so he had the opportunity. If he truly had dangerous plants in his greenhouse, he had the means. And if he was obsessed with Vicky, as some people believed, he had the motive.

As Dad liked to say, "if" was the biggest two letter word in the English language. So, if Porter wasn't the murderer, who was? Ozzy? It seemed like a stretch to me, but, to him, maybe five thousand dollars was an amount worthy of committing murder. The means and opportunity seemed to be lacking, though. Well, I'd talk to Shirley first. Based on how that conversation went, I'd figure out what to do next.

My third suspect, Gary Napier, had motive in spades. A few minutes of research at the county assessor's office would confirm Gary's claim about the home's ownership status. If his name was on the deed, that left him in line to receive all the proceeds from the sale of the house.

Another thought popped into my head as I worked shampoo into my hair. Did Vicky have a will? If so, who was in line to inherit her estate? If she didn't have a will, her estate would have to go through probate. What would be involved with that? I'd have to ask Jeanette about a will and keep my fingers crossed one could be found. That would sure make things a little simpler.

As I rinsed off the shampoo, I ruminated over Gary's means and opportunity. Just because he claimed he came to town after the call with Matt didn't make it true. What if he was having money problems and saw the house as his way out of debt? Until I established his whereabouts the day of Vicky's murder, I couldn't rule him out.

Matt might not have been willing to completely rule out Brent, but I was. I knew Brent as well as I knew anyone outside my immediate family and Sloane. He said he didn't do it. I believed him one hundred percent. It was simply a matter of time until Matt confirmed his indisputable innocence.

That left me with three credible suspects. While I got dressed, I formulated a plan. Since all signs pointed at Porter, I'd focus on him first.

I dillydallied on my way to church so I could join Mom just in time to grab a spot and sit. She hugged me when I reached the top step of the building's entrance but was frowning.

I wasn't out of her doghouse.

"I haven't had to call you from the hospital yet. That's a good thing, right?" I scrunched up my nose and crossed my eyes.

Mom rolled her eyes. Mission accomplished at diffusing her frustration with me.

"You, my dear little one, should be the poster child of why a parent never stops worrying." She put her arm through mine. "Shall we ask for some divine intervention?"

Since I was back in investigator mode, I made a point of scanning the pews to see who else was attending Mass. I never knew when something important would catch my attention, so I was always in observation mode. That was one benefit of the attention to detail Dad had ingrained in me from a young age.

Or maybe it was a curse. Sometimes, it was hard to tell.

None of my suspects were in attendance. That didn't mean much, since a half dozen churches could be found within a mile of my apartment. Porter and Ozzy could be members of another denomination, and Gary didn't even live here anymore.

With nobody to keep an eye on, I cleared my mind and spent the hour-long service meditating. I also asked Dad for the divine intervention Mom mentioned. I was pretty sure I was going to need all the help I could get.

When Mass was over, Mom and I went to the Brown County Diner for brunch. The place was buzzing with the after-church crowd, which was normal. What wasn't normal was being served coffee by the mayor herself, Angela Miller.

Angela owned the diner and ran it with her husband, Claude. For years he supervised the kitchen while she oversaw the dining room. Many scoffed when she ran for mayor because she put in so many hours at the diner. There was no way she would put the community above her business, they said. And then when she was elected mayor, a lot of those same naysayers wondered how she would cope juggling two full-time jobs.

In my book, she was handling both jobs with the skill and aplomb of Phryne Fisher, the fictional Australian detective. She did this by limiting her work at the diner to weekends. During the week, and after the diner closed on Saturday and Sunday, she put on her mayor hat. Friends and family had stepped in to fill her shoes at the restaurant, but it was always reassuring to see her in her light blue shirt and white apron, a pot of coffee in one hand and an order pad in the other.

"What can I get you ladies on this fine morning?" Angela poured us each a cup of coffee and left the pot on the table. The woman knew me.

"Can you tell us when Chief Roberson plans to arrest Mr. Rasmussen?" Mom stared at me as she poured sweetener in her coffee.

Patience, Allie. She wants to keep you safe.

"I wish I could." Angela shook her head. "What an awful thing. Vicky was such a kind woman, and Porter, well..."

"Well what?" My clue radar rocketed up to eleven. If anyone outside of the police had information, it would be the mayor.

"Slow your roll, Allie. He's a good man and deserves a thorough and impartial investigation. Enough of this unpleasant talk. What are you having for breakfast?"

We gave her our orders. Western omelet for Mom and a Belgian waffle with a side of turkey bacon for me.

While we waited, Mom filled me in on her latest activities. She'd struggled, both emotionally and physically, after Dad passed away. Over the past few months, though, she seemed to have found her footing again, as evidence that she hadn't misplaced her car keys since Luke and Sloane hosted a Super Bowl party.

"I have some news." Her cheeks got red as she stirred her coffee. "You have to promise you won't say anything to Luke and Rachel, okay?"

"Deal." I kept my voice neutral.

Mom didn't like to confide in one of her kids at the exclusion of the others. As a family physician, she'd spent her career earning the trust of her patients by being honest. If you created a Venn diagram of Mom and secrets, the circles wouldn't come within a mile of each other.

"After the game yesterday, I went to dinner with Rachel and the kiddos. While we were waiting to be seated, a gentleman struck up a conversation with me." She smiled. "He asked me if I'd like to meet him for a cup of coffee."

"OMG, seriously? What did you say?"

Dad had been the love of Mom's life. They'd been more passionate about each other with each passing year. The fact she'd go out on a date with someone else had never occurred to me. Sure, I wanted her to be happy, but I wasn't ready for this.

"Told him I'd think about it." She took a drink of her coffee, never breaking eye contact with me. "After I got his number."

"Mom." Now my cheeks were getting hot. My dear, widowed mother was becoming part of the dating scene. Maybe. It was inconceivable.

"Don't 'Mom' me. You and your brother have been after me for months to get out of the house more often. Well, this may be a chance to do just that."

"Did Rachel see you talking with this man? What did she say?"

"That it was nobody's business but my own." She shrugged. "Maybe you could take a lesson from your sister when it comes to discretion, yeah?"

Angela delivered our meals, which gave me time to regroup. Mom was right. Luke and I had made suggestions to make sure she didn't spend every evening alone with nothing to keep her company but Sudoku puzzles and her thoughts. This was about her, not me, after all.

"You know we want you to be happy, right? If having coffee with this guy makes you happy, go for it."

Mom's shoulders dropped and her jaw unclenched. She smiled, too.

Then it hit me. She wanted my approval, or at least my acceptance. Given how joined at the hip Dad and I had been, it was reasonable to assume I'd be the most resistant to Mom having another man in her life.

She was right.

Nobody would replace Walter Cobb, literary agent, hero, father. But he was gone. To deny Mom the opportunity for some happiness, even something as simple as having a cup of coffee with someone, was wrong. It wasn't only wrong, it was selfish. I didn't want to be selfish.

I cut into my waffle. As steam rose and tickled my nostrils, I gave Mom a long look. "Do I know this man? What's his name? How old is he? What are his intentions? Does he know you have a daughter who's a superhero known as the Kickboxing Crusader?"

Mom covered her mouth with her hand to prevent omelet being sprayed all over the table. Once she swallowed, she let out a long laugh. I joined her and reached across the table to give her hand a squeeze.

Moments like these were magical. I'd had countless of them with Dad over the years. With Mom, not as often. Since his passing, they were becoming more common, and I treasured each one of them. It filled me with joy to have one now.

Mom ignored my questions and started talking about the twins' next game. I wasn't letting her off the hook that easily.

"Ahem, it's rude to ignore someone when they've asked you a question. You taught me that."

"I did." She chewed on a forkful of omelet and gazed around the room as if she hadn't a care in the world. At this point, she was torturing me on purpose.

"So?"

She put down her fork. "Patience, little one. For now, I choose not to answer. I haven't said yes, after all."

She was good, maybe a little too good for my comfort level.

"Fine. I'll get my answers from Rachel. She'll tell me." It was my last play, and I was desperate.

"Don't bother. She was busy with Tristan and Theresa when my friend and I were chatting. She's more in the dark than you are."

Checkmate.

"Well done." I lifted my coffee cup to her. "I accept defeat. For now."

After breakfast, Mom and I readied to go our separate ways. She was taking the twins into Columbus to see the latest hit animated film. Then they were going to her house to make homemade pizza. While T and T loved spending time with their grandma, it also gave Rachel a break from the pressures of single motherhood. It was a win for everyone.

I gave Mom a hug and admonished her not to eat too much popcorn and spoil her appetite.

My walk home gave me the alone time I needed to ponder Mom's news. On the one hand, I had enough going on in my own life. I didn't want to think about Mom creating a profile on an online dating site. Or downing shots with the senior singles club that met once a month at Hoosiers, the local sports bar. Or taking a bus trip with a bunch of silver tigers for a weekend trip to a casino for gambling and who knew what else.

The string of troubling visions made me shudder. I'd deal with Mom as an eligible woman when, and if, I had to. Not a nanosecond before.

For now, I had more pressing issues on my plate. Like figuring out what I was going to say to the murder suspect I was going to be visiting in a few hours.

Chapter Nine

When I got home from my morning with Mom. I found a note from Brent. He had a few things he wanted to do at the library and would be back by five. Sammy's dog crate was empty. It wouldn't be surprising if I found out Brent had taken his four-legged buddy to the library to serve as a therapy dog of sorts.

"Just you and me this afternoon. Let's see how much we can get done." I gave Ursi a couple of kitty treats and returned to my laptop. Work to pay the bills first. Work to catch a killer second.

Two hours later, I hit send on an e-mail to a client regarding the manuscript I'd been editing. Overall, the story was strong, but I wanted a stronger motivation behind the protagonist's choice to put her life on the line.

The irony of making that request wasn't lost on me.

Relieved that I had at least a modicum of self-awareness, I fetched Ursi's harness and leash.

"Up for a little sleuthing?"

The cat trotted to the door then sat and stared at me with unblinking eyes, radiating an aura of impatience. She was ready for action.

The sky was the color of dull slate as we exited my building. A breeze from the north had grown in force, too. Rain was on the way. I flipped up the collar of my jacket. If we were lucky, we'd be back home before the showers arrived. Man, I was getting tired of lousy weather.

I'd never visited Porter's house before. With his years in the hardware business, I'd assumed it would be flawless. When Ursi and I rounded a bend in the road and my gaze fell upon the home in question, my assumption was confirmed.

The Rasmussen home was an A-frame structure with cedar shingles and redwood siding. A split-rail fence ran along the perimeter of the property. There was an opening in the fencing big enough for an impressive path of flagstone pavers that ran from the sidewalk to the front step. Flower beds lined either side of the path. A soft glow emanated from a lamp in the front window.

As if a director had asked for increased tension, the wind died down, leaving the clicks of Ursi's claws on the stone the only sound.

"Here goes nothing, girl." For good luck, I picked up Ursi and pressed a front paw against the button for the doorbell. A booming *ding-dong-ding* made Ursi pin her ears back flat as I stepped backward. It was so loud I wondered, for a moment, if Porter was hard of hearing.

When there was no answer after a couple of minutes, I was ready to admit defeat and head home. I was turning away from the door when it opened with a quiet *whoosh*.

"Miss Cobb, this is a surprise." Porter removed dirt-covered work gloves and offered to shake hands.

"Please, call me Allie." Sweat broke out on my brow as the man stared at me, brushing spots of dirt from his gray sweatshirt. "I wanted to stop by. To see how you're doing with…you know, everything going on."

"You mean being accused of poisoning the town's beloved librarian?" He looked at Ursi, who was sniffing the air. "I was working in the greenhouse. You're welcome to join me if you aren't afraid of being murdered."

"Of course not." A nervous laugh escaped as I scratched Ursi under her chin. "Is it okay if my cat, Ursula, comes along?"

"By all means."

A scent of spiced potpourri tickled my senses as we followed him through the living room. It was painted a shade of yellow that called to mind an early morning sunrise. Framed photographs of flowers hung on the walls, the colors so vibrant I wanted to reach out and caress the petals. Gardening magazines were stacked on an end table next to a burgundy recliner.

From there, we passed into the kitchen. Stainless steel appliances coordinated with black, granite countertops to give the room a classy feel. The black-and-white checkerboard tile was spotless.

As we exited through the back doorway, I was left with a singular impression of Porter's home. It was stylish but not ostentatious. Contemporary yet timeless.

There were also no dishes in the sink, no unopened mail on the kitchen island. Nothing was out of place. As much as I liked the décor, I couldn't help but wonder whether Porter was obsessive when it came to keeping house.

If so, was he obsessive about anything else?

The backyard belonged on the cover of *Better Homes and Gardens*. A greenhouse stood in one corner of the yard. A wooden shed painted deep forest green occupied another corner. In the center of the yard, an ornate stone birdbath gave the local avian population a place to get a drink.

The grass had a newly mown smell and a healthy, vibrant green color. A glance over my shoulder toward the house brought me to a halt.

"You even have roses?" Flower beds on either side of the back door contained a half-dozen rose bushes.

We stared at the bare, thorny bushes. In a few months, they'd no doubt be bursting with glorious petals in shades from red to white to maybe even yellow.

"My wife was named Rose. I grew them in her honor." He wiped something from his eye as his voice caught. "She loved the smell but was wary of the thorns. She was always encouraging me to figure out a way to grow thornless roses. I never managed to pull off a completely thornless rosebush."

How could a man so devoted to his wife that he grew flowers dedicated to her be a murderer? Like an incomplete sentence fragment, the idea didn't make sense. Then again, if he cared for someone so much that he was willing to tend to a high-maintenance and prickly flower, maybe over-the-top obsession wasn't out of the question.

Porter cleared his throat. He was at the greenhouse's doorway with his bushy, gray eyebrows raised. Evidently, while I'd been gawking at the bare rose bushes, he'd moved on. After a quick look at Ursi to make sure she wasn't doing anything untoward in the yard, I gave her leash a gentle tug and double-timed it to catch up with him.

The greenhouse was made entirely of glass. I tapped on a pane to make sure. Metal strips connected the panes, which were about two square feet in size. Ornamental stone pavers lined the bottom edge of the structure, which gave it a clean, finished touch.

We strolled down the middle of the structure. Raised, wooden planter beds about four feet in height ran along each side of us from the front to the back of the building. Above us, potted ferns so green they'd make St. Patrick proud hung from hooks bolted to the metal connecting strips.

To my right, three orchids were in full bloom. I ran my fingers across one of the flower's delicate petals. It was as white as fine bone china. "They're beautiful."

Ursi gave a bossy *meow*, so I picked her up and let her sniff the flowers.

Her tiny nostrils flared back and forth as a paw reached toward the plant. I pulled her away and set her back down, my cheeks warming at the thought of my cat damaging one of his gorgeous plants.

"Sorry about that. I guess she liked it. Didn't want her to get her claws or teeth into it. I've heard orchids are poisonous to pets."

Porter bent over and offered his palm to Ursi. After she gave it a sniff, she rubbed her head against his knuckles and plopped down at his feet. With a chuckle, he scratched her between the ears.

"That's not really true. This is a moth orchid, which is perfectly safe. There are some varieties of orchid that would leave Miss Ursula with an upset tummy, but that's about it. No harm, no foul." He straightened up and slipped his gloves back on. "I hope you don't mind if I work while we talk. What can I do for you?"

"I wanted to see how you're holding up. I know what it's like being accused of taking someone's life. How frightening that is."

"Ah, yes. Georgie Alonso." Using a hand spade, he stabbed at the black soil and turned it over. "Nasty business, but some might say he got what was coming to him."

I took a step back. Sure, it was no secret Georgie had been a louse, but, in my book, it was bad manners to speak ill of the dead. Was that a sign Porter was callous enough to be a murderer? Maybe. Time to try a different line of questioning.

"I heard the police think Vicky was poisoned."

"Indeed." He pulled some seedlings from a flat and worked them into the soil he'd turned. "And that, my friend, is why Occam's razor puts me in a difficult position."

Occam's razor. I sidled along an edge of one of the planter boxes for a better look around while I dredged up the term from the cobweb-filled crannies of my college years. After a minute of concentration, and not seeing anything suspicious, I snapped my fingers.

"It's the principle in problem solving that says the simplest solution to a problem is usually the right one. The fewer assumptions you have to make, the better."

While I basked in my moment of victory, Porter nudged Ursi away from a partially covered pile of roots near his feet. He adjusted the tarp to cover them completely.

"Exactly. I was at the library before you were. Thanks to my career, I have easy access to poisonous materials. Only two assumptions are needed for Chief Roberson to decide I'm the killer."

The matter-of-fact way Porter stated the case against him made me shudder. It was cold and analytical. There was no emotion, as if he was resigned to a fate as a convicted murderer.

Why was I here, then? If Porter was convinced he was going to be convicted of murdering Vicky, wasn't that game, set, and match?

No. Forget Occam's razor. If I'd learned anything since my return home from New York, it was that things weren't always what they seemed. There was more to this story. I felt it in my bones.

"If you don't mind me asking, what poisonous materials do you have access to these days?" I picked up Ursi, who had settled down on the tarp and was grooming herself. All this talk of poisons made me worried for her safety. Or maybe I was paranoid. Probably a little of both.

"Some of the flowers I grow may be poisonous when ingested in sufficient quantities." He stabbed another area of soil and worked it until he seemed satisfied it was ready to be home to more flowers.

Intriguing. "If they're poisonous, why do you grow them?" I moved to the center of the aisle, just to be sure. No sense in taking a chance of getting something harmful on my clothes.

He sighed and leaned on the planter box, looking me straight in the eyes. "Many reasons, actually. Azaleas are potentially harmful. They were also Vicky's favorite flower. I grew them for her. Monkshood is another. The vibrant blue coloring of the flower has won me a few awards at the county fair. They're not harmful in and of themselves. In fact, you can buy both of these specimens at any decent garden center."

Porter's passion for his plants came through loud and clear. It made sense, too. Vicky liked a particular flower. He wanted her to like him, so he grew that flower. By the same token, he always entered his flowers in the county 4-H fair. If a particular flower increased his odds of winning, it was logical to grow it.

Everything fit. Again.

"You don't seem to be working very hard to prove your innocence."

He pointed the spade at me like a weapon. "What would you have me do? Parade up and down in front of the municipal building with a megaphone shouting at anyone who will listen I didn't do it? I cared for Vicky. I wouldn't want to hurt her."

His hands dropped to his sides as he shook his head. "I've told the chief I'm innocent and hired a lawyer. My kids believe me. I have faith in the legal system. Beyond that, it's in God's hands."

Porter returned to his work. With his back to me, the message was as clear as the building's glass tiles. Our conversation was over.

J.C. Kenney

I thanked him for his time and made a quiet exit.

On the walk home, I tried to make sense of the enigma that was Porter Rasmussen. One moment he was Henry Jekyll, and the next he was Edward Hyde. While the mood swings were unnerving, I could empathize with what he was going through. He'd lost the object of his affection and then was accused of committing the crime.

That was a devastating one-two punch.

Did it clear him of murder, though? While Ursi and I waited at a four-way stop, the answer was obvious.

No.

It was the pile of roots he covered with the tarp that bothered me. Porter hadn't seemed to mind Ursi sniffing at other plants. Were those roots dangerous, like the azaleas and monkshood he mentioned? If so, how could a prosecutor prove the poison used to kill Vicky came from one of them? I needed to figure out a way to get my hands on some samples.

As we crossed the street, an encouraging thought popped into my head. Maybe, in this case, the Occam's razor theory did apply. Maybe Porter was the murderer and I wouldn't have to go snooping around town, desperate to dig up clues, to build a case.

I blew out a long tension-releasing breath. With everything else I had going on, a quick, simple investigation sounded pretty good. If only things were ever that easy.

Chapter Ten

Brent's truck was nowhere to be seen when we reached my building. My heart swelled at the thought of how much my beau cared for the library and the community. And he wasn't even a Rushing Creek resident.

Yet.

At the top of the stairs, I looked at my bike. A thin layer of dust covered the seat. Ursi sniffed at cobwebs that had formed between the spokes of the rear wheel. I hadn't been out on my two-wheeled steed in over a week.

"I'm slacking, girl. Where does the time go?"

Ursi looked up and rubbed a cobweb from her nose. I laughed as I took a picture of her cleaning efforts. Life was never boring with her.

I took a minute to wipe the dust off the seat, and the cat, and we headed into the apartment. I poured Ursi an extra serving of dry food. It had been a long walk, and I had to jump out of her way when she attacked the bowl.

Pleased that we'd gotten home without getting rained on and that my kitty wasn't going to die from malnutrition, I wrote down some observations of my chat with Porter. The big takeaway from my visit was a question. Did Porter's knowledge of poisonous plants mean he was the murderer?

The clock brought my musings to an end. It was half past four. The library closed at five, so Brent would be home soon. We hadn't had nearly enough quality time since I returned from the conference. I could change that, though, and went to the kitchen.

I lagged way behind Brent when it came to culinary skills. The man was an absolute wizard in the kitchen and could turn a can of chunk chicken, dry pasta, and frozen veggies into a gourmet feast.

Me, not so much. It wasn't that I couldn't cook. To me, cooking for one was more trouble than it was worth. I usually ended up with more leftovers than I wanted, and I felt bad throwing out stuff I never got around to eating.

During the last holiday season, I'd whined to Rachel how envious I was of her kitchen talents. After reminding me she spent countless hours around food because of her job, she agreed to give me cooking lessons.

Now was a chance to put those lessons to the test.

By the time Brent and Sammy arrived, I had a red sauce simmering in a pot, glazed chicken breasts and jasmine rice in the oven, and green beans grilling in a skillet.

"Wow." Brent hugged me from behind and kissed me on the neck. "Smells amazing. To what do I owe such a feast?"

"I wanted to do something nice before you go." I gave him a spoon to sample the sauce. "What do you think?"

He dipped the spoon into the sauce then brought it to his nose. "Nice smoky aroma with a hint of chipotle seasoning."

"Yes." I bounced up and down on my tiptoes. It made my day when he recognized the seasonings I'd used.

He put the spoon in his mouth and closed his eyes. After a few moments, while my heart stopped beating, he put his hand over his heart. "That is the best sauce I've tasted in ages. Brava."

My heart soared. While I hadn't discussed my cooking lessons with Brent, he was aware of them.

He was also appreciative and encouraging without being condescending. When I got something right, he told me what he liked about it and why. When I missed the mark, he offered constructive criticism, discussing what I'd done that resulted in a less-than-satisfactory result. Then he'd offer suggestions to avoid those letdowns in the future.

He didn't offer false praise, which was fine in my book. I wanted to become a good cook, both for him as well as for myself. When he complimented my cooking, I'd earned it, which left me as euphoric as when Dorothy made it back home to Kansas.

When he was finished sampling, Brent set the table and got drinks. I arranged our meals on stoneware plates I'd purchased from one of the artisans in town. Once I was satisfied with the meal's presentation, I posted a picture on social media. My colleagues back in New York City wouldn't believe it without proof.

After giving Ursi and Sammy a few morsels of the chicken, I took a seat at the kitchen table with a satisfied sigh. During difficult times like these, I needed to enjoy the happy moments.

As he poured the sauce over his chicken and rice, Brent filled me in on the latest at the library. Two of the employees were going to take on more hours so the library could maintain its regular schedule. While it was only a short-term solution, the goal was to ensure patrons saw as little change as possible.

Also, a posting for a head librarian would go up at the end of the week. Evidently, the five library board members were unanimous in their belief that it would be inappropriate to open the job for applications without giving the town some time to mourn Vicky's passing.

"What's that mean for you?" A twinge of regret dashed through me as I munched on some roasted green beans. My question might have seemed cold or calculating, but the fact was Brent was eminently qualified for the position, he knew the staff, and was well thought of in the community. If I couldn't have my beloved Mrs. Napier back, I wanted Brent running the library.

"I'll have to submit my resume just like anyone else. The board knows about my interest in the position." He shrugged as he chewed on a piece of chicken. "Hopefully, the past few days showed them what I can do. If it doesn't help, that's fine. Sticking around was the right thing to do."

My heart went out to him. Brent and Vicky had become friends. Losing her was hurting him, too. The composure he'd shown these past few days was inspiring. Hopefully, it hadn't gone unnoticed.

"Have you shared that Vicky told you she wanted you to take over for her?"

"I brought it up with a couple of the board members today. They didn't know anything. That confirms Vicky never said anything to them."

I sagged back into my chair. Brent had been so excited Vicky had wanted him to succeed her. Yet nobody but him knew of her wishes. Sure, he could tell people that's what she wanted, but who would believe him?

And if he revealed the conversation, what would the community and, more importantly, the police think? At best, it seemed like an opportunistic gambit to get the inside track to a position he coveted. At worst, it could renew suspicions that perhaps Brent knew more about Vicky's demise than he'd been letting on.

I knew better, but other people didn't.

"What about Freddie? She's the board president, after all. Seems like if Vicky was going to tell someone, Freddie would have been the first one." I let a piece of chicken melt in my mouth. Between the excellent results of my cooking and the suggestion about Freddie, my adrenaline kicked in. I leaned forward and raised my eyebrows, confident I'd just provided the key to Brent's dilemma.

He shook his head. "She was at the restaurant all day. The other board members said they'd talk to her about it. I'm not hopeful, though."

I gave his hand a squeeze. "No big deal. I'll see if I can get over to Marinara's tomorrow and talk to her."

With that issue settled, Brent asked me about my visit with Porter. While we finished dinner, I gave him a detailed report, even checking my notes to make sure I didn't miss anything. As we cleared the table, I asked him what he thought.

"His knowledge of poisonous plants definitely makes him look more like the murderer." He was silent while he loaded the plates and utensils into the dishwasher. "Do you think the police have a sample of those dead plants you mentioned? I can't imagine he'd be dumb enough to keep his source materials around, but you never know, right?"

"Right." I pulled out my phone and called Matt, chuckling at the fact I had the Rushing Creek Police Chief on speed dial. What an odd history I'd had with my former brother-in-law over the past couple of years.

He answered after the first ring. "What now, Allie?"

"Brent needs to head home tonight." I winked at my boyfriend. "He wants to talk to you before he goes. To make sure the two of you are on the same page."

Matt's world-weary sigh seemed overly dramatic, but he promised he'd be there in ten minutes.

Then again, I couldn't criticize the man in good conscience since I was luring him to the apartment on false pretenses. I didn't want him to blow us off when we brought up the plants in Porter's greenhouse. It would be much tougher for him to do so in person.

By the time Matt knocked on the door, we had a plan. First came the snickerdoodles I'd baked for dessert.

I offered him some cookies while he and Brent got situated at the table. He raised an eyebrow but accepted them.

"Thanks for coming by, Chief." Brent inhaled a snickerdoodle. They were his favorite. "I wanted to make sure you were okay with me leaving town tonight."

Matt opened his trusty notebook. "I'll need your phone number and a work address and phone number there." He scribbled down the information Brent recited. "Oh, and next of kin in case I can't reach you."

Brent blinked twice. "Is that really necessary? I mean, can't Allie vouch for me that I won't leave the country or anything."

"Until I can completely rule you out, yes, it's necessary." Matt rubbed his forehead. "Besides, it's protocol and I don't want to be accused of playing favorites."

"If you insist." He gave Matt the contact information for his parents, who lived in Cincinnati. "You won't call them unless you have to, right?" He nodded as he ate a bite of cookie. "What else do you want to tell me, Allie?"

"Oh." My cheeks got hot. The question was unexpected and had me on the defensive. "What makes you think there's anything else?"

Matt leaned back in his chair until the front two legs were off the ground. "Come on, guys. A little credit please? I am a cop, after all."

He eased the chair back so all four legs were touching the hardwood floor. "Brent could have given me all of this information over the phone. And while the cookies are good, I know when someone wants to talk in person. So, spill it so I can get out of here early enough to see the kids before they go to bed."

"I went to see Porter today."

Using my notebook once again, to make sure I didn't miss anything, I recounted my visit. My goal was to have the narrative stick to the facts. Matt could draw his own conclusions. I had mine already.

"We executed a search warrant at Porter's property yesterday." While he finished his cookie, Matt flipped through his notebook. "There wasn't a pile of dead flowers in the greenhouse when my team searched it."

We were silent for a moment as the information sank in, the only sound coming from Sammy as he snored his way through a nap.

"So, you're saying he didn't do it, then?" Brent drummed his fingers on his thigh. I sympathized with my boyfriend's distress.

"Take a deep breath before you hyperventilate, Brent. I'm not saying anything like that." Matt bent over to scratch Ursi's ears. "What I am saying is Porter's knowledge of plants is relevant. Could he have used something he grew to poison Vicky? It's possible."

"But the other day you said she was poisoned." Brent removed his glasses and rubbed his forehead.

"I did. And she was. Toxicology takes time, though. Until I get the test results, I won't know what substance was used."

"What's next, then?" With my hopes for a simple, open-and-shut case disappearing as fast as the plate of cookies, I wanted to know how Matt planned to proceed. I'd come up with my own plan, but knowledge was power. And knowing the chief's course of action was very powerful.

"Don't worry. We're not just going to sit back and wait for the test results. We have a few other leads we're following up on."

"Great. Why don't you tell me what they are, and I'll help." I flipped to a blank page in my notebook. It was white, with "The Cobb Literary Agency" and the website address inscribed in Kelly green. I'd given away dozens at the conference. Every time somebody took one, I gave myself an imaginary high five.

Matt pushed back his chair. "I don't think so."

"Why not?" My protest carried an undercurrent of righteous indignation as I got to my feet.

"The mayor has asked me, in the interest of keeping you safe, not to share information regarding any ongoing investigations with you." He stood, using his entire twelve-inch height advantage over me to make his point clear. "Before you hunt her down and give her a piece of your mind, think for a second. She cares about you. She doesn't want you to get hurt. I don't want you to get hurt, either."

"Same here." Brent looked me in the eyes and held my gaze until I looked out the window.

Matt put his hand on my shoulder. "We all know you won't stop looking into this. Be careful, okay?"

I returned my gaze to him and nodded.

He gave my shoulder a friendly punch, like when we were kids. "Tell you what. I'll pay Porter a visit and see if I can get a look at those plants. I'll have Jeanette investigate the flower breeds you mentioned. It can't hurt getting up to speed in case they turn up in the toxicology report."

I walked Matt down the stairs and out of the building to have a word with him alone. Our conversation had, no doubt, frustrated Brent and I didn't want him any more agitated with a three-hour drive ahead of him.

"Level with me, Matt. What's your gut tell you?"

He removed his Rushing Creek Police Department baseball cap and ran his fingers through his hair. Gray strands, each one a reminder of the pressures he lived under as a policeman and a father, shone in the light cast by the streetlamps.

"My gut tells me Porter did it. My head tells me not to listen to my gut. Regardless, we'll catch the killer. Fair enough?"

"Yeah, fair enough." I went back inside.

I ascended the stairs at a languid pace so I had time to make sure I had a big smile for Brent. He deserved a positive sendoff, not one to give him worry-filled, sleepless nights.

Determined to exude a positive vibe, I put the rest of the cookies in a plastic bag and hummed an upbeat jazz tune Brent liked as I helped him gather his things. He was a light traveler, so the biggest challenge was breaking down Sammy's crate while the doggo kept trying to get in the middle of our labor.

"He doesn't want to leave. I don't want to, either."

I wrapped my arms around Brent and gave him a kiss. "I don't want you to leave either. Everything'll work out fine. Promise."

I refused to let him go until he gave me a genuine smile. When he was ready to go, I walked him to his truck. Sammy jumped into the cab the moment the driver's door was opened, but Brent hesitated.

"I'm going to hit you up on Skype every night at seven. If you don't answer, I'm getting in the truck and driving here. You're too—"

I cut him off by grabbing his jacket and pulling him in to a long kiss.

"I'll be fine. You can help me out by having your resume ready to go when the job is posted." I gave him a friendly pat on his backside. "Now get going. I want you home before it gets too late."

"Yes, ma'am." He saluted, then gave me another kiss. As the truck rumbled to life, he lowered the window. "Seven o'clock. Every night. Be there or be square."

"Whatever, nerd." I blew him a kiss as the truck pulled away.

It was reassuring that Brent was more worried about my safety than I was.

My footfalls echoed on the concrete as I walked back to the building's front door. Ghostly images formed in the bookstore's window, making the hair on the back of my neck stand on end.

Once inside, I leaned against the door and wiped a bead of sweat from my brow. Maybe I was more distressed than I wanted to admit. As I climbed the stairs, I hoped I was wrong about that.

Chapter Eleven

The next day, the alarm clock rattled me out of bed at six. A new work week meant a jam-packed schedule, and then some. I started the day with a thirty-minute kickboxing session to sharpen my mind and get the blood flowing.

While I cooled down after the workout, I started a pot of coffee and made an omelet with peppers and mushrooms. At Sloane's urging, and with Rachel's guidance, I was making more healthy choices when I cooked for myself.

It was especially hard in the morning, because I loved simple things like bagels slathered with cream cheese and mixed fruit. Sadly, the carbs and sugars those kinds of meals contained were stark reminders that I couldn't eat like I was still in college. Thank goodness for Rachel's lessons, which were helping me eat low-sugar and fresh meals whenever possible.

The Rushing Creek farmer's market wouldn't open for another few weeks, but the grocery had fresh produce, which Rachel had assured me was of excellent quality. The thought that I might be turning into a food snob now that I was in my thirties made me laugh.

"No food snob here. Just trying to stay healthy so I can take care of you, little girl." I picked up a yawning Ursi and danced with her over to her food bowl.

She responded to my antics by letting out an annoyed *rowr* and pushing away from me with her leg.

She could act standoffish all she wanted. The way she rubbed her head against my leg before attacking her breakfast of diced chicken chunks told me all I needed to know.

Over breakfast, I responded to e-mails that had stacked up over the weekend. As crazy as the upcoming week was threatening to be, I needed to stay on top of work.

Once my tummy was full, I hit the shower. I got dressed in a teal, cable-knit sweater Rachel had given to me for my birthday and black yoga pants. The outfit was comfortable and looked nice. The sweater's bright color made me think of spring and made me feel I could take on the world.

Monday was my day to check on the status of queries. Editors responded to my queries, which typically consisted of an e-mail to the editor, along with a synopsis of the book and a series proposal if the author was writing a series, on their own individual schedules. The usual response was either a request for the full manuscript or a polite no thank you. When editors didn't respond within a week, I always followed up. Today, it took a couple of hours and two mugs of coffee to check in on those outstanding queries.

When that task was complete, I turned my attention to queries authors had sent to me, looking for someone to represent their manuscript. I had an e-mail address dedicated solely to receiving unsolicited queries. The in-box filled up faster than a rain barrel in a downpour, so I had to be sure to go through it at least twice a week.

Ninety minutes and sixty-eight queries later, it was mission accomplished. I'd responded to three authors by asking them to send me their complete manuscript. The rest received my standard rejection e-mail. It was always important to be picky with queries. If I didn't think I'd fall in love with a story, I wouldn't be able to present it to an editor with the enthusiasm it deserved.

Besides, I'd reached the point where I no longer had to aggressively add to my author list. My first couple of years running the Cobb Literary Agency had been all about growth—signing authors and getting them good publication contracts. Now, I was moving into a new phase. My objective had changed to stabilization—keeping the authors I'd signed and having the agency grow as their careers progressed.

I was representing forty-three authors. It was a roster that varied from multi-bestselling thriller author Malcolm Blackstone to a nineteen-year-old woman I'd signed only two weeks ago. She'd written a wonderfully unique young adult fantasy set on Jupiter. I had out-of-this-world hopes for it.

My goal was to top out at sixty authors. I wasn't confident I could give each of my authors the attention they deserved if I exceeded that figure and didn't have help. Even if I found an intern (and after that first interview, I wasn't confident in success), I wanted to stay around that figure for a while.

With intern help, I'd be able to offer my less-experienced authors extra support as they learned the ins and outs of the publishing world. It would also give me more time to strategize with more seasoned authors how to keep their careers moving in the direction they wanted.

It was almost eleven when I kicked away from my desk. The casters squeaked as the chair rolled me across the hardwood floor. I didn't stop until I bumped against the bookcase against the opposite wall. It was a fun way to end a productive morning.

"Time for a walk, girl." My eyes and brain needed a break, so I put Ursi's harness on her and we headed outside.

An unfamiliar guy with red hair and glasses was putting out new items in the sock store that occupied the first-floor space across the hall from Renee's bookstore. I waved to him as we passed by the store. He smiled and waved back.

A warm feeling enveloped me as we continued down the sidewalk. Even a brisk breeze that smacked us in the face when we turned the corner couldn't dampen my mood. The exchange was the best of Rushing Creek. When you crossed paths with somebody, you offered a cheerful greeting or waved. Maybe it was old fashioned, compared to the hustle and bustle of life on Manhattan's streets, but it was genuine. A reminder that people were, in fact, basically good. Most of them, at least.

The ones that weren't murderers.

Even though I'd had a stellar morning in the productivity category, I still had a full afternoon of work in front of me. With that in mind, Ursi and I made our walk a simple fifteen-minute stroll through the neighborhood.

I returned to the apartment invigorated from the walk, and I got back to work by editing a client's rom-com manuscript. Ursi curled up on a seat cushion the twins had placed under my desk and went right to sleep.

I had a great job.

An hour later, I'd read fifty pages and made only a handful of comments and corrections. It was a good sign for the manuscript as a whole. This author had a keen eye for detail, which meant I'd likely breeze through the rest of the story in a few hours.

Thanks to the strong manuscript, I got to take a break from the day job earlier than planned. That was good because it meant I could spend more time working on the list of murder suspects than I'd budgeted.

Since the easy-peasy, open-and-shut case I'd hoped for wasn't going to happen, I needed to put some serious thought into it. To help me focus, I added some peppermint essential oil to a diffuser I kept in the kitchen, threw together a chicken Caesar salad for dinner, and returned to detective work.

My credible suspects were Porter, Ozzy, and Gary. I added Brent to the group, not because I thought he was a suspect, but because Matt hadn't completely ruled him out.

It didn't hurt to include Brent. It was simply part of the system I'd developed. I was being thorough and methodical. Including all reasonable suspects forced me to examine all possibilities with a clear, impartial mind. When Sloane's father, Thornwell, had been murdered, fingers were pointed at her. I got involved first to clear her name, and second to catch the killer. At the time, I still included Sloane among my suspect list.

The approach had worked twice before. Hopefully, it would work again. The suspects got their own page in the notebook. Each page was divided into three columns. Each column was given its own heading—motive, means, and opportunity. I checked my notes and filled in as much as I could for all four suspects.

When I was finished filling in the columns, I took a break to massage my aching hand. I'd tensed up during the task and gripped the pen way too hard. As I worked the pain away, I studied my handiwork. The conclusion was inescapable.

Porter was the most likely murderer. By a mile.

There was much information to be gathered, though. I knew virtually nothing about Gary outside of what I learned during our conversation. I knew enough about Ozzy, and his Vesuvius-like temper, to consider him a credible suspect. My opinion of the man didn't amount to much, though. What I needed were facts.

When it came to proving Brent's innocence, I needed one thing. A witness. If there was someone who could place him during the time between the library closing and when I got home, he'd be in the clear. That was proving to be easier said than done, though.

I glanced at the clock. It was a little after four. A memorial service in Vicky's honor was being held in front of the library at five.

I headed for the bedroom to change into more formal clothes. After a few minutes of debate, I picked out a white blouse and dress slacks with a black and gray herringbone pattern. With the sun out and the temperature in the low sixties, I finished the ensemble with a gray wool blazer and a pair of black flats. Even though I was playing no part in the service, it was important to show Vicky the respect she deserved by dressing up.

With an extra handful of tissues stuffed into my pocket, I gave Ursi some dry food for dinner and headed out the door.

The scene in front of the library was breathtaking. A raised platform had been erected in front of the library's entrance. It was about two feet high and fifteen feet across. The flowers and stuffed toys that mourners had brought to the library were displayed across the front edge. White, ceramic pillars stood at each corner of the platform. Candles burned inside etched crystal hurricane lamps that were nestled atop the pillars.

The pièce de résistance was a theater-like curtain behind the platform. It was yellow—Vicky's favorite color. The posters signed by the library visitors were attached to the curtain. There were so many that they stretched all the way from one end to the other.

A stool had been placed in the center of the platform. It was the stool Vicky sat on while she checked out patrons' books. It was perfect.

I wiped away a tear with one of the tissues. The service hadn't even started and I was on the verge of a full-blown meltdown. I closed my eyes and hugged myself. I hadn't yet grieved over Vicky's death. I vowed not to until I found her killer.

And brought the guilty party to justice.

As the time for the service drew near, the crowd grew. Silver-haired grandmothers held hands with fidgety preschoolers. Men from the state park, still in their green and brown uniforms, stood in a group to the left of the platform, chatting with Luke and his Rushing Creek Parks Department crew. Even a pair of squirrels dashed down a nearby tree, across the grass, and up another tree.

Freddie kicked off the service with a heartfelt talk that opened the faucets. A string of local dignitaries, including Mayor Angela and the superintendent of Rushing Creek schools, shared moving and sometimes humorous stories about the community's beloved librarian. By the time the service concluded with the high school choir's performance of "River Deep, Mountain High," Vicky's favorite song, I'd used up every last bit of my tissue supply.

I gravitated toward the platform when the service concluded. As I took a picture with my phone of a stuffed lion wearing a bow tie, a shadow fell across the platform.

"Thanks for coming, Allie." Freddie gave my shoulder a squeeze.

"Wouldn't have missed it." I faced her. "Your words were beautiful."

"That's high praise, coming from a literary agent."

We laughed.

"She was my friend. Did you know we met in college?"

Vicky had often spoken of how close they were, but that bit of information was new to me. I shook my head.

"Oh, yeah. We were on the same dorm floor. She was studying library science. I was a business major. We started hanging out when our floor went to football games together. Plus, she had a job at the library and knew the best places for study groups to get together."

Images of a teenaged Vicky, with her dark hair pulled back in a ponytail, helping fellow students navigate the nine-story Indiana University library came to mind. I blinked away another tear.

"So, how did both of you end up here?" Vicky had told me one time she'd convinced Freddie to move to Rushing Creek, but I was curious about the details.

"Vicky is, was, a year older than me. She got the job at the library here right out of college. I visited her a few times, and I fell in love with the town." She ran her fingers over the lion's head. "My dad owned a pub, so I grew up wanting my own restaurant. Every time I came to see her, she pointed out places she said were perfect for me. When she showed me the storefront that became Marinara's, it was love at first sight. She even gave me a tip about the house I ended up buying."

Freddie's house was down the street from Vicky's. I made a mental note to ask her if she'd seen or heard anything unusual in the neighborhood the morning of the murder. Or even the night before. Maybe she knew something helpful and didn't realize it. That would have to wait for another time, though. I couldn't live with myself asking too many pointed questions right now.

The love-at-first-sight comment gave me an idea, though. I wanted to hear more happy stories, but this was an opportunity I couldn't pass up.

"Did you know Gary was in town over the weekend?"

Her eyebrows shot up. "I hadn't heard that. Probably just as well nobody told me. I never liked him. Any idea why he was in town?"

I recounted my conversation with the man.

"It seems shady that the deed never got changed and now that Vicky's gone, he gets the proceeds from the sale of the house." I scheduled a reminder in my phone to prompt me to visit the assessor's office. A check of the property records would confirm the names on the deed and whether there was a mortgage on the property.

Freddie moved a few of the stuffed animals and took a seat. Her lips were pursed as she wrapped her fingers around the edge of the platform.

"I know this is a lot to dump on you, especially right now, but do you think Gary could be the murderer?" I sat next to her and put a hand on her shoulder. "Any thoughts or suspicions you can tell me would be helpful."

"Gary was a self-centered jerk who only cared about himself. Sure, he came across as a good, reliable husband. That was all a façade. The fact that he ran out on Vicky instead of getting tested to see if he was the reason they couldn't have kids should tell you all you need to know about him."

As she spoke, Freddie's cheeks took on a crimson shade. The anger was understandable.

From what I could remember, Vicky ignored the behind-the-back whispering. All she said was that sometimes things between people didn't work out. At least that was all she said to me. Freddie's tone let me know Vicky had told her friends much more than she was willing to share with a ten-year-old girl.

"You think he could have done it?" Good Lord, I was talking about murder like we were discussing the weather forecast.

She tilted her head to the side. I held my breath as she pondered my statement.

After what seemed like hours, she took a deep breath. "Yes. If what you told me about the house is true, then yes, I do."

I let out the breath I was holding. I had my suspicions before, but they'd seemed far-fetched. Now, not so much. I needed more to go on, though.

"Why do you think that?"

"I guess it comes down to this. If he was willing to leave his wife instead of facing his own potential impotence, I bet he'd be willing to kill if it meant he'd get that house. It's a matter of self-centeredness."

"What can you tell me about him?" If I could find out more about the man, I might be able to figure out how he could have pulled off the murder.

"He was a pharmaceutical sales rep—at least he was back then. Maybe you could talk to your mom or someone at the hospital. They might know if he's still doing that."

"I'll do that. Anything else you can think of?" I wanted to get inside his head. What were his interests, his spending habits? Things like that.

"He was on the road a lot for his job." She snapped her fingers. "He also had a thing for European cars. He got a different one very year."

Aha. Now I had something to work with. A taste in expensive vehicles might lead to a desperate need for cash, especially if he got something extravagant and couldn't keep up with the payments.

Trouble with making a car payment might be an indicator of bigger money problems, like struggles keeping up with a mortgage. Losing one's house. That sounded like motivation for murder to me.

The crowd had dispersed during our chat. They'd been replaced by workers who were taking down the set. My time was about up.

"Thanks, Freddie. I appreciate it."

"My pleasure." She let out a short laugh and got to her feet. "Not really, but you know what I mean. If it helps catch Vicky's killer, I'm happy we had this chat."

"Me, too." My promise to Brent popped into my head as we shook hands. "By the way, I understand you'll be posting Vicky's position at the end of the week."

"That's right. I hope Brent wasn't just being nice when he said he was going to apply."

"Nope. He's looking forward to being considered for the position. Did, ah, Vicky ever talk to you about a succession plan? You know, for when it came time to retire, or…" I couldn't bring myself to finish the question.

"Every now and then we talked about what we wanted to do when we retired. It was never anything serious, though. Things like moving to Fiji and spending the rest of our lives drinking mai tais while a cabana boy tended to our every whim." She chuckled, though the smile didn't reach her eyes.

I gave Freddie a hug. I didn't know her well and knew full well some people weren't huggers, but she looked like she needed one.

After the embrace, Freddie gave me a big smile. "Thanks. I needed that. Don't forget my offer for breadsticks on the house."

We said our goodbyes and I made my way home. I was so focused on writing notes into my phone, I cracked my knee against a fire hydrant and almost bonked my nose against a light pole. That was okay. Ice and a couple of Advil and I'd be fine.

More importantly, I had a lead on Gary.

Chapter Twelve

I made a beeline for my case notebook the moment I was inside the apartment. Ursi yowled in indignation at me when I didn't give her something to eat the moment I walked through the door.

"Give me a minute, Miss Bossypants. I need to get this down before I forget." My pen flew across the page as I transferred my notes from phone to page. The more I wrote, the more Gary looked like a credible suspect.

As I worked on a to-do list of Gary-related leads to follow, my feline bumped her head against my shin and let out a muffled meow, like her mouth was full. I ignored her until she put her paw on my leg and gently dug her claws into my flesh. *Ouch.*

That got my attention.

"All right, you win." I rolled my chair away from the desk. The nanosecond I laid eyes on Ursi, I froze.

She had something small and furry in her mouth. I closed my eyes for a few seconds, hoping when I opened them, the fur would really be a collection of dust bunnies from under the bookcases.

No such luck.

With her tail straight as a flagpole, she trotted toward me. At the foot of the chair, she sat and, radiating with pride, dropped a dead mouse at my feet. *Meow.*

I hated mice. Growing up, I'd mostly ignored them. Living in an old house close to a patch of woods meant a few showed up in the basement every year when the temperature dropped. Dad would set out the traps, and in a week or so, the varmints were no more to be seen.

It was when I got to New York that I grew to loathe the creatures. To be fair, it wasn't mice I loathed. It was their rodent cousin the rat.

One night, a few weeks after moving to New York, I got up to go to the bathroom. I turned on a light and right there, in the middle of the hallway, a big, fat, scary rat was gnawing on a chicken bone it had scavenged from my trash. It looked at me with its beady midnight black eyes and seemed to sneer at me before it scurried away, the bone still in its mouth.

A scream loud enough to wake the whole ten-story apartment building escaped my lips as I collapsed against the wall. It took a full five minutes before my heart stopped pounding against my ribcage like a jackhammer and my ragged breathing returned to normal.

Once I calmed down, I went to the kitchen to find the contents of the trash can strewn all over the floor. With a growl, I fetched a broom and cleaned up the mess.

Unable to get back to sleep, I spent the rest of the night packing my things. Three days later, I moved into a new apartment building. The rent was a hundred dollars a month higher, but well worth it as the landlord provided me documentation that the place had been pest-free for ten years.

I never fully recovered from that scare. To this day, every time I saw a mouse, the disgusting face of that rat flashed before my eyes.

Ursi wasn't trying to frighten me, though. I knew enough about cat behavior to appreciate her act of giving me a present. It was kind of a gross present, but the way she was sitting so erect made it clear she was proud of herself.

"What a ferocious hunter you are." I scratched her head as I kept up a steady stream of compliments. This was the first mouse she'd brought me in the three years we'd been living together. The least I could do was act appreciative.

A few minutes of lavish praise and ear scratching made Ursi happy, so, after a quick rub of her head against my ankle, she sauntered off to the kitchen. When she was out of sight, I leapt from my chair, grabbed a half-dozen tissues from the box on my desk, and wrapped up the creature until it was a little mouse mummy.

Crisis over.

I tossed a couple of kitty treats to my live-in predator and, while she was distracted, dumped the mouse into the trash can in the corner of the kitchen. After feeding my little huntress, I removed the bag from the can and took it to the dumpster, even though it was only half full. I was in no mood for taking chances that Ursi's present was still alive.

After a ham and Colby sandwich on wheat toast for dinner, I was right back out the door. I had my first meeting with the Rushing Creek 9/11 Memorial Planning Committee.

Every year, the committee held a ceremony on the county courthouse grounds in the middle of town to commemorate that history-altering day. Over the years, the committee had run out of ideas how to keep the observance fresh and engaging. Even though I didn't live in New York on the day the towers came down, I was there when the new World Trade Center opened. Because of that, folks had asked me to join the committee, believing my years in New York could bring new ideas to the committee.

I had my doubts about having something to offer, but as I stepped outside, I vowed to participate in the meeting in good faith. Who knew, maybe I'd have something of value to add, after all.

If nothing else, I could always try to pump the committee members for information about my murder suspects. Good Lord, I was becoming way too jaded.

The meeting was being held in the private room at the Rushing Creek Public House. When I told my sister I was joining the committee, she insisted the pub host the gathering.

She greeted me with a hug when I arrived and even escorted me to the back, where the private room was located.

"What's with the red-carpet treatment?" I navigated around a four-seater table and came to a stop.

The entrance to the room was ten feet away. My stomach had gotten jumpier with each step I'd taken through the restaurant. I wiped my palms on my jeans to try them out.

"I know Mom cornered you into joining this group. I also know you're not a fan of joining committees."

"So, you're going to sit in for me?"

Rachel and I shared a difficult past. Since I'd returned to Rushing Creek, our relationship had improved from barely tolerating each other to getting along most of the time.

Growing up, the two of us couldn't have been more different. Two years ahead of me in school, she was a glamorous cheerleader who hung out with the cool kids. I was a bookish brainiac with only one real friend—Sloane. Since I was so different, Rachel and her friends made fun of me and made it clear in no uncertain terms that I wasn't welcome among them.

Over the years, I went from wanting to be like Rachel to resenting her. She and her friends looked down on me, simply because I didn't share their interests. Because I was different. By the time I graduated from high school, I despised my sister, who was shallow and vain in my view. She, in turn, thought I was a stuck-up, pseudo-intellectual snob and had no problem sharing that opinion with everyone.

When I moved to New York, I thought I'd never speak to Rachel again. Life had other things in mind, though. Traumatic events like her divorce and then our father's cancer battle opened the doors for communication. We began to exchange text messages, which over time led to a few phone calls.

With our teen years behind us, we both came to realize, and regret, the pain we'd caused each other. The wounds were deep, though. Repairing those wounds was going to take a long time.

The improvement had occurred in baby steps through small gestures. Was this Rachel's latest kind gesture?

"Heck, no." She snorted. "I figured if I didn't get you into that room, you'd come up with a way to weasel out of it."

"Oh. Well then." The words stung, not because they were hurtful, but because they were true.

I looked toward the front of the restaurant. "If I make a break for it, you'll chase me down, won't you?" Despite my desire to sound serious, I cracked a smile.

Rachel placed her hand against the wall. My escape route was blocked. "I'll tackle you before you take two steps."

We broke into a fit of giggles that eventually led to some curious stares from nearby diners.

"Let me introduce you to the committee." She draped her arm around my shoulders. "I promise they won't bite."

The chair of the committee was a man named Jack Rogers, the middle school science teacher. He was also a veteran who'd enlisted in the army after graduating from Rushing Creek High School in 2004. After two tours in the Middle East, he returned to Rushing Creek and a well-deserved hero's welcome. He used the GI Bill to get a degree in elementary education and had been teaching kids the scientific method ever since.

"Welcome to the group, Allie." With a big smile, he shook my hand with a little more enthusiasm than usual. "We're stoked to have you join us."

His dark hair was cropped short, no doubt a remnant of his time in the service. A bodybuilder's physique that went with the hairstyle made me think he could return to active duty at the drop of a hat. He had penetrating green eyes that sparkled but also told of unimaginable horrors he must have seen overseas.

I was thankful for Jack, and people like him.

The enthusiastic greeting left me a little dazed, so I resorted to nodding and saying hi as Jack introduced me to the other four committee members. Two were women. One, who was named Ashley, had auburn hair that looked like it came from a bottle.

The other was Vivian Franklin, a retired woman who worked part-time at the library. With snow-white hair and reading glasses that hung on a sparkly necklace around her neck, she looked right out of a casting call for an older librarian.

The final two members were guys, one named Bob, the other named Mike. Bob sported a shaved head and had colorful tattoos covering both of his arms.

Mike had a bushy, hipster beard. Between the beard and his red-and-black flannel shirt, I imagined his music collection being filled with Mumford & Sons and the Avett Brothers. Then again, I liked both of those bands, so hopefully Mike and I would get along just fine.

With introductions concluded, Rachel made her exit with a promise to return with complimentary soft drinks and appetizers. My sister was smart. Not only was she fulfilling her civic duty by letting the committee use the room, she knew how to take advantage of an advertising opportunity.

There was no doubt in my mind the committee members would share how well they were treated at the Rushing Creek Public House. The word-of-mouth advertising would prove to be priceless. The generosity she showed tonight would be recouped in a couple of weeks. It was a win for all involved.

Seeing Rachel's business acumen firsthand made me proud to be her little sister. I sat in my chair a little straighter throughout the meeting. And made a note to compliment her on her astuteness.

Jack brought the meeting to order by unfurling a little flag and asking us to all rise and recite the national anthem. Until that moment, I hadn't fully appreciated the importance the man put on the committee. When we finished, his eyes were watery. Now, I knew better.

I gave my fellow committee members background about my time in New York and then we got down to business. The five veterans of the group were unanimous in their opinion that the existing ceremony needed a complete overhaul. The goal for tonight's meeting was to spend the hour brainstorming.

Since I was the newbie, I offered to take notes.

Bob shook his head. "Thanks, Allie, but tonight we really want your input, okay? Since you lived in New York, we want you to tell us how people there observe 9/11 since the day it happened, okay?"

"Alrighty, then." I searched my memory banks for a couple of minutes. I'd seen that day observed in so many forms and fashions during my decade in the Big Apple, it was hard to know where to begin. I started with my first year there.

At first, the others stuck to nodding their heads and saying, "Uh-huh." That changed when Vivian asked a question about a song I'd mentioned, the gorgeously moving "Empire State of Mind" by Alicia Keys. After that, it was like someone had opened the barn door and the horses had barreled out.

Once the conversation and ideas began flowing, the only time the discussion came to a halt was when Rachel, assisted by a server, brought in the drinks and food.

I wasn't sure whether the room became silent because of the food or because of the server. The food consisted of a plate of Rachel's famous six-inch tall supreme nachos, along with a sampler platter of wings, potato skins, carrots, celery, cherry tomatoes, and a variety of dipping sauces. My stomach growled the moment the aroma of the nachos reached my nostrils.

The thing, or more precisely person, that stopped me from attacking the delightful Mexican dish was the server. Her skin was the color of bone china. The whiteness of it was exacerbated by the girl's jet-black hair, which was shaved above her left ear; she had matching nail polish. The goth look was completed by her use of thick, black eyeliner and a black teardrop tattoo at the corner of one eye.

"Diet Pepsi for you, Miss Cobb." The young woman smiled as she handed me a glass filled with the fizzy, dark soda. A silver stud nose ring glittered in the light as she moved past me.

I looked from my glass to Rachel. She'd evidently been watching me because, when our gazes met, she ran her fingers along the collar of her blouse then started doing something on her phone.

A second later, my phone buzzed. It was a text from Rachel that said the look on my face was priceless.

The others were digging into the food, so Rachel and her helper made a quiet exit while I sipped my drink and munched on a handful of cheese-laden tortilla chips.

After a few moments of relative quiet, which was interrupted only by a request for a napkin or dining utensil, Jack brought us back on task by asking for more ideas. The food disappeared as the ideas kept flying.

Ninety minutes after the meeting began, Jack brought the meeting to a close. We'd come up with fifty ideas of things to incorporate into the service. Some, like inviting former President George W. Bush to speak, were a little far-fetched. Others, such as Vivian's suggestion to pass out cupcakes decorated with red, white, and blue icing, were much more doable.

Poor Ashley, who had been taking notes by hand, flexed her fingers and grimaced. I took a travel-sized bottle of Advil from my purse and offered her one.

"I feel for you. Sometimes it takes me hours to complete my clients' royalty statements, and when I finish, my hands always ache. I think a lot of it comes from the stress of double and triple checking my calculations."

"You're a lifesaver." She accepted the bottle without a moment's hesitation. "This is my fifth year on the committee. It feels like I took more notes tonight than all the other meetings combined."

"You probably did." Jack gathered his things and gave her shoulder a light pat as he went around the table to thank each of us individually. "Great meeting, everyone. You all have your assignments. We'll reconvene in a month. On a lighter note, who wants a drink? I'm buying."

Everyone else in the group said yes, so I promised I'd join them in a minute after I tidied up the room a bit. The others offered to help, but I insisted they go get their drinks. I wanted some time alone to decompress from the meeting.

And formulate questions to ask the group about Vicky's murder.

Once I was satisfied with a coherent, and subtle, line of questions in my head, I joined the group. They were seated at a round table near the front picture window. A glass of white wine was waiting for me.

It looked like getting involved in a local committee wasn't such a bad thing, after all.

Jack lifted his glass. "To us, and the promise of the best nine-eleven ceremony Rushing Creek has ever seen."

Amid a chorus of cheers, we clinked glasses. I took a sip of my wine. While I rolled the fruity Moscato around my tongue and over my taste buds, I debated how to bring up my first question.

Vivian beat me to the punch by asking if I knew how the investigation was going.

"I know how close you and Vicky were. I thought between that and your ex-brother-in-law being police chief, you might know something." The white-haired woman put down her mixed drink. Her hands were shaking.

If my sixth sense for investigation was right, she'd been waiting all evening to ask the question. Well, she'd opened the door for me. It would be rude not to walk through.

"The chief has a few suspects. They believe she was poisoned." I left it at that. Better to offer them a few breadcrumbs and see where it took me.

"I thought they arrested someone already." Bob pointed at Vivian. "Someone you work with at the library, wasn't it?"

"You must mean Porter Rasmussen." I spoke up to keep Vivian from answering. The goal was to control the conversation. "He was taken in for questioning but hasn't been charged with anything."

"Anything, yet." Ashley leaned forward, as if to share a well-kept secret. "I have a friend who works for the fire department. According to her, it's only a matter of time until they arrest him. He's as guilty as sin."

"Why do you say that?" One of the things I'd learned about conducting an investigation was to use open-ended questions whenever possible. It allowed a witness to tell the story without them thinking I was looking for a specific answer. It wasn't a foolproof approach, but, in a situation like now, it usually worked.

The redhead's lips curved up at the ends in a menace-filled smile. "The guy's a legend in gardening circles around here. He probably cooked up some poison from the flowers he grows. Did you know there are, like, over a hundred flower species that are poisonous to humans? I looked it up. I'll bet you guys another drink some of the flowers he's grown are like that and he's got a bunch of other poisons hidden somewhere in his house."

"Come on, Ashley." Jack gave her a long look. "You sound like you've been talking to Maybelle Schuman."

"Maybe I have and maybe I haven't. Just because she embellishes her stories sometimes doesn't mean she's wrong on this one."

Maybelle's rumormongering was a thing of legend in Rushing Creek. If I wasn't careful, the conversation would descend into the morass of gossip and innuendo.

"I'm sure you crossed paths with Porter at the library, Vivian. What do you think of him?" I sipped my wine.

Everyone at our table turned their focus on her. The conversation was back where I wanted it.

"I usually work in the afternoons, so I didn't see him much. When I did, he always seemed harmless enough." She ran a hand down the sleeve of her blouse. "He was quiet. Kind of lonely. Which makes sense, I guess, since he's a widower."

"Or a killer." Mike put up his hands like he was surrendering as we turned our gazes toward him. "I'm just saying the guy fits the personality type."

Jack shook his head. "You've been watching too many cop shows. I saw a lot of sketchy-looking souls when I was in Iraq who were our allies. I wouldn't be so quick to judge."

Interesting. The military veteran coming to the defense of the accused. Maybe it was nothing, but I made a mental note to get Jack's take on the murder later. His military background would give him insight I could never possess.

The discussion continued until our glasses were empty. When Rachel came by to ask if anyone wanted another, I shook my head. I'd had enough. The others followed my lead, so Jack paid the bill and we made our goodbyes.

I stepped from the warm light of the pub into the chilliness of a dark, spring night. As was typical for a Monday night in the off-season, traffic was nonexistent. The stars above twinkled like tiny cousins of the nearby streetlights that illuminated my walk home. The stillness of the night amplified my footfalls. It seemed like a gun was going off every time I took a step.

Replaying the conversation in my head as I strolled north on the Boulevard, identifying the group's consensus was easy enough. Porter used the poison from his flowers to kill Vicky.

There'd been no consensus on why he did it, though. In fact, the group didn't seem overly concerned about a motive.

That bothered me. I'd learned many things about human behavior in recent years. One of them was always to look for a motive behind one's actions. Porter had the means and he had the opportunity. Did he have the motive, though?

He had a crush on Vicky. She was leaving town. Love often made people do crazy things. Especially lonely people.

But kill her? I wasn't convinced yet.

Chapter Thirteen

I slept the sleep of the dead Monday night and didn't open my eyes until Ursi roused me from blissful slumber by batting at my nose.

"Okay, I'm up." After a long yawn, I sat up and rubbed the sleep out of my eyes. Only then did my alarm attract my attention. The persistent *beep, beep, beep* had been going off for a half hour. That woke me up.

I silenced the clock radio with a flick of the wrist and vaulted out of bed. It was a trick I learned living in a dorm during my college years. I preferred morning classes. My roomies, not so much. Born of equal parts necessity and courtesy, I became adept at getting moving in the morning while not disturbing anyone else's slumber.

As I poured Ursi some dry food and started a pot of coffee, a small laugh escaped me. Sure, yesterday had been a busy and productive day, but to sleep through the alarm for so long Ursi got tired of waiting for me? That was a new record in the slumber category.

While an English muffin toasted, I fetched my phone to check for any agency emergencies that needed my immediate attention. Unless I let my authors know I was going to be unavailable for a period of time, I responded to all messages within a day.

There were no urgent e-mails, but a text from Rachel caught my attention. And then made my jaw drop.

Goth Girl from the restaurant wanted to interview for the intern position.

Okay, that was unexpected. Usually, the only time Rachel and I texted was to discuss something family related. Plus, if the young woman had wanted to meet me, why hadn't Rachel introduced us at the pub?

The coffee's pot's gurgling came to an end, so I poured a mug of the liquid gold into my Wonder Woman mug. The chocolaty aroma heightened my senses as I responded that I'd be happy to chat with her. After all, if my first interview was any indication, I was going to have to expand my candidate pool.

The first part of my morning was consumed by preparing the manuscripts of two clients to go out on query. The authors, both of whom wrote thrillers, and I had agreed to submit the query materials, which included a cover e-mail and two-page synopsis, to editors at ten big publishing houses. By the time I sent the materials, which were accompanied by a personalized cover e-mail, and set up a spreadsheet to track the status of each submission, it was after ten.

When I hit send on the final e-mail, I got to my feet and did a happy dance from my office into the living room. Ursi was watching the world from her favorite perch, so I bopped over to her, raised one paw, and gave her a high five.

"Progress, girl. It's a beautiful thing."

She responded to my enthusiasm by yawning and turning her backside to me.

"Killjoy. Fine. I'm going out and you're not invited."

Nothing had changed overnight to sway my nagging doubt about Porter being the murderer. Gary still seemed suspicious and the nasty e-mail exchanges between Ozzy and Vicky concerned me. Ozzy and my friend Shirley had become cozy over the past few months. While I was happy for my friend, I couldn't deny concern for her well-being, should she get into an argument with the man.

How solid was my friendship with Shirley? I was about to find out.

It was a beautiful day as I left my building with a wave to Renee. Downtown Rushing Creek was bathed in a golden glow of sunshine and warmth that its citizens hadn't enjoyed in months. To revel in the conditions to the max, I removed my jacket and whistled a bouncy tune from the musical *Waitress* as I bebopped my way to Soaps and Scents.

Shirley was ringing up a sale when I entered the shop. We exchanged hellos, then I wandered up and down the aisles while I waited for her to finish. Halfway down the natural soap aisle, I stopped to breathe in the lovely aroma. The scent of lavender enveloped me and conjured images of lying in a field of freshly mown grass with a book by my side as the sun smiled down upon me.

"Allie, my dear." Shirley gave me a hug. "To what do I owe the pleasure?"

I sniffed a creamy sample of soap. The vanilla aroma was heavenly. "Can't a girl just come in and check out your new products?"

"Of course she can. But you were in here two weeks ago, I believe, and loaded up on enough things to last you months. I don't want you going bankrupt on account of my shop."

It was always fun to exchange friendly banter with Shirley. Though she was my mom's age and looked like she'd just arrived from a Grateful Dead concert, there was no generation gap between us.

We were friends.

And that made the reason for my visit even more troubling. So, instead of prolonging the agony, I ripped off the proverbial bandage.

"It's about Ozzy." I looked around to make sure nobody was within earshot then told her about the disturbing e-mail exchanges. "Has he ever mentioned being angry with the library, or Vicky in particular?"

"Never. It's like I tell everyone, his bark is worse than his bite." She chewed on her lower lip for a moment. "This is about the murder, isn't it?"

"I'm afraid so. His language in the e-mails is pretty shocking. It worried me. For you. In case he ever got angry with you."

I pulled up one of the e-mails on my phone. I'd forwarded it from the library account to my personal account just in case.

As she read it, she frowned. "I see. Well, I can see your point, given how he comes across to some people. Let's talk to him about it."

Shirley told a part-time helper she'd be back in a little bit and led me out the door. On our way to Ozzy's shop, I filled her in on the general context of the issue. By the time we crossed the threshold, Shirley had turned into an angry bull. Ozzy was the red cape.

"Oswald Eugene Metcalf, I'd like a word with you." Shirley paused for two seconds, while she glared at her boyfriend, then marched back outside.

Oswald Eugene Metcalf? I'd never heard anyone use Ozzy's full name before. As he scurried after Shirley, with his eyes as big as dinner plates, the cantankerous, intimidating man was nowhere to be found.

I had to put my hand over my mouth to keep from laughing. By the time I caught up to them, I was no longer smiling.

Shirley was reading him the riot act. When she finished, she brushed her long, gray hair from her face and planted her hands on her hips. It was a commanding side of her I'd never seen before. And one I didn't want to be on the wrong end of.

"Well? What do you have to say for yourself?" Shirley tilted her head forward to give the impression of an old-time school teacher staring down a troublemaking student.

"Sure, things got a little heated, but it took me weeks to make those carvings. They were some of my best work ever."

"What Allie told me is true, then."

"More or less. Look, Vicky and I agreed on a price and I started the work. A few weeks later, she told me there was a problem with the number I quoted. By that time, I was too far down the road on the project to stop, so I held up my end of the bargain."

"By finishing the carvings." In response to my interruption, Ozzy gave me a look so menacing, I took a step back.

"Yeah. Then that woman tried to screw me over, so I sold the pieces." He pointed a varnish-stained finger at me. "But I never laid a hand on her. And I sure as all get out didn't kill her."

"What makes you say that?" Shirley's scolding tone had been replaced by one of astonishment.

Ozzy tilted his head in my direction. "Because that busybody's here. I figured it was only a matter of time until she came after me claiming I killed someone."

Despite my blood reaching boiling state in an instant, I held my tongue. I would only pour gas on the fire if I responded to the slanderous accusation.

"*She* is my friend. You don't have to like her, but you do have to treat her with respect."

Ozzy tapped his foot and shoved his hands into the pockets of his canvas woodworking apron. Something in the direction opposite of me seemed to catch his attention.

The pause in the verbal volleyball gave me an opening. "Since you didn't do it, who do you think did?"

I crossed my fingers. Hopefully, my choice of "since" instead of "if" would make a favorable impression.

"Not Rasmussen. He doesn't have the guts for something that ruthless. Her ex-husband's another matter. If I was a betting man, I'd put my money on him."

"Why do you say that?"

"Gary Napier is as slippery as a greased pig. He's been divorced for years, but he never looked into the deed situation until now? When, suddenly, he'll get all the money when the house sells?" Porter shook his head. "No. If he had really cared about making sure the deed was right, he would have done it already."

It was the same conclusion I'd drawn. This was the most civil verbal exchange I'd ever had with Ozzy. I saw a lot of merit to his analysis, too. Porter was still the most likely suspect, but Gary definitely merited further investigation. While I was in the woodworker's good graces, maybe I could get his take on a few other things.

I asked him a few more questions about Gary and Porter. How well did he know them? Did he have recent interactions with either of them? After he answered them, I asked if I had more inquiries, would he be willing to talk to me further?

At first he grumbled about me needing to stop sticking my nose where it didn't belong. When Shirley cleared her throat, he stopped mid-grumble.

"Okay, but don't bother me when I'm helping a customer. Some of us have to work for a living."

Taking the high road, I brushed aside the swipe at my career and promised to do so. After shaking hands with Ozzy, I gave Shirley a hug and thanked them for both their time and candor.

I wanted to get my thoughts down on paper, so I headed for the Brown County Diner. It was a short jaunt, only three blocks, but by the time I arrived, I was convinced of Ozzy's innocence.

It wasn't that I believed his denial of any involvement in Vicky's murder. It was more that, with each passing day, evidence continued to mount around Porter and Gary. Sure, it was circumstantial evidence, but I didn't doubt that it would be enough to lead to an arrest soon.

The diner's aluminum door handle sent a shiver through me when my fingers touched its warm surface. The warmth was exhilarating. I took it as a sign of good things to come.

My exhilaration was replaced by ravishing hunger the moment I stepped into the diner. The mouthwatering aroma of rhubarb pie, right out of the oven, greeted me and wrapped me in a blanket of blissful memories.

Rhubarb pie had been Dad's favorite. Growing up, pretty much any time my father liked something, I chose to like it, too. Becoming a fan of rhubarb pie wasn't easy, though. The tart taste that was reminiscent of sour, green apples took some getting used to. Eventually, I learned that adding a couple of oversized scoops of ice cream to my pie made it rather enjoyable.

Okay, maybe the ice cream made it more tolerable. Over time, though, I came to realize it wasn't the pie that mattered. It was the time spent with Dad that mattered.

Nobody else in the family would come within ten feet of a piece of rhubarb pie, so that meant when Dad brought one home, I was going to have time alone with my other hero. Just the old man and me. The books we discussed, the problems we solved, the memories we created over pieces of that baked good would stay with me forever. And with them, Dad would stay with me for the rest of my days.

With heartwarming memories swirling around in my head like fireflies on a summer evening, I didn't notice Jeanette until I was almost seated in a booth by the window. She was sipping coffee and munching on French fries while she watched something on her phone. She was so engrossed in whatever was on the screen that she hadn't seen me. It was time to change that.

The timing was perfect. I trusted Jeanette with every fiber of my being. She would be the perfect sounding board as I hashed out my thoughts about the investigation.

I slid into the seat across from her and reached for a fry. My fingers were mere inches from my goal when she clamped a hand around my wrist.

"It's rude to take a fry from a friend." Her gaze was still locked on her phone. "And it's dumb to try to steal from a cop who's on her lunch break."

"Um. How about I buy you another order to make up for my indiscretion." Jeanette loved the diner's French fries almost as much as I loved their coffee.

"That's acceptable." She released my wrist and shifted her gaze to me. With a wink and a smile, she tossed a fry in my direction. "What's up, A.C.?"

"Nothing much." I doused the fry with pepper and popped it in my mouth. "Just out and about talking to people, investigating murder. You know, the usual stuff."

"Care to share your intel with your best friend in blue?"

"Sure." After I ordered coffee and a salad, along with two orders of fries, I filled Jeanette in on my morning.

"Interesting." Jeanette stole back a fry. Then she took another. "That's your penalty for theft."

I pushed my plate toward her. "What do I get for giving you all of these?"

Jeanette raised an eyebrow.

"Keep this between us?" When I nodded, she pulled the plate the rest of the way toward her. "We got the preliminary toxicology results. The report confirms she was poisoned. By a natural substance."

This time it was my turn to be surprised. Not by the information, but by Jeanette's willingness to share it. She'd been reprimanded in the past for sharing information with me. Since the information had helped with the capture of murder suspects, she hadn't been seriously penalized.

She was ambitious, though, and wanted to go places in her career. That meant she would probably look for a position in a larger city in the near future. Black marks on her record wouldn't help her in any future searches. To avoid getting any more, she'd been less forthcoming with police intel recently.

"Sure makes it sound like Porter's your perp. Are you guys going to make an arrest?"

"Not yet. The evidence is still circumstantial at this point, and you know how Matt is on a murder case."

I did, indeed. Matt was an excellent cop and good police chief. He didn't tolerate mischief in his town and wouldn't hesitate to throw a vandal or petty thief behind bars. With Rushing Creek so dependent on tourism, the man was acutely aware of the importance of bringing the hammer down on misdemeanor crime. If the community ever lost its reputation for safety and quaintness, it would take massive efforts to get it back.

Police Chief Matt Roberson's main goal was to make sure that reputation stayed intact. If that meant slapping on the handcuffs first and asking questions later, so be it. The business community appreciated it and the residents felt safer because of it.

Felony crimes were a different matter.

Matt also freely acknowledged Rushing Creek PD lacked the resources a department in a larger city had. He didn't use it as a reason to complain. He used it as motivation to deploy the resources at his disposal in the most effective way possible.

That meant the department took a slow and methodical approach when the matter involved life and death. Matt didn't want to make a mistake that would require backtracking. Starting over meant spending money the department didn't have.

If it took longer to make an arrest than some people liked, that was their problem. What mattered was that once the Rushing Creek Police Department arrested a suspect in a felony crime, that suspect ended up going to prison.

I took a long drink of my coffee. "What happens next?"

"We'll keep an eye on Rasmussen while we work on connecting him to the poisoning. In the meantime, I'll take a closer look at the ex-husband. Don't want to leave any stone unturned."

Rationally, I agreed with the plan. Emotionally, I didn't. The thought of letting a killer remain free, even for a day, turned my stomach. I needed to figure out a way to force the issue.

To make sure Vicky's murderer didn't have the chance to disappear before an arrest could be made.

Chapter Fourteen

I'd seen—and felt—firsthand the results that came with giving a murder suspect a chance to escape. The result wasn't pretty. In fact, the result could be quite painful. Because of that, I couldn't stand by, with my hands in my pockets, while a killer remained loose on the streets of my beloved hometown.

It didn't help that after parting ways with Jeanette, I'd interviewed another intern candidate. The meeting started out well enough but took a nosedive when the woman, a retired teacher, said she wouldn't be able to work on books that contained sex scenes or profanity.

It was an objection I completely understood. Every reader had their likes and dislikes to which they were entitled. Shoot, Sloane had never been much of a reader until I turned her onto cozy mysteries. After reading her first Miss Marple novel, she was hooked on the genre.

"I like the puzzle without the blood and gore. There's enough of that in the real world," she'd told me one time as she helped herself to my collection of *The Cat Who* books. She never returned the books, but Luke had let me know she still read them, especially when she was stressed about something.

The thing was, as an agent who represented writers who wrote in a variety of genres, my portfolio included manuscripts with sex and violence. It was part of the business. I couldn't have an assistant pick and choose what he or she wanted to read. If a story was good enough for me to represent it, it was good enough for an intern to work on it. Every single one of my authors deserved nothing less.

To counter my dwindling intern prospects, I texted Rachel with instructions on how the young woman from the pub could submit her resume.

I was editing a police procedural manuscript when the resume arrived. There wasn't much to it. The candidate was a high school graduate named Calypso Bosley who professed a love for classic literature. She said she'd recently moved to town. The best way to reach her was via e-mail or her cell number.

The resume seemed a little odd, but it was error-free. That was a start. If she really did love classic literature, I'd be able to call her out on it in a manner of minutes. I sent Calypso a text that I could meet her Friday afternoon.

As afternoon turned to evening, I grew more antsy. Despite immersing myself in work, then taking Ursi for a walk, I couldn't get Porter off my mind. When night had fallen, I gave in to my fixation and decided to pay Porter another visit.

To be accurate, I wasn't interested in talking to the man again. I was interested in checking out his greenhouse and shed. Porter struck me as the kind of person who loved his flowers with such a passion that he wouldn't destroy them. Even if he used some of them to commit a murder, he'd find a way to preserve them.

Hopefully, that meant there were clues to be found.

"Time to play cat burglar again, girl." I filled Ursi's dinner bowl, gave her a few extra kitty treats as I swore her to secrecy, and changed into my ninja outfit.

It was the same black head-to-toe ensemble I'd worn on a previous caper. That adventure had worked out in the end, so I had high hopes this one would, too. Of course, my trusty lockpick and penlight helped my confidence. I was a woman who believed in the right tool for the right job, after all.

After three deep breaths, I kissed Ursi on the head, asked her to wish me good luck, and slipped out my back window onto the fire escape.

With the assurance that came from pulling off this stunt before, I glided down the metal stairs and dropped the last few feet to the ground without making a sound. A few quick steps had me at the gate of the building's tiny courtyard. As I opened the gate, a light from above stopped me cold. It was coming from the apartment on the third floor across from me.

I'd never seen that light on at this time of day.

Emulating Ursi as best as I could, I slipped through the opening quickly and quietly. With my heart in my throat, I leaned against the wooden privacy fence and closed the gate with my foot.

As long as I'd lived in my apartment, the sock shop across the hall from Renee's had used that space to store excess inventory. There was no reason for that light to be on at this time of night. Unless someone from the store had left it on.

Or someone was up there right now. Someone who might have seen me.

There was work to be done, so I set the troubling issue aside. If the light was still on when I returned, I'd bring it to Renee's attention tomorrow.

I gave the fence three taps for good luck, took a deep breath, and set off for Porter's house. Since I was on foot, it was easy to stick to the shadows. One time, though, I had to take cover behind an oak tree to keep from getting caught in a truck's headlights and ended up with mud-covered hands.

A few incident-free minutes later, I arrived at my destination. It was dark. With only pinpricks of starlight to illuminate the property, the place had an abandoned vibe. It made me sad.

Then I remembered the man inside might have murdered my hero.

I understood why Matt wanted to wait for more evidence before formally charging Porter with murder. I didn't agree with it. That meant finding hard evidence that would lead to Porter's arrest.

Now.

With my mission clear, I dashed around the side of the house to the backyard. The split rail fence was no match for me. I vaulted over the top horizontal rail with the ease of Wonder Woman.

Then it was decision time. Greenhouse or storage shed?

I headed for the shed. Luck was with me because the padlock on the shed doors used a key instead of a combination. It was time to, once again, use my trusty lock pick.

Picking a padlock wasn't quite the same as picking a door lock, but the difference didn't make me sweat. With my heart beating at a steady rhythm, I slipped on gloves and got to work.

I didn't want to draw attention to myself, so I left the penlight in my pocket and worked the lock strictly by feel. After a minute of manipulating the locking mechanism without success, a neighbor's dog let out a deep-throated series of barks. I dove to the ground and slapped my hand over my mouth to keep myself quiet.

When no lights came on, I got up on one knee and resumed my task, my heart now beating at a jogger's pace instead of a more sedate walker's. In fewer than sixty seconds, the lock was picked. I allowed myself a chuckle as I slipped inside the shed. Who knew a skill borne of desperation in New York years ago would be critical to snooping around in Rushing Creek?

My penlight provided illumination as I poked around the shed. It contained the usual things. In the center of the shed, like a luxury sedan at a high-end auto dealership, a spotless riding mower sat, waiting for action. On the far wall, lawn tools powered by small engines hung from nails. Bags of grass seed and lawn fertilizer lined the base of the wall to my right. To my left, rakes in assorted sizes leaned against each other as they towered over a couple of red, plastic gas cans. Smaller tools had made themselves at home on a wooden shelf that ran throughout the interior of the shed at eye level.

Disappointment grew as I analyzed every item in the shed with a close examination. Porter certainly took care of his things. The sharp edges of every cutting tool were covered with a thin sheen of lubricant. If something was metallic, it shone like polished silver in the penlight's beam.

If Porter was hiding something, it wasn't in the shed.

As if on cue, my phone vibrated. It had been an hour since I left the apartment. The longer I stuck around, the greater my odds were of getting caught. I'd spent time on the wrong side of Rushing Creek PD's interrogation room table before. I didn't want to do it again.

Time to move.

I opened the shed door a crack. The house was still dark. I locked the shed back up and scuttled across the lawn on all fours until I'd plastered my back against a greenhouse wall.

My heart was banging against my ribcage while blood was pounding in my ears. I closed my eyes and took deep, slow breaths to get my nerves back under control. As the jackhammer in my chest eased back to a rhythmic, normal *thump-thump*, I dried my sweaty palms on my yoga pants and marveled at the insanity of my situation.

Rational Allie said it was time to stop pushing my luck and get the heck out of Porter's back yard. Vicky's murder was a matter for the police, not me. Matt and his team were good cops, smart cops, who would make an arrest at the appropriate time. Justice would be served. My presence here would only screw things up.

Emotional Allie insisted the opposite was true. That the Kickboxing Crusader wouldn't leave the job unfinished. I'd promised to do everything in my power to bring Vicky's killer to justice. That meant getting inside the greenhouse and getting a look around.

Emotional Allie won.

I focused on the brightest star in the sky. "You can do this. For Vicky."

On all fours, I crept to the greenhouse's door. It was locked. The lock wasn't much more than a decoration, though, so I got inside the building in less time than it took to say supercalifragilisticexpialidocious.

The shed had provided concealment from the outside I currently lacked. With nothing but glass surrounding me, I was as vulnerable to keen eyes as a free-range chicken was to a fox. It didn't matter. Since I didn't have Ursi's gift of night vision, illumination was a necessity.

I clicked the penlight on and held my breath.

No dogs barked and no house lights flashed on, so I got to work. Pointing the beam at the floor minimized the illumination but made for slow going. I wasn't sure what I was looking for. Sure, a small, glass bottle with a skull-and-crossbones label on it would have been helpful, but I wasn't counting on striking that pot of gold. I was hoping I'd recognize a clue when I saw it.

With more patience than it took to get the twins to eat their vegetables when they stayed over, I made my way down the greenhouse's center aisle. Other than the flowers themselves, the only things of note to my right were two plastic jugs of fertilizer and twenty-pound bags of potting soil, stacked four high.

A little table was at the end of the aisle. Pruning shears, a hand spade, and other garden implements were lined up in a neat row on the wooden surface, next to a brass watering can that looked to be a century old. Green garden hoses were wrapped up at the base of the table, one on each side.

I peeked inside the can. It was empty. A long sniff confirmed there were no noxious odors, either. So far, I'd come up with a big fat nothing.

A sinking feeling was growing in my gut as I bent down for a closer look at the hoses. Maybe this was nothing more than a fool's errand. It would be easy enough to call it quits and make a quiet exit. Nobody would be the wiser.

Except me.

Now wasn't the time to quit on Vicky. Ten, maybe fifteen minutes more and I'd be on my way. I turned off the light and started to stand so I could stretch my back muscles. As I did so, disaster struck.

My elbow struck the watering can. In the darkness, I couldn't see it fall, but the clank, crash, and clang as it fell left no doubt what I'd done.

With my heart in my throat, I scrambled for the can, dropping the penlight in the process. Under my breath, I cursed my foolishness as I felt around in the dark. The split second I wrapped my hands around the spout, things went from bad to worse.

The dog started barking again. This time it kept up its *woof, woof, woof* until a light came on in Porter's house.

Indecision left me rooted in place, just like the plants surrounding me. Make a break for it or find a place to hide? I pawed around on the floor until I corralled my penlight. The seconds it took seemed like hours, but leaving it behind would be way too risky.

With it back in my possession, I got down on all fours to keep out of sight and moved toward the front of the greenhouse. My fingers were within inches of the escape when the back door of the house flew open with a bang.

I retreated, dropping a few curse words as I scuttled around, desperate to find something, anything to give me cover. The beam of Porter's flashlight flashed above my head as he shouted at the dog to be quiet. It responded to his shouts with more barking, as if to say *hey, dummy, there's a prowler in your greenhouse.*

The exchange bought me a few seconds. I dove into a space between the floor and the underneath surface of the raised beds and wormed my way behind a collection of plastic flower pots that were covered in cobwebs. The stench of compost filled my nostrils as I curled myself into a tight ball. An invisibility cloak would have really come in handy at the moment.

My heart was pounding out a rhythm that would rival a bass drum as the door opened. Surely, Porter could hear my heartbeat, even if he couldn't see me.

"Hello? Who's there?" The man's speech was slurred, as if he'd been drinking. "I've got a gun and I'm not afraid to use it."

A tiny click was followed by the greenhouse being bathed in a dim, yellow light. *Fabulous.* Someone who'd had too much to drink and was armed was looking for me. I shuddered at the thought of what would happen should he find me.

Thanks to a lucky break, the light left me in the shadows. At least I had that going for me.

I took small, light breaths to keep from making noise and sent up a prayer that he'd overlook me. The irony of asking for divine intervention in the middle of a break-in wasn't lost on me. Still, I was ready to take any help I could get.

Porter was making his way down the aisle at a sloth's pace. The time taken between steps seemed to be hours. As he moved, he maintained a running dialogue with himself. The words didn't make much sense, but at least they served to muffle the sounds of my breathing.

Before long, he left my limited field of vision. All I could do was remain as still as a corpse and wait him out. It was a thought that made my blood run cold.

"What do we have here?" Porter had come to a stop right in front of me. His tan chinos were mere inches from my face. The sour scent of cheap whiskey and sweat emanating from him made me want to gag.

"Can't have this now, can we?" He moved away, only to return a few moments later.

I squeezed my eyes shut and asked my maker to forgive my transgressions. This was it. The man had murdered my hero and was about to do the same to me.

A soft thump right above my head almost pulled a scream from me, but I managed to keep silent. Then came a metallic *snip*. It was followed by more of the same. A few seconds later, green leaves floated to the floor.

Holy horticulture! He was pruning the flowers right above me.

My hip was broadcasting waves of pain to let me know it had reached its limit of being in such an awkward position. Yet, adjusting myself, even a fraction of an inch, was out of the question.

When I thought things couldn't go downhill any further, sweat began dripping down my nose, tickling my nostrils. If my predicament didn't change soon, a sneeze, and my exposure, was inevitable.

"Much better." Another handful of leaves drifted to the floor as Porter shuffled away, his brown loafers scraping against the hard-packed, gravel floor.

A few seconds later, he passed me as he made his way back in the direction of the door.

"Must have been a squirrel or something. Well, goodnight my lovelies. See you in the morning." The lights went out and Porter made his exit.

I let out a long breath and let my head fall back against the wall. My vision blurred as tears formed. That was too close.

Way too close.

A little later, the back door to Porter's house slammed shut. Once again, I was alone in the darkness. Thanks to the flowers mere inches above me, I'd escaped detection.

I crawled out from my hiding place and made for the door, ignoring the protests from my hip and shoulder. After counting to three to build up my courage, I slipped out of the greenhouse and headed straight for home.

When my building came into view, I vowed never to try such a foolish stunt again. Whether I could hold myself to it was another thing entirely.

Chapter Fifteen

Despite employing melatonin, smooth jazz, and bergamot oil, sleep was slow in coming. When I eventually did nod off, I had nightmares of my hair being cut off by garden shears, then being stuffed into a garbage bag and dumped in a landfill.

When the alarm went off, I was groggy from sleep deprivation but also agitated due to my misadventure's lack of success. To remedy the situation, I headed for my spare room at the back of the apartment for a kickboxing session.

The exercise was good for me both physically and mentally. While I broke a good sweat, my mind cleared and let ideas come to the surface. Sure, it was frustrating I'd failed to find evidence to definitively tie Porter to Vicky's murder. That failure provided the opportunity to consider other possibilities. After all, the evidence was all circumstantial so far.

As I pounded the leather bag with right-left-right combinations, my conversation with Ozzy came to mind. Despite the man's crusty attitude, he knew a lot about Rushing Creek. I would be foolish to dismiss his analysis.

What if Ozzy was right? Could Gary really be the murderer? One thing was for sure. If I was Gary, I'd be keeping a low profile as the evidence stacked up against Porter. As far as I knew, there'd been no sign of Vicky's ex since I'd seen him at the restaurant.

Was that a coincidence? I gave the bag a roundhouse kick with my left leg and arrived at a decision at the same time. Matt taught me not to believe in coincidences, especially when murder was involved.

I had home ownership research to do.

Since it was the second week of April, royalty payments for the first quarter of the year had arrived from publishers. My clients worked hard and deserved their money. No matter what, they came first. I spent a couple of hours processing the payments. Despite my desire to investigate Gary, that task could wait.

When that was complete, I posted a message on the private agency social media page that I'd be making author royalty payments in a few days. Doing that always made me feel like a million bucks. My authors worked hard. It was fulfilling to see them, literally, rewarded for their labor. It was one of the things that served as a reminder I had the greatest job in the world.

I wanted to keep the positive mojo going, so I gave Ursi some kitty treats, grabbed my laptop, and hopped on my bike for a ride to the library. Sure, I could have done my research from the comfort of my couch, with Ursi snuggled by my side. Instead, I thought it would be a nice gesture to visit the library. The Wi-Fi signal was more than adequate for my research purposes, and I could offer the staff some moral support.

The hugs the staff gave me when I entered the building confirmed I'd made the right choice. They were grieving, too, and deserved whatever help I could give them. Even something as small as a pat on the back and a kind word.

A group of gray-haired senior citizens was discussing their latest book club choice as I wound my way to a research spot. They were talking about *Red Gale Gamble*, the latest novel by my thriller-writing client Malcolm Blackstone. The train of positivity was full steam ahead today.

Once I found a spot to my liking, I got to work. The first step was to confirm the ownership status of Vicky's house. A five-minute search of the assessor's office records verified Gary's claim. Both he and Vicky were still listed as owners of the property. I wouldn't have believed it if I hadn't been staring at an electronic version of the property card.

With that task complete, I wanted to learn about the man. The challenge I faced was the lack of online information about him. It was easy enough to confirm his current job on LinkedIn and current address with a Google search, but information that mattered to me was less easy to obtain.

I wanted to know more about the circumstances that led to the divorce and, more specifically, anything to confirm whether the deed issue really was an oversight. Luck was with me when I came across an article the *Brown County Beacon* had published. Evidently, since Vicky was the town's librarian, the paper's editor at the time thought her personal life was a matter of public interest.

The report was rife with gossip and allegations attributed to anonymous sources. Drinking, infidelity, and money problems came up at one point or another. It was so bad, by the time I finished the slimy piece, I wanted to take a shower.

I was also infuriated that such a horrible piece had made it to publication. The *Beacon*'s journalistic standards had certainly changed over time. For the better, thank goodness.

Neither Vicky nor Gary were portrayed in a positive light, but she came out looking a lot better than he did. While she was portrayed as a cold, distant spouse, he came across as a carousing spendthrift.

And there it was. Gary was allegedly a big spender. If it was true back then, maybe it was true today. I tapped my knuckles on the arm of my chair as I considered what to do next. I wanted to get a look at the man's current bank records. That was going to be easier said than done, though.

I wandered through the stacks to stretch my legs while I debated the merits of going to the police with my latest concerns about Gary. Matt had already promised he'd look into the man. It wouldn't help the situation to make a nuisance of myself. Maybe it was best to leave it to the pros.

For now, at least.

Having decided to put Gary on the back burner for the time being, I started back to my chair. In the fiction section, I stopped to chat with Ashton Bergman, one of the part-time employees. When I said hi, she looked at me with puffy, red-rimmed eyes.

"Tough day, huh?"

"Crying at work. I know, real professional." She wiped her eyes with a tissue. "I thought I was doing better. I even thought I was done crying. Guess I was wrong."

Ashton was a few years younger than I was. She and her husband had a son, Wyatt, who played soccer with the twins. I didn't know the woman well, but Rachel was constantly raving about her organizational skills as the team mom.

Between her perfectly manicured nails, flawless complexion, and glamorous long, brown hair, she looked like a totally together mother of the new millennium. Breaking down at work didn't seem to be in her nature, so her current state had me concerned.

"I understand." I put my hand on her forearm and gave it a little squeeze. "Vicky was special to everyone. Is there anything I can do?"

"No." She leaned against the shelves and knocked a John Grisham novel to the floor.

I grabbed it and slid it back into position. "Old habits die hard."

She laughed, which lightened the mood. Humor was definitely good for the soul.

"You know, there is something you can do." She wrapped her arms around herself. "It's Vicky's office. This morning we got word from the library board to have someone clear it out. I drew the short straw."

It was my turn to lean against the shelves for support, as my legs had turned to rubber at the news. To have to go through Vicky's things, separating personal from business items, wouldn't be a pleasant task for anyone who knew the woman.

On the other hand, for the right person, it could be an opportunity for a final conversation of sorts with her. A chance to reflect on the past and relish the memories created with Rushing Creek's beloved librarian.

I was the right person.

"Tell you what, Ashton." I took her by the arm and led her toward the break room. "Why don't you get yourself something to drink. I'll take care of Vicky's office."

A few minutes later, I grasped the aluminum door handle. It was cold to the touch. A shiver went through me as the implication of what I was about to take on sunk in.

The room on the other side of the wooden door held too many memories to count. To put things in boxes for transfer to Vicky's house, or worse, to be thrown away, seemed like desecration, like taking a sledge hammer to the sanctuary at church.

But it would provide the catharsis I needed. At some point, I had to accept that she was gone. No matter how hard I tried to reel in her killer, I couldn't bring her back. Besides, she didn't need my help where she was now.

I needed hers, though. I needed some way to say goodbye in my own way. Catching her killer might give me a sense of vengeance, but it wouldn't help me say farewell. To let go, once and for all. If going through the things in her office couldn't do it, nothing would.

Here goes. With a gentle push, the door swung open without a sound. It was dark and gloomy until I switched on the overhead lights. The room hadn't changed much since I'd last been in it. Some papers on her desk had been rearranged and a few of the filing cabinet drawers hadn't been fully closed.

The police had been respectful in their search the day of the murder. I made a mental note to relay my appreciation to Matt.

Somebody had left a few cardboard boxes in a corner, so I grabbed one and filled it with new books that needed to be entered into the library's system. A tear came to my eye when I came across half a dozen novels written by my authors. Supporting my authors by purchasing their books was supporting my career. It was yet another way the woman had been looking out for me.

When I was certain there were no more books to be added to the system, I took the box to Ashton. She thanked me when I told her what to do with them. I understood. She wasn't grateful for being given work to do. She appreciated my help in completing her assignment and letting her get the credit. It did my heart good to help her, so it was a win for both of us.

Dealing with the books was a no-brainer, but I was uncertain what to do when I returned to the office. As my gaze went from one side of the cluttered room to the other, my shoulders sagged. Over thirty years of documents, mementos, and knickknacks had accumulated in here, and I'd volunteered to remove them.

Vicky's desk was as good a starting point as any, so I eased into the desk chair and put all of the papers in a single pile. That tiny act gave me an idea. Personal items would go in one box. Office supplies would go in another for later reuse by the library. Items that could be thrown away would go in a trash bag. Everything else would be labeled with Post-It notes, their fate to be decided by the library staff.

With my plan in place, I started with the top, right-hand drawer of Vicky's desk. It was filled with pens, paper clips, and other random office supplies, so I made quick work of it. The second drawer held two collapsible umbrellas and a dozen disposable rain ponchos.

I laughed and let a tear run down my cheek. Vicky was always prepared for the unexpected in case one of her employees or patrons wasn't. God love her. I was going to miss her.

The bottom drawer was chock full of extension cords, all tangled together. It was an odd sight. I'd always known Vicky to treat library property with care. It was a shame I couldn't ask her about the mess.

Once I had the cords wound up and bound with Velcro strips, I dropped them in the box with the office supplies. With the cords removed, I found a cedar curio box in the drawer with Vicky's name engraved on the lid in gold script. A warm memory of a winter night long ago came to me. I'd given the box to her for Christmas my senior year of high school to thank her for all she'd done for me.

For years, it had sat in a place of honor, right next to her nameplate. It was shocking I hadn't noticed she'd moved it. I couldn't deny the pang of disappointment that ran through me as I tried to imagine what convinced her to hide it under a bunch of extension cords. Oh well, yet another mystery involving my hero that would remain unanswered.

I started to put the box among her personal items when curiosity got the best of me. She used to keep peppermints in it. Did she still do so? Like a little kid sneaking a sweet before dinner, anticipation built up inside as I lifted the lid.

Huh. Instead of candy, the only thing in the box was a wad of aluminum foil in a shape that resembled one of those energy bars Sloane ate before a run. I picked it up. Its weight confirmed this wasn't simply a wadded-up ball of aluminum foil.

Something was inside the foil wrapping.

The hair on the back of my neck rose to attention. Was this a clue? Using a pencil and a pair of scissors so I didn't leave more of my fingerprints, I peeled back the aluminum foil and found a layer of parchment paper. I'd seen similar paper at Rachel's restaurant.

Whatever was wrapped within the parchment paper was soft. It wasn't a collection of rare and valuable jewels or gold coins. The thought of Vicky as a jewel thief made me chuckle and eased the tension that had been building in my neck.

Using the same method I'd followed with the aluminum foil, I unwrapped the parchment paper.

"No way." After all that effort at being careful, all I found was a plastic bag containing green plant material that looked like Italian spices.

I sat back and scratched a mosquito bite on my arm. Why would anyone keep a wrapped-up stash of spices in their desk drawer? If they were expensive spices, then I guess that might make sense if one wrapped them up at home. But at the office? No.

After a closer look, I had a brain blast. Taking even more care than before, I opened the bag and sniffed. Woo boy. That wasn't the aroma of oregano, basil, or thyme. Unless I was mistaken, it was the aroma of something way illegal.

It was the aroma of marijuana.

I zipped the bag shut and looked toward the door to make sure nobody had seen me. The implications of my discovery brought on a massive headache. I'd just opened a ten-foot-high can of worms. A question came up that made me sweat.

What should I do next?

Chapter Sixteen

The closest I'd ever been to marijuana in my life was smelling it and seeing people smoke it while I lived in New York. While weed was becoming legal in more states every year it seemed, in Indiana it was still illegal. On account of that, since moving to Rushing Creek, I hadn't come across it other than noticing a whiff or two emanating from tourists during the summer. So, I wasn't convinced my suspicion was right.

I knew someone who could tell me, though.

A half hour later, I was in Mom's office.

"It's definitely marijuana. No doubt about it." She pushed the bag across her desk toward me. "And stop shaking. I'll file this under doctor-patient confidentiality."

I sat on my hands to stop the trembling. It worked. Sort of.

"But why would she have it, Mom?" I bit the inside of my cheek by accident and let out a howl. The pain radiating from my mouth didn't help my agitated state. "Vicky was as straight as an arrow. The craziest I ever saw her get was when she had a second glass of champagne at my apartment open house."

"I don't know. Maybe—"

"Could she have gotten a prescription for it? From, I don't know," I waved my hands around in circles as I tried to come up with something, "an osteopath or someone like that?"

Mom rolled her eyes as she tried, and failed, to suppress a chuckle. As my cheeks got hot, her smile turned into a frown.

"Nobody can prescribe it legally here. There is a pill that contains THC, the active ingredient, for lack of a better term, in marijuana. I've never written a script for it, but I know a couple of colleagues who have."

I tapped the bag. "That obviously doesn't apply here. Is there anything else you can think of?"

"It's not out of the realm of possibility she went out of state to get it. Some states where it's legal are within easy driving distance." She frowned. "I know she took something nonprescription for a touch of arthritis in her knees, but she never complained about anything worse than that. Overall, she was in fine health."

"So, what are you saying?" I forced myself to keep my voice level. "You think she was a closet dope smoker?"

Mom put up her hands. "Not at all. What I am saying is we shouldn't jump to any conclusions."

I massaged my neck muscles. The tension was killing me. The circumstances surrounding Vicky's death were crazy enough. Now, this discovery made it darn near impossible not to conjure up wild scenarios.

"You don't think this has anything to do with her murder?"

"I don't know, Allie." Mom took a drink from a bottle of sparkling water. "I've got an appointment in a few minutes, so I need to go. I think you should see the police about this. Right now."

Mom had always been the clearheaded one in the family. When she gave advice, it was unwise to ignore it. I'd made enough unwise decisions in the past few days.

"I will. Promise me one thing?" I remained silent until she nodded. "Keep this between the two of us? I don't want Vicky's reputation tarnished when she can't defend herself."

"Like I said, I'll consider this a matter of doctor-patient confidentiality."

I gave Mom a hug while I thanked for her help and understanding. Once I was back outside, I took a moment to collect my thoughts.

My hero, Vicky Napier, a dope smoker? It didn't make sense. Of course it didn't, because I didn't know the whole story. There could have been a perfectly reasonable explanation, in Vicky's mind at least, for her to have the pot.

Maybe she used it to help with pain or some other medical issue I didn't know about. Or maybe she had gotten it for a friend who used it for pain management. My not knowing the reason for her possession of it was of vital importance here. After all, why risk tarnishing a wonderful woman's reputation when I didn't have all the facts?

My internal debate came to an abrupt halt when my phone buzzed. It was an appointment reminder. I had another intern interview in thirty minutes.

"Seriously?" I shook my fist at the clear, blue sky. It wasn't falling, but at times it seemed like it.

There was no way I was going to turn in the marijuana without being able to explain in detail how it came into my possession. That meant giving it to Matt or Jeanette and nobody else. My visit to the police station would have to wait.

Since I was getting around on two wheels instead of two feet, I made it home in plenty of time to hide my discovery, change into a nicer outfit, and get downstairs to Renee's for some coffee before the interview started.

A handful of customers browsed the aisles while Renee, in a black peasant dress with red and silver accents, added books to the fiction shelves. Syncopated, piano-heavy jazz flowed from the speakers. I helped myself to a cup.

"Look at you. Quite the no-nonsense ensemble. Planning on taking over the world?" Renee offered me a packet of sweetener.

"Just the publishing world. You can have the rest." In a lime green oxford shirt, gray slacks, and black flats, I wanted to convey a professional message during the interview. Based on my friend's comment, it was mission accomplished.

We chatted while I waited for my interviewee to arrive. Business had been brisk all day, which made Renee happy.

"Which reminds me, I signed a contract to replace the roof. They should start work next month. I'll let you know when I have a firm start date." Renee flicked a piece of black fuzz from her sleeve. "It'll be a relief to finally have that taken care of."

A new roof had been at the top of my landlord's wish list since before I moved in. The current one wasn't leaking, but it was over twenty years old. We'd often talked about the replacement fund she'd been building ever since she bought the building ten years ago.

Chatting about the roof made me think of the third floor. And the mysterious light that had been on. Should I ask about? If I did, would Renee want to know details? That could put me on the spot as to what I was doing when I saw it.

Well, nothing ventured, nothing gained.

"Are you doing any—"

"Excuse me, Miss Cobb?"

I turned to find a tall woman with short, brown hair standing a few feet away from me.

"I'm Brandy Whitaker. I'm here for the interview."

I didn't want to be rude to Brandy, so the question about the light would have to wait.

"Wonderful meeting you." I shook her hand.

Renee poured her a cup of coffee while we exchanged pleasantries.

The woman chattered nonstop as we walked to the back of the store and got seated. I'd never had someone fangirl over me, so I didn't know what it was like. This had to be close, though.

"I can't believe I'm actually having coffee with the Kickboxing Crusader."

The mention of the crime fighting nickname Sloane had given me made me wince. I'd gotten used to it as a joke among family and friends, but its use by people I didn't know made me uncomfortable.

"I've looked over your resume."

Brandy was practically bouncing up and down in her seat, so I focused on my interview checklist to minimize the distractions.

"I see you're an adjunct professor of English. Tell me about that."

"Sure, but can I get a selfie with you first?" Before I could protest, she had her arm around me and her camera in front of us. "Smile."

She was quick. I had to give her that. I scratched an eyebrow as I regathered my thoughts. "Now, about your teaching experience."

"Right." Her focus was on her phone. No doubt, the picture was going to be on the web in minutes. "I teach English as a Second Language to adults at the community college in Columbus. This semester, I'm teaching night classes twice a week."

Okay, Brandy was stretching the rubber band of truth, but not enough to make it snap. To teach a class like that, she had to have a strong background in two languages. That was a promising start.

"And what made you interested in the position?"

"Working with you." She leaned toward me. "By the way, I heard you're looking into the librarian's murder. Is it true?"

Good Lord, this woman wasn't interested in working in the publishing industry. She seemed to have this misguided idea I lived this Wonder Woman–like double life as a literary agent by day and crime fighter by night. If only I was as glamorous as Lynda Carter or Gal Gadot, the actors who'd played Wonder Woman.

Despite every effort I made to limit the discussion to the intern position, the conversation invariably turned to my history of solving mysteries. The realization was crushing. Given Brandy's background, I'd begun the interview with high hopes. With each question and each rambling, off-point answer, those hopes died a slow, pitiful death.

When the interview reached the thirty-minute mark, I brought it to a close.

"Great. Do I have the job? I can start anytime." She gave me a soft punch to the shoulder. "You and me. We'll make a great pair, like a modern Holmes and Watson."

It took one hundred percent effort from every fiber in my body to refrain from cringing. At least I had a ready-made excuse to let her down softly.

"I'm still conducting interviews. I'll be in touch when they're complete."

I shook her hand and escorted her out the door. The second she was out of sight, I leaned against a wall and blew out a long breath.

"I take it the search continues?" Renee glanced at me from the sale she was ringing up.

"Yep. One more to go." I left it at that. There was no need to be unkind.

Since Renee was busy with customers, I headed upstairs. With my question about the mystery light still on my mind, I bypassed my apartment and climbed the steps to the third floor.

A fine layer of dust covered the corridor's hardwood floor. The unadorned walls took on a grayish sheen in the meager light that penetrated the dirty window behind me. A trail of footprints from the stairs to the door to my left were the only indication of activity up here.

In the time I'd lived in my apartment, I'd been aware of the third floor but hadn't given it any thought. It was like the Soldiers and Sailors Monument in downtown Indianapolis. I knew it was there, but it didn't affect my life, so I never gave it any thought.

Renee told me when I moved in that she had plans to eventually renovate the third-floor apartments but wanted to replace the roof first. Maybe she'd been up here the night I saw the light.

I wandered toward the window at the far end of the hall, my footfalls echoing as if I was in a subterranean cave. When I reached the end, I leaned on the windowsill and peered out. The view of the courtyard below wasn't that much different than the view from my fire escape.

Green, wall-to-wall, all-weather carpeting took the place of grass. A gas grill, its lid open, had been wheeled against the fence that bordered the alley. Someone had set up a game of cornhole but hadn't bothered to put it away. Plastic deck chairs were situated in a shallow U-shape, apparently to watch the cornhole game.

After a glance over my shoulder to make sure I was alone, I undid the latch. Dirt, wood, and old paint conspired to make an awful screech as I forced up the window. After leaning on the frame to catch my breath, I poked my head out to get a look around.

Visions of me taking the place of a bird in a cuckoo clock made me laugh. What did I think I was doing? I had no business being up here. Sure, Renee had never prohibited me from visiting the third floor, but I couldn't escape the feeling I was trespassing.

Well, I was here, so it would be a waste of time, and effort, to simply slip back inside and return to my apartment. With that in mind, I leaned out as far as I could to see if I could get a look into the apartment to my left.

The light was off. With no illumination, I couldn't see anything. Maybe I'd have better luck next time.

Someone had turned off the light, though. That must have meant something. I just didn't know what. Or maybe I was just getting paranoid.

With a growl, I scooched back in and closed the window. *Ugh.* My hands were filthy and I'd gotten cobwebs in my hair. On top of that, my blouse was covered with grime. Hopefully, a trip through the washer and dryer would get the stains out. It was one of my favorite tops. I didn't want to have to throw it away because of my own carelessness.

I brushed what gunk I could off my hands and marched downstairs like I snooped around the third floor all the time. Ursi met me when I opened my door. She gave me a quick sniff, pinned her ears back, and turned away from me.

"Happy to see you, too." I rolled my eyes and headed to the bathroom. "I get it. I was sticking my nose where it didn't need to be and got all filthy."

After cleaning up, I made my way to the kitchen for some dinner. Ursi wound her way around my legs and started running her motor the second I opened a can of fancy, soft food.

"My apologies for coming home so gross." I put her food bowl on the floor.

Ursi gave me a *meh* and attacked her dinner. Evidently it was apology accepted.

The marijuana from Vicky's desk was weighing heavy on my mind, so I texted Ashton to apologize for my hasty exit and to let her know I'd return in the morning to finish the job. Nobody else was getting a look in there until I had a chance to give it a thorough once-over.

God only knew what else was in there.

After chatting with Brent and promising all was well, I fell into bed early and drifted off to sleep with Ursi curled up at my feet and Janet Evanovich's latest on my lap. Holy cow, what a day.

The next day, I strode into the library as the doors opened. After exchanging pleasantries with Ashton and the rest of the staff, I made a beeline for Vicky's office. A disturbing thought had occurred to me while I'd been getting dressed. What if there was more marijuana stashed around Vicky's office? Or at her house, even? There'd been no word of anything being found, but maybe the police were keeping that quiet.

I held my breath as I opened the door. The room was as I'd left it.

Maybe I was letting my imagination run wild by worrying about problems that didn't exist. It had become an occupational hazard. I'd had a hyperactive imagination my entire life. While it had served me well as an agent, as an investigator, it had its plusses and its minuses.

Finding the room as I'd left it was a huge relief. I let out a long, tension-relieving breath and thanked the stars for my good fortune. It was time to get to work.

I finished the desk in short order. After that, I turned my attention to the first of the filing cabinets. The top drawer was packed with purchase orders. I stuck a Post-It note on the front of the drawer so the staff would know what it contained.

The drawer below was much the same. Evidently, the document retention policy Vicky followed was to keep every single document.

The next one down housed folders containing spreadsheets and similar budget-related documents. Except for the last folder.

It held an aluminum foil package just like I'd found yesterday.

My heart rate hit maximum race speed as I yanked open the other drawers. One package had been bad enough. Two was outright worrisome. A third turned up in the bottom drawer of the middle cabinet.

Now I was sweating.

As if I were searching for a ticking time bomb, I went from cabinet to cabinet, shelf to shelf, hoping and praying the bomb wouldn't be there. I even got on my hands and knees to check under the credenza.

Right when I thought there was nowhere else to look, I noticed a sliver of space between the filing cabinets and the wall. It wasn't more than a couple of inches wide.

But it was wide enough to serve as a hiding place for package number four.

Enough was enough. It was time to call the police.

Chapter Seventeen

"Hey, Allie. What's up?" Jeanette's voice was cheery. Like she was having a good day.

And I was about to ruin it.

"Can you come see me at the library? And bring Matt if he's available?"

My efforts to keep my voice neutral were utter failures because Jeanette went into serious cop mode in an instant.

"What's going on? Is it an emergency? Are there injuries?"

"No. It's nothing like that. I, uh, found some things in Vicky Napier's office." In stop-and-start fashion, thanks to being totally unnerved, I told Jeanette about offering to clean out the office and my subsequent findings.

"Stay right where you are. We'll be there in five."

Now all I could do was wait. And let the chips fall where they might.

A few minutes later, there was a knock on the door. Before I'd had a chance to answer, the door swung open and Matt entered. Jeanette was right behind him, with her evidence technician kit in hand.

The police chief's eyes were blazing as he marched to within inches of me. He stood there, glaring at me, until the door closed with a click.

"Officer Wilkerson, will you repeat to me the conversation you had a few minutes ago with Miss Cobb?"

Miss Cobb? Matt never called me that. This wasn't good.

His gaze held me rooted in place as Jeanette recounted our phone call. When she finished, he opened his notebook.

"Is that an accurate version of what you said to Officer Wilkerson?" When I nodded, his focus, finally, shifted from me to the notebook. "Can you point to where these items are?"

At my direction, Jeanette, with gloved hands, retrieved the evidence. She opened one package and gave it a sniff.

"Marijuana. No doubt about it." She dropped each of the packages into their own paper evidence bag and made notes on each of them.

"I want a detailed sweep of this room. Call in backup if you need it." Matt turned his attention back to me. "You found another one of these yesterday? Where is it?"

With a wince, I confessed it was at my apartment. "I'm sorry. I know I should have called you. I panicked. Vicky was my hero. I didn't want to believe she'd have anything to do with something illegal."

I'd messed with evidence and compromised a crime scene. On top of that, I'd delayed reporting what I'd found by almost twenty-four hours. If there was ever a time for Matt to be justified in yelling at me, then slapping handcuffs on me and hauling me off to jail, this was it.

The explosion never came.

Instead, he leaned on the edge of the desk and rubbed his eyes. "You couldn't leave well enough alone, could you?"

"Look." My embarrassment was turning to anger. Sure, I'd messed up, but I was still going to stand up for myself. "I *was* leaving well enough alone. I only found the pot because I was doing Ashton a favor. Seems to me your team should have been more thorough when they searched the library. Or did they even conduct a search?"

Matt swallowed as he scribbled down something. Jeanette was seemingly too engrossed in her evidence collection work to get drawn into the debate. Their silence spoke volumes.

They must have completed only a cursory search of the office.

This wasn't the time to press my advantage. What mattered was getting to the bottom of the situation.

"Is this the drawer where you found the package yesterday?" Jeanette was by the desk, down on one knee. When I nodded, she put a yellow evidence marker by the drawer pull. "I'll finish searching the room and check for prints where Allie found the evidence. Work for you, Chief?"

Matt nodded and adjusted his Rushing Creek PD baseball cap. I was still in his doghouse, but calling his team out on their major oversight had knocked him off his high horse. For now, we'd reached détente.

"What haven't you told me?" He cracked the smallest hint of a smile. The man knew me well. He'd learned, sometimes the hard way, there was usually more to my stories than I let on initially.

Since this was one of those times, and I was still in jeopardy of being arrested for withholding evidence or something worse, I told him about my visit to Mom's office. A knock on the door brought my report to a halt.

"As much as you'd like me to, I can't cover for Vicky. This information will have to go into a police report. All of it. Be right back." Matt stepped outside, closing the door behind him.

I dropped curse words as I flopped into Vicky's desk chair. "I hit a new high mark in stupidity this time, didn't I?"

Jeanette, who was burrowing her way through a box of paperbacks that had been marked for the book sale, shrugged. "I don't know. Facing a killer alone in a hotel room's pretty tough to top in that category."

There was no malice or ill intent in Jeanette's tone. She was simply stating the truth. It was a tough point to argue. Still.

"I don't know. I thought walking down a dark alley at night while a murderer was on the loose was pretty inadvisable."

"Copy that." Jeanette went to a box of hardbacks for the sale. "Then again, chasing a truck being driven by a suspected murderer through town on your bike is a solid contender for the Foolish Amateur Crime Fighting Award."

"Yeah, well, sometimes the Kickboxing Crusader has to put herself at peril in the pursuit of truth, justice, and the American way."

Jeanette laughed so hard, she snorted. That was one of the many great things about her. She knew the value of a joke, especially in anxiety-filled moments.

"I thought you hated that nickname?" She picked up a massive Stephen King novel, gave it a shake and, when nothing fell out, returned it to the box.

"I do. But I figure now is as good a time as any to bring up my past exploits on behalf of the greater good. You know, like Frozone from *The Incredibles*."

"Here's the deal." Jeanette removed her gloves. "Were you foolish, dumb, reckless? Yes. Did you break the law when you decided to keep the weed you found yesterday? I'm afraid so, but a good defense attorney could probably get you off."

I opened my mouth, but Jeanette put her hand up to stop me.

"Let me finish." She stared at the floor. "Matt's angry, but he's less mad at you than he is at himself and the department. We should have been more thorough when we searched the library. He's the one who's going to have to deal with any blowback from this."

Jeanette's words were reassuring and let me return to why she and Matt were here in the first place.

"All this marijuana has to be connected to the murder, doesn't it?"

"Maybe, maybe not." Matt closed the door behind him. "I've been persuaded to keep the library open while Officer Wilkerson continues her work. Allie, you and I are going to continue our conversation elsewhere."

He opened the door. "Shall we?"

With my head held high in defiance of Matt, I strolled out of the office. Determined to maintain my poise, I avoided eye contact with the dozen or so patrons and staff who had gathered by the checkout counter.

Their whispered conversations made my ears burn, but I wasn't in handcuffs, so I stopped new rumors from getting out of the gate. A few feet from the exit, I turned to him.

"Thank you for your quick response to my call, Chief. I appreciate your help." Without waiting for a response, I pushed open the door and headed for my bike.

"Not so fast." Matt wrapped a hand around my upper arm. "Clever stunt, but we still need to talk. Wheel your bike over to my cruiser and then we'll go someplace less conspicuous."

Twenty minutes later, after a stop at my apartment to pick up the last of the contraband, we were seated in a booth at the back of Big Al's Diner. It was my favorite restaurant. Matt knew that, so he must want something.

"This is less conspicuous than the library?" I raised an eyebrow as I stirred sweetener into my coffee.

"I know you like this place, so it's more conducive to an honest conversation, then." He took a sip of his coffee. "Why do you think your discovery is connected to Napier's murder and not something else?"

"I wish I had something concrete to give you, but all I've got is a feeling. I knew the woman, Matt. Between the disorienting effect it has, and the gunk that would be left in her lungs, I simply can't imagine her smoking dope." I pointed my spoon at him. "For the sake of argument, if she was smoking it, why hide it in a public building? Wouldn't it have made more sense to keep her stash at home?"

Matt ran his fingers through his hair. "You ask better questions than a couple of people on my team. If you tell anyone I said that, I'll toss you behind bars and throw away the key."

I made a motion like I was zipping my lips shut. Then I crossed my heart. I didn't want to end up in jail, even if Matt's comment had been made in jest. It couldn't hurt to be on the safe side. Just in case.

"Seriously, though, I don't have answers to your questions." He tapped his pencil on the tabletop. "I'll make the usual inquiries, but it doesn't make any sense."

"Maybe you could have a word with my old friend Willie Hammond?" I chuckled. Willie and I were far from friends. He and Al were brothers. Their last name was about all they had in common, though. Al was gregarious and kind to a fault. Willie was calculated and shady. The fact that Willie was involved with illegal gambling made me think even less of the man.

"Nah, after everything that went down last September, Willie knows I'm keeping my eye on him. Besides, I've never heard of him being connected with drugs." He finished his coffee and poured himself another cup.

"I'll follow up with the other doctors in town. See if Vicky had been seeing any of them. I don't know. With all the hippie artists who live around here and love to smoke a joint from time to time, God only knows where she got it."

"But what if she got it by accident? What if Porter's been growing weed and some found its way into the library?"

I slapped my hand on the table as an idea bloomed like an orchid in Porter's greenhouse. I'd always thought Porter's motive was weak. Sure, he had a crush on Vicky, but she'd never shown any interest in him. No, instead of unrequited love, I had a much more powerful motive.

"I'll bet you he was dealing to the employees, maybe even to some library patrons. Something happened and Vicky found out. She hid the weed until she could do something about it, probably talk to him, but he killed her to keep his operation under wraps."

Matt stared at me while he stirred his coffee. The classic-style soda pop clock on the wall ticked, ticked, ticked as the seconds passed. After what seemed like hours, he took a drink.

"It's possible. I'm not sure how plausible it is, though. We searched his property from top to bottom. If there was a dope-dealing operation going on, we didn't find any evidence of it."

He jotted down a few things in his notebook. "Tell you what I'll do. I'll have someone take another look at Porter's file. It's a long shot, but maybe he owns property somewhere that could be used for what you're suggesting."

I almost jumped out of my seat. "Yes. Thank you so much. I appreciate it."

"Don't get your hopes up, though. And promise me you'll stay out of trouble for a change, okay?"

"I'll try." I took a drink. "I don't mean to be a pain. I just want whoever did this caught. ASAP."

"I know. We all do. That's why I need you to help me by not withholding information or evidence. My team and I can't do our jobs when you pull stunts like you did with that package."

My cheeks got hot at the gentle admonishment. To cover my embarrassment, I brought my coffee cup to my lips and held it there, pretending to take a long drink.

Matt was right. There was no denying it.

The publishing industry had taught me the importance of patience. I believed in it. A book was ready when it was ready, and not a day before. It was a lesson I preached to my authors, especially my new ones, on a regular basis. Rushing through a manuscript or accepting a publishing deal without thinking over the terms of the agreement could lead to disappointment some time down the road.

When it came to my personal life, patience was something for which I had little use. Especially when friends and family were involved.

So, I finished my coffee and reiterated my pledge to behave myself. That didn't mean I wouldn't keep snooping, though.

Especially since the snooping I was going to do would be from the safety of my apartment.

After a quick pedal home, I settled in on the couch, with Ursi snuggled next to me and my computer on my lap. I had no doubt Matt would follow up as promised, but I couldn't deny my confidence in his team was a little shaken. Maybe I was being unfair, but since they missed the weed in Vicky's office, what else could they have missed?

The thought of Porter growing marijuana in secret someplace intrigued me. It was a longshot, but I wanted to see if there were any property records under a name associated with his old lawn and garden business.

One of the great things about living in the twenty-first century was the ability to search for property records of a potential murderer while scratching my kitty's ears. How Trixie Belden was able to solve all those cases without the internet was beyond me. I wouldn't trade life in the twenty-first century for anything.

A visit to the secretary of state's site confirmed the corporate name of Porter's old business, PRLG Industries, Inc. Not the most distinctive name, but it gave me something to go on. That was, assuming I was right that the initials stood for Porter Rasmussen Lawn and Garden Industries.

With that information in hand, I paid another cyberspace visit to the county assessor's office for a property records search. As the minutes went by, my hopes of making a hit faded away. After an hour of searching, using various permutations of Porter's and the company's name, I waved the white flag.

"No luck, girl."

I held Ursi against my chest as I scratched under her chin. Her purring eased my disappointment. The upside was that I didn't have to worry about the waters being muddied by another surprise discovery.

At least, that was the hope.

Chapter Eighteen

My displeasure at failing to find evidence Porter owned property under another name where he could be growing pot was eventually replaced by relief.

I'd done all I could. The next steps were up to the Rushing Creek Police, not me.

Which was good since my plans for tonight were focused on the Fearless Foursome.

The Fearless Foursome was a group formed in the aftermath of the murder of Rushing Creek resident Georgie Alonso. The membership consisted of me, my bestie Sloane, Jeanette, and another friend, Lori Cannon.

We were all personally connected to the two murders committed in Rushing Creek in the last couple of years. Sloane's father, Thornwell, had been knocked unconscious and dumped in the Rushing Creek to drown. Lori's boyfriend, Georgie, who was also the father of her little girl Brittany, had been suffocated under a pile of landscaping mulch.

At Sloane's request, I investigated her dad's murder. My impetus for looking into Georgie's murder was even more personal. For a while, I was the main suspect.

By virtue of her job, Jeanette worked on both investigations. She became a dear friend in the process.

Even though we all knew each other beforehand, the group had formed quite by accident. I'd noticed Lori having trouble coping in the aftermath of Georgie's death, so I suggested she talk to Sloane, figuring my bestie might be able to help Lori in a way nobody else in Rushing Creek could.

Jeanette and I had been exercising together and would often unwind after our walks with a cold drink at the pub. One night, we saw Sloane and Lori there. They invited us to join them, and the conversation turned to the coping mechanisms each of us used in the aftermath of traumatic experiences.

Each of us brought a different perspective to the table. The discussion proved to be more helpful than a cup of coffee first thing in the morning. Over the course of that evening, we laughed, cried, and formed a bond stronger than the one shared by Harry, Hermione, and Ron in the Harry Potter books.

Since then, we'd gotten together once a month for dinner and conversation. Topics of discussion usually centered around everyday things like Jeanette's dating life and the challenges Lori faced getting her finicky daughter to eat anything other than chicken nuggets and steamed carrots.

We always made sure every member of our group had time to open up about what she was feeling, though. Our get-togethers were safe spaces, where feelings, often raw ones, could be shared in a caring, confidential, and supportive environment.

Tonight was my night to host the Fearless Foursome, so, after checking work e-mails and assuring Brent I was safe and sound, I got the apartment ready. Thanks to Mom, I'd learned the value of neatness, so there wasn't a lot of hard work involved. At an early age, she'd instilled in me the importance of picking up after myself. To this day, I never started work without making my bed and putting clean clothes away instead of letting them stack up on a chair someplace.

A little bit later, I wiped my hands.

"I think we're ready. What about you, girl?"

My kitty sniffed at her litter box, looked at me, yawned, and plopped down on the floor to clean her paw.

"Fair enough. I'm sure our guests will appreciate your efforts to clean up for them." I went to the bedroom to change, whistling a bouncy Jason Mraz tune.

I was filling my ice bucket when there were three rapid knocks on the door, followed by someone calling out my name. This was repeated two more times.

"Coming, Sloane." My bestie's use of the same knock that Sheldon from *The Big Bang Theory* used tickled me to no end. She might have the body of a thirty-one-year-old, but she had the youthful heart and soul of a preteen. That was one of the many reasons I loved her.

"Sloanie Baloney." I wrapped my arms around her as soon as the door was open. She'd been traveling since Saturday, and I'd missed her wonderfully upbeat disposition during these dark days.

She handed a me a plastic grocery bag containing two-liter soda and called out for Ursi. A second later, my fur baby appeared and wound herself through Sloane's legs.

"Hey, sista. Tell your mom I'm not going to talk to her whenever she calls me by that dorky nickname." Sloane took Ursi in her arms and nuzzled with her as Ursi started purring loud enough to rattle the windows.

I let out a loud, drama-filled huff. "And please tell your aunt Sloane I will stop calling her that as soon as she stops calling me the Kickboxing Crusader."

Sloane looked at me out of the corner of her eye and grinned. The back-and-forth needling was all in fun, a hallmark of a lifetime spent as best friends. After pretending to put her ear close to Ursi's mouth, she returned the cat to the floor.

"Ursi told me to consider your truce offering and to get back to you later with a counter proposal. In the meantime, we're to set aside our dispute in the name of having a good time tonight." She sashayed over to the coffee table and took a couple of chips from a ceramic serving bowl. "She also said to remind you that, while she likes you, she adores me."

"Ungrateful feline." I stuck out my tongue at Ursi, who simply strolled away with her tail held high.

I waved for Sloane to join me in the kitchen while I poured her a ginger ale. "How's training going?"

Her career as a trail runner had reached the point where she was competing as a professional. She wasn't making much money as a pro athlete, but that wasn't the point.

What mattered was she was living out her dream. I'd known her all my life, and the one thing Sloane wanted was to be a runner. As a little girl, she ran for fun. As she got older, running became an escape from the dysfunction in her home. Now she was running because she was good at it.

One of the best, in fact.

The previous November, she'd competed in the national trail running championship, finishing second in her class and fourth overall among female competitors. That performance had put her in the mix to be selected to represent the U.S. at the world championships.

"It's good. I've got a couple of high school kids that want to start training with me. It's fun to be spreading the gospel of trail running."

The report filled my heart with joy. My bestie was happy doing what she loved. These were exciting times, indeed

A bit later, Lori arrived with a plate of homemade cookies and a bottle of Moscato.

"Brittany's spending the night with her grandmother, so Mama's ready for a glass of wine." She handed me her things, kicked off her four-inch heels, and plopped down in a chair in the living room. "Or two."

"Kiddo having trouble sleeping again?" Sloane took a seat next to Lori.

One of the things we often talked about during these get-togethers was our collective battle against insomnia. Lori had it the worst since Brittany often had nightmares due to missing her dad.

"She was doing really good." Lori accepted a glass of wine from me and took a drink. "No problems for three weeks. Then a boy at school started making fun of her for having a father who'd been murdered. Now we're back to square one."

"That stinks," Sloane and I said in unison. And it did. Big time.

Brittany had suffered enough trauma by losing her father. She was only six, for crying out loud. The last thing she needed was to be traumatized all over again by unthinking and cruel children.

"While I'm mad at the boy, I'm really angry at his parents. The things he said to Brittany were clearly learned." She took another drink. "I don't understand why there's so much hate in the world."

A knock on the door signaled Jeanette's arrival. I went to get it.

"I have connections at the police department. I could have one of my friends in blue pay this kid's parents a visit." Sloane put her arm around Lori as our young friend laughed. That was my bestie at her finest, bringing a little sunshine to the world.

I opened the door and was met with the glorious aroma of Italian cooking.

"Dinner has arrived." Jeanette motored into the kitchen and put her mouthwatering contribution on the counter. "Two pizzas, a couple orders of breadsticks, and an extra-large bowl of Marinara's salad. Let the festivities commence."

While I hung up Jeanette's jacket, my friends attacked the feast. The group had reached an agreement that the host was responsible for snacks, one person took care of dessert, the third brought drinks, and the fourth member of our merry band provided dinner.

We all loved Marinara's, so when Jeanette had asked if it would be okay if she did that instead of cooking something, the response was a resounding yes.

"Great call, Jeanette. I vote we have Marinara's every time from now on. I'll try to talk Freddie into making us a couple of her deep-dish pies," Sloane said through a mouthful of breadstick.

"I thought they only made deep dish on the weekends?" I folded my slice of pizza long ways, à la New York style. My decade in the City had turned me into a devoted fan of thin pizza. And one who thought fans of Chicago-style, deep-dish pizza were Philistines.

"That's because it's your turn for dinner next month." Lori ignored my question while she drizzled French dressing on her salad. "No weaseling out. Besides, I hear you make an amazing chili. You could do that."

"Who said I make an amazing chili?"

Lori grinned. "Your husband. He brags about you every time he comes into the bank. It's always Sloane did this amazing thing and Sloane did that amazing thing. I think he kinda likes you."

Sloane's cheeks turned beet red. She and my brother Luke had only been married for six months, so she was still getting used to being talked about by her husband.

"I heard he gives you foot massages after your long runs." Jeanette winked at me as Sloane's eyes got wide. The teasing was in full swing.

"All I know is that brother of mine better be doing those things." I leaned toward Sloane. "And a whole lot more, if you know what I mean."

We three who were dishing it out burst into laughter when Sloane put her hands over her ears and closed her eyes. She didn't open them until we quieted down.

"You three are monsters. But you're right. I am pretty amazing."

We broke into another round of laughter as Sloane got up and gave each of us fist bumps. I was in the company of good friends and dining on good food. Life couldn't get better.

It was an evening full of positivity as good things were happening to all of us. My agency was growing. Matt had approved Jeanette's request to attend an advanced evidence technician certificate course. Lori was in line for a promotion at the bank. The arc of Sloane's trail running career was continuing upward.

Even with all the good news, our meetings had a purpose, so I asked if anyone had something they wanted to get off their chest.

Lori cleared her throat. "I, um, heard the police found weed in Vicky's office. Is that really true?"

I clamped my mouth shut and looked at Jeanette. Since the contraband was in police custody, this was Jeanette's call. My work investigating the murder was over.

"News sure travels fast." Jeanette rubbed her eyes. "It's true. That's why I was late getting here. At this point, we're investigating all possible connections between the murder and the marijuana. Beyond that, I can't comment."

"Good old Mrs. Napier? A pothead? No way." Sloane removed the band holding her ponytail in place. She hadn't used the library as much as I had when we were growing up, but she shared my affection for the woman.

Jeanette put up her hands. "Nobody's saying she smoked pot."

"The security guard at the bank said it's connected to her murder. Is it?" Lori's brows were furrowed. She and Brittany went to the library twice a month. I sympathized with her concern.

"At this point, we simply don't know, so we're not ruling anything out."

I seized the opening my police friend had provided. "I've got an idea. Why don't we do a little brainstorming. See if we can come up with some ideas of why the pot was there."

An hour later, our flow of ideas had run dry. Despite my high hopes, we kept coming back to the theories Matt, Jeanette, and I had already discussed. Lori and Sloane were convinced the pot was somehow connected to Porter. There was no scenario we could come up with that brought Gary into the mix. When I mentioned Ozzy, the others chuckled and shook their heads.

"Allie, at this point, I think you need to let it go. Jeanette kinda knows her stuff, after all." Sloane dipped her pizza crust into a cup of cheese sauce that had come with the breadsticks.

"Kind of?" Jeanette threw an unopened packet of red peppers at Sloane. "More like mostly. On good days, at least. Speaking of which, my day starts early tomorrow. Time for me to fly."

Lori and Sloane agreed it was time to call it a night. As I stifled a yawn, I had to agree they were right.

Jeanette offered to walk Lori to her car. Sloane volunteered to stick around and help me clean up. I was delighted to accept. Any time spent with Sloane was time well spent.

After she put the plates and empty cups in the dishwasher, Sloane leaned against the counter, her brows creased. "I don't care what Jeanette says. There is *no way* in the world that pot belonged to Mrs. Napier. It had to be some kind of mix-up."

"Agreed. It kills me to think about the rumors Maybelle's probably already spreading. Can't wait for the police to prove her wrong, though." I put the leftover breadsticks in a plastic freezer bag and handed it to Sloane.

"What do you think happened? It's not like that stuff just walked into her office." She rinsed out the empty two-liter bottles and dropped them in the recycle bin next to the trash can.

"I don't know. It's a mystery. The police will figure it out, though."

"You sure? You're not exactly known for waiting for Rushing Creek's finest to do the job when someone's been killed."

"True, but this time around, the evidence is pretty strong against Porter."
I leaned against the fridge and drummed my fingers against its steel surface.

"Pretty strong, huh? You're not convinced he's the killer, are you?"

"You know me way too well. No. I'm not convinced he did it, but what am I supposed to do? Matt's following up on my suspicions about Gary Napier, and he promised to go through his file on Porter again. I'm at a dead end."

"If you say so." Sloane's phone buzzed. "Gotta dash. I've got a call with a race promoter on the West Coast about doing some promotional stuff for her event."

"Awesome." I gave her a hug. "I'm so proud of you. Living the dream, just like you talked about when we were young."

"I've had a lot of support, especially from you when there wasn't anyone else. I'll never forget that, you know." We walked to the front door. "One other thing I'll never forget is how you wouldn't give up tracking down my dad's killer, even when it put you in the hospital."

"You think I should keep investigating."

Sloane never told anybody what she thought they should do. Her approach was to make suggestions until the person caught on to what she was saying. It was a nonconfrontational approach she learned growing up in a household with an alcoholic father and a distant mother.

"I think you're not satisfied with the situation. So, the question for you is whether you're okay with leaving things to Matt or if you need to keep digging." She opened the door. "Love ya, kiddo. Whatever you decide, it'll be the right one. I'm sure of that."

After another hug, Sloane hollered goodbye to Ursi and took off. As I drifted toward the kitchen, I considered my bestie's words. She knew me better than anybody, even Mom. She knew I wouldn't be happy sitting on the sidelines like a spectator at one of the twins' soccer matches, waiting for Matt to make an arrest.

She was right.

If only I could figure out what to do next.

Chapter Nineteen

Before I was going to do anything, I needed to finish cleaning up the kitchen. Jeanette had taken the leftover pizza home, so I folded the remaining pizza box in half and put it in a trash bag. After that, in went the bags the breadsticks came in.

I was about to rinse the empty cheese and marinara sauce cups for recycling when something made me stop. At first, I couldn't figure out what had caught my eye. After a few seconds of staring at the trash, something rang a bell. Brownish paper was sticking out of one of the bags.

Brownish paper that looked familiar.

Seconds later, I had the paper in question out of the trash and smoothed out on the kitchen counter. The shade, a light brown, was right. I rubbed a corner between my fingers and thumb. The wax-like coating was smooth against my thumb. A closer inspection of the paper's surface made the hair on the back of my neck stand on end. I'd seen paper just like this. Felt it, too.

It was the same paper used as the wrapping for the marijuana in Vicky's office. Had to be. I fetched my case notebook. Sloane was right. I wasn't ready to give up.

And now I had something to go on.

Step one—get my thoughts recorded before jumping to any conclusions. The paper in my hand was definitely from Marinara's. The paper used to wrap the pot was the same.

No, it appeared to be the same. Did that mean Freddie was somehow involved?

That idea was absurd. The woman had owned that restaurant for decades. It was a favorite of tourists and locals alike. As for Freddie, her position as library board chair was more than honorary. She'd worked hand in hand with Vicky to keep the library up to date. The women had been friends, for crying out load. The murderer wasn't Freddie.

The pot had to be connected to someone who worked for Freddie.

But what was the connection to Vicky?

I took a deep breath to gather my wits. Logic and patience were paramount. And a focused mind.

The latest rule in Allie's book of amateur investigating—don't go to the police if all you have is a hunch. I wasn't going to bother Matt unless I could bring him a tangible lead to follow. The parchment paper on the table by my notebook seemed the same as what was wrapped around the pot.

Seemed the same.

The difference between seeming to be the same and being the same was as wide as One World Trade Center was tall. That was a huge problem. Even if testing proved the paper was manufactured at the same location at the same time, that didn't necessarily mean they both came from Marinara's.

After all, Rachel used similar baking material at the pub. There were probably a dozen or more businesses around town that used the paper. So, what did it mean?

Ursi jumped onto my lap and bumped her head against my hand. It was past my bedtime, and she was ready to head to bed.

"Sorry, girl." I scratched her head, then under her chin. "Got a new puzzle piece. I'm not sure where it fits."

My senses were tingling. A clue was right in front of me. All I had to do was work the puzzle. Identify the pieces. Organize those pieces in an orderly fashion. Study the pieces to see which loops went into the correct sockets.

Then stand back to see what secret the completed puzzle would reveal.

One might conclude the paper situation was a coincidence. If I did that, I could call it a night and get a solid eight hours of sleep before hitting the ground running tomorrow.

There was a problem. I didn't believe in coincidences. There was a connection, a missing piece to the puzzle. Maybe it was in my case notebook.

I went to the first page and studied every word, every observation, every supposition I'd recorded. Nothing jumped out at me. In a fit of frustration, I slammed the notebook shut, sending Ursi scrambling to the bedroom. The clue was somewhere among the pages, though. The tingling sensation confirmed it.

Too wide awake to even think about turning in, I brewed some coffee. While the pot gurgled, I closed my eyes and meditated, giving my brain a rest. By the time I took my seat again, with a chocolaty aroma from the dark roast emanating from my Wonder Woman mug, my head was clear.

Since my first review had proven to be fruitless, my second attempt needed a different approach. Before I got back to work, I looked around. Ursi hadn't returned.

Great. She'd no doubt had enough of me and was curled up right in the middle of my bed. At least that spot would be warm when I eventually got there.

"You can do this, Allie. For Vicky." I took a big gulp of coffee and started anew.

This time, instead of reading each word, I simply gazed at each page, like it was a work of art. I let my subconscious guide me, confident that if I stayed calm, the puzzle piece would reveal itself, like a stunning swirl of vivid color on a canvas of muted earth tones.

I devoted a minimum of two minutes to each page. On the seventh page, something caught my eye.

The library break room.

More specifically, the contents of the fridge when I visited the first time after the murder. My notes indicated all liquid containers had been removed because of the suspicion of poison. Something about the fridge, though.

"Aha!" I snapped my fingers as the imaginary light bulb above my head switched on.

There had been a Marinara's pizza box in the fridge. I closed my eyes and replayed the scene in my head.

At the time, I'd assumed the remains of the deep-dish pie was someone's lunch. What if that someone was Vicky? And instead of lunch, it had been her dinner?

Marinara's delivered. What if she'd ordered the pizza because she was working late and somehow the pizza she ordered came with something that wasn't supposed to be there?

A theory that completely exonerated Porter came together. The driver, who also sold drugs, delivered Vicky's pizza. At some point during the exchange, the marijuana ended up in the library. Maybe the driver dropped it on his way out the door and didn't notice until too late.

At some point that evening, Vicky must have found the pot and then hid each package in a different place for some reason.

I saw two scenarios. In the first one, she found the pot, panicked when she realized what she'd stumbled upon, and hid it in random places until she felt safe enough to go to the police.

In the second, instead of panicking, she hid the packages in random different locations with the intent of keeping them safe until someone suspicious showed up. Then she could put a face and name with the pot when she contacted the police.

For the same reason, neither situation satisfied me. Why didn't she contact the police when she found the marijuana and turn it over to them? Her choice to hold onto the packages had been reckless.

And put her at risk.

Which led me to consider the ramifications of that fateful choice. By now, I was miles away from facts and completely into conjecture, but I stayed with it. I wanted to present a complete narrative to Matt.

At some point, the drug dealer must have returned to the library and confronted Vicky. Since I found the pot, she must have denied having it. When she didn't cooperate, someone, the dealer himself or maybe his boss, must have decided to kill her.

Porter had claimed Vicky was the only person at the library when he arrived the morning she was killed. What if the murderer got into the library, poisoned Vicky's drink, and got back out of there before Porter arrived? Implausible? Yes.

But not impossible.

An alternative scenario popped into my head. What if Porter had been in cahoots with the drug dealers and he poisoned her at their direction?

"Nah." Despite my earlier research into Porter's potential secret properties, that supposition didn't feel right. There was nobody around to debate the point, but I was confident in it, regardless.

Porter had a crush on Vicky. He wanted them to be together. The explanation that if he couldn't have her, nobody would have her made way more sense than an alliance with drug dealers. It was too far-fetched for my liking.

That left me with the pizza delivery driver.

I went to my suspect page and added a new line. The motive was easy enough. He wanted his marijuana back. The means didn't take much thought, either. From what I'd read, drug rings were ruthless. It didn't seem like much of a stretch for someone in that trade to have poison close at hand.

Opportunity seemed straightforward enough. The killer, probably someone different from the dope dealer, waited for Vicky to arrive at the library and approached her with some innocuous-sounding story. She doubtlessly let the person in. It was a well-known fact Vicky drank tea all day long, so when the opportunity presented itself, the killer put the poison in her drink, then got out of there. Then Porter showed up. He was too late to save her but was perfectly placed to take the fall.

Wow. I'd woven quite the tale. Would Matt buy it? I'd have to figure out a way to make sure he did.

Chapter Twenty

Slate gray skies loomed overhead as I left my building a few minutes before eight. Matt would be arriving at his office soon, and I wanted to catch him before he got too tied up to see me. We had much to discuss. And much to plan.

Hopefully.

I flipped up the hood of my jacket as raindrops as cold as ice began to fall. A shiver ran through me. If the dismal weather was any indication of my day to come, I was in trouble.

While I waited for the light at the Boulevard to turn green, I reminded myself that a little discomfort was a small price to pay for bringing justice to Rushing Creek. If that sounded overly dramatic to some people, so be it. Vicky was a treasure to my community, a true superhero without a cape.

Once the light turned green, I trotted across the street, weaving my way around a puddle formed by a storm drain clogged with leaves. I made a mental note to mention it to the mayor's assistant. Things like that looked bad to tourists. I was always happy to help my community in ways besides solving murders.

By the time I pulled open the door to the police department, the rain had stopped. The sky was still foreboding, but I took the precipitation coming to an end as a good sign.

One of the weirdly good things about my history of solving murders was my ability to breeze into and out of the police chief's office without anyone batting an eye. It was empowering, but I wished I didn't have to do it.

Jeanette was on the phone, so I gave her a wave instead of stopping at her desk to say hi. Besides, despite my lack of one hundred percent confidence in my plan, Matt deserved to hear everything first.

I knocked on his door's window. He wasn't on the phone, so I entered without waiting for an invitation.

"Morning, Chief. I've got something you need to see." I slipped into the chair across from him and opened my backpack.

Matt rolled his eyes and sighed. "I'm busy, Allie. Besides, I thought we agreed you were done being Agatha Raisin."

"If you're going to needle me, you'll have to do better than that. Aggie's older than me and British. Besides, while the show's a hoot, the books are better."

"Is it encoded in your DNA to say the books are better?" He put up his hands. "Never mind. I know the answer. What news do I allegedly want to hear?"

"I think I have a lead for you on the marijuana packaging." I placed the parchment paper on his desk. "This came from Marinara's. They wrap their breadsticks with it. I'd bet my lunch money this came from the same source as the marijuana wrapping."

In the blink of an eye, Matt's demeanor changed from annoyed to completely engaged. He leaned forward to get a close look at the paper. After a minute of intense study, he consulted his notebook.

"Interesting." He pressed a button on his phone. "Jeanette, could you join us, please? And bring your E.T. kit."

While we waited, he stared at the clue, scratching his chin. His silence had me on edge so much, I almost jumped out of my chair when Jeanette knocked on the door.

When she entered, Matt pointed at the parchment paper. "What do you make of this, Officer?"

The formality was unnerving. It was also a sign to both of us Matt meant business. I'd made a calculated gamble by presenting the paper as part of the marijuana investigation. I'd figured if he bit on that, I could use the opening to tell him my new theory.

And my plan to catch the killer.

Using a pair of tweezers from her evidence technician kit, Jeanette held the paper to the light. "Common parchment paper. Used in baking. Similar in color and texture to the material used in the marijuana packing."

"Agreed. Allie says this came from Marinara's. Can you compare it to a piece from the library? See if it's close enough to warrant further analysis."

"On it, Chief." With a nod to each of us, Jeanette dropped the paper into an evidence bag and left, closing the door behind her.

"Thanks for bringing this in." He leaned back and put his hands behind his head. "Now, tell me your theory."

Excellent. I told him about Jeanette picking up dinner from Marinara's for our get-together, then went to my light bulb moment and finally to my conclusion. He took notes and gave me an occasional "uh-huh" and "okay" but offered no other comment other than that.

"I'm convinced there's a connection between the pot and Vicky's murder." I shook my head. "I haven't found the piece connecting them, though."

"That's okay. I'll pay Marinara's a visit and ask Freddie who delivered pizzas to the library in the last week."

"I thought of that. What if the driver denies any knowledge of the marijuana? Then you're back to square one."

"Maybe. Maybe not. This is a lead I have to follow up on. Besides, when needed, my interrogation techniques are much more effective at withdrawing information than what you've experienced."

There was an edge in Matt's voice I hadn't heard in a long time. It was intimidating and threatening. It made me happy I wasn't the delivery driver.

His current demeanor notwithstanding, it was time to suggest an alternative course of action. One with which he probably wouldn't be thrilled.

"What if the dealer's connection is worse than you? You can threaten jail time, but they can threaten worse."

"That's when I get the prosecutor involved. Let the perp plead down to a lesser charge in exchange for giving up his supplier." He rapped his knuckles on the desktop two times. "No muss, no fuss."

Shoot. Hadn't thought of that. I scratched my forehead to buy some time to regroup. "Okay, but what if you can't get the perp to talk? You can only hold him so long before you have to release him, right?"

Matt crossed his arms and frowned. "And I suppose you have a better idea?"

"Since you asked." I got up to stretch my legs. And to go through my pitch in my head a final time.

Vicky must have been looking down upon me from above, because there was a knock on the door. It was Jeanette. Matt waved her in. If she was back already, it had to be good news. At least, I hoped it was good news.

"Sorry for the interruption, Chief, but I thought you'd want to know. A preliminary check indicates the parchment paper from last night is the same paper from the first package Allie found. Permission to run additional tests?"

"Interesting." Matt rubbed his hands together. "You may be on to something, Allie. Make it so, Jeanette."

"Chief, is it okay if she stays? I'd like her to hear my suggestion, too." It would be easier for Matt to reject my suggestion if he was the only one in the room. If she thought my idea had merit, he might be willing to try it out.

He gestured toward another visitor chair in a corner of the office.

It was time to present my case like I was pitching a book I loved to an on-the-fence editor. "With the information you have, Chief, it makes perfect sense to contact Marinara's. The problem lies in the fact that, barring a confession, there's nothing to connect the delivery driver to the marijuana."

"I'm afraid she's right, Chief. The only fingerprints I came up with belong to Allie and Vicky Napier." Jeanette had her own little notebook out. "Whoever else handled them used gloves."

"So, what if you set a trap for the perp at the library?"

Matt tilted his head back and stared at the ceiling. "A trap? Seriously? You've been watching too much *Scooby-Doo* with the twins."

"Word's already out that marijuana was found at the library. Outside of this building, nobody knows how much, though. Am I right?"

After an exchange of glances, Matt and Jeanette nodded.

"It's common knowledge I've been clearing out Vicky's office. I can make sure people know I'll be at the library again tonight. After closing time. By myself."

"Maybe I haven't had enough caffeine, but I'm not following." Jeanette tapped a pencil on the cover of her notebook. "Why would anybody care about that?"

"I get it." Matt touched his finger to his nose then pointed it at me. "Very clever. You want to lure the perp back to the library. Catch him in the act of trying to retrieve his contraband. With you as the bait, no doubt."

"Exactly." I pounded my fist on the arm of the chair as adrenaline surged through me. My plan was coming together. "Think of me as a confidential informant, or something like that."

I opened my notebook to a page where I'd sketched out the library. "Here's what I thought we could do. First—"

"No."

I waved his interruption away. He just needed to see more of what I had in mind, so I began describing the building's layout.

A large hand came down on top of my map with a smack. "I said no, Allie. This is a police matter. I appreciate you wanting to help, but this isn't your job. It's ours. You've almost gotten yourself killed playing cop. No more."

At first, my brain didn't make sense of his words. He wouldn't even let me lay out the plan? It was a good plan.

Then it dawned on me once I paid attention to what he'd said. It wasn't the plan Matt was worried about, it was my safety. It was his job as police chief to protect me from harm, not put me in harm's way.

"Okay. I get it. You don't want me getting hurt. I'll admit I haven't always used good judgment in the past. This time will be different. Especially because I want to use backup."

Matt opened his mouth, but Jeanette headed him off.

"Hear her out, Chief. I agree, she's gone off half-cocked in the past. She's got good instincts, though."

It was all I could do to stop myself from rounding on Jeanette. Half-cocked? That was a bit harsh.

"Fine. Let me hear it." Matt flipped his notebook to a new page.

"The first thing I want to do is arrange a visit with an old friend." Once I had their attention, neither Matt nor Jeanette spoke a word until I'd taken them through the scenario from start to finish. They'd both taken copious notes, though.

The silence was deafening while I waited for a response. Matt was scratching his forehead and frowning as he studied his notes. Jeanette went to the map of Rushing Creek on the wall and stared at it. After tracing her finger along the Boulevard as it ran through town, she turned around.

"It might work, Chief." In rapid succession, she ticked off a handful of points supporting my idea.

Matt drummed his fingers on the desk. It was a good sign he hadn't rebuffed Jeanette outright. The final decision was his and his alone, though.

"Tell you what. Tommy's on duty tonight. I'll put him on this." He held up his index finger. "Tonight only. If nothing happens, that's it."

I sprang out of my chair, the sweet taste of justice already on my tongue. "Thanks, Matt. You won't regret this."

"I hope not. Now, get out of here before I change my mind. I'll brief Tommy when he reports for his shift."

Another of Allie's Rules for Investigating—when the police chief tells you to do something after agreeing to your plan, you do it. With a plan in place, I headed out the door.

After a glance over my shoulder to make sure Matt hadn't changed his mind and was coming to get me, I e-mailed the library to let them know I'd be back in the evening to finish my project. Seconds later, I got a reply from Vivian thanking me for helping out and promising to let the evening shift know they should expect to see me. It was *so* helpful to know the people there.

With that piece of the puzzle in place, it was time to find Rushing Creek's preeminent rumormonger.

It was only a little after nine in the morning, which meant it was too early for Maybelle to be holding court outside the pharmacy. Even though living in a small town often meant others knew my business, it also meant I knew theirs. Case in point, since it was Friday, she'd be having coffee at the diner.

I found her seated at a booth with two of her retired teacher friends. After getting a cup of coffee to go, I wandered in her direction, pretending to be checking my phone.

"Allie Cobb, what are you up to this morning?" Maybelle made room on her side of the booth and patted the open spot.

Perfect. I joined the women and got the conversation going with the normal small talk.

It wasn't long before Maybelle put her hand on mine and patted it in a motherly fashion. "I understand you've been helping out at the library. I simply can't believe the news about Vicky." She shook her head. "I never figured her for a drug user. It's scandalous."

The other women nodded their heads in agreement.

I bit my tongue. Maybelle had provided the opening I needed, though.

"It's very sad. The police say there was only the one package, so I guess it could be worse."

"One package?" Maybelle raised her eyebrows. "I heard they found more than that."

"It was just the one." I took a drink of my coffee.

All three were leaning toward me. Like fish caught on a line, now all I had to do was reel them in.

"At least I hope so. I need to go back there tonight to finish cleaning out Vicky's office. I'd hate to come across more."

They leaned back, each nodding and exchanging knowing glances. I wasn't a mind reader, but I didn't have to be one. They knew my history as a crime solver and knew I had reliable contacts within the police department.

They'd bought the story hook, line, and sinker.

"Isn't returning to the library dangerous? I mean, after what you found? Who knows what else might be there?" Maybelle ran a hand over her gray hair, as if she was preparing to start the rumor mill yet again.

"From what I understand, they did a thorough search of Vicky's office. I'm sure they found all there was to be found." I glanced at my phone.

"I'm sorry, ladies, but I have to get back to my office for a call. It was great chatting with you."

I made for the door with a smile. Word of our discussion would be out before lunchtime. My plan was officially in motion.

Chapter Twenty-One

When it came time to meet my maker, one of the things I was going to have to answer for was my behavior toward Maybelle Schuman. She wasn't a bad person. She just had a lot of time on her hands.

I firmly believed she didn't consider her gossip hurtful. It seemed that talking about people was a way for her to stay connected to the community. With her children in other parts of the country and her husband deceased, the retired teacher clearly wanted to stay a part of the Rushing Creek fabric. So, she chose to gossip.

Countless times over the years, I could have called her out about the damage her storytelling did to innocent people. Yet I'd always held my tongue. At first it was out of respect for all she'd given to my hometown. In the past couple of years, it morphed into a way to pump her for information.

Today, I'd taken it a step further. I was using the woman to spread my lies. I could try to rationalize it until the day I died, but it was still a smarmy means to an end. If the end resulted in catching a murderer, I could live with the consequences of my dubious behavior.

And ask for forgiveness next time I was at church.

With some time to kill before I put step two into place, I headed to the apartment for some agent work. Besides, I'd told the women I was going home and wanted to look convincing.

At noon there was a knock on the door.

I welcomed Sloane with a big hug. "Right on time."

"I didn't think getting together for lunch was a big deal. Do you know something I don't?" My bestie's eyes went wide as she put her hands over her mouth. "Ohmigod, you're pregnant. Congrats!"

Before I could correct her, Sloane had thrown her arms around me and was jumping up and down.

"Sloane. Sloane." It wasn't until I shouted her name that she stopped bouncing me up and down like a pogo stick. I held my excitable, wonderful friend still until she was looking me in the eyes. "I'm not pregnant."

"Oh." She tucked a strand of her brown hair behind her ear and plopped down on the couch. "Well, that's good. I mean, you and Brent aren't even engaged, much less married. Your mom would have gone through the roof. You have been practicing safe sex, though. Haven't you?"

I did a face palm as my cheeks turned into two blast furnaces. This was clearly what I got for my underhanded behavior with Maybelle.

"We're not discussing family planning right now. I need your help with something else. Something important."

Ursi jumped onto Sloane's lap and started rubbing the side of her head against Sloane's hand.

"Family planning's important. After all, you're on the wrong side of thirty. That biological clock's ticking away. Isn't that right, Ursula? Your mommy needs to be thinking about these things."

My traitorous feline responded with a full-throated *meow* and gave me an accusatory, unblinking stare. She wouldn't be getting any kitty treats for a while.

"We'll talk about that later, Sloane. For now, I need you to focus. I need your help to catch Vicky's killer. Tonight."

Sloane's hands, which had been scratching Ursi behind her ears, stopped mid-scratch. "You've never asked me to help with one of your investigations before. Do I have to do anything dangerous?"

"Depends on if you consider having lunch at the pub dangerous." I told her my plan for the trap at the library and how she could help with it by discussing certain parts of it with me over lunch. The discussion would be just loud enough for nearby diners to overhear us, which was what I wanted.

"Wow. Are you sure about this? Your plan for lunch seems okay, but tonight sounds pretty risky." Her voice went up at the end. She did that when she was worried about something.

"We'll be at the pub for lunch. It'll be fine. Tonight, Tommy Abbott will be parked close to the library for backup. Matt's having us use a two-way communication setup." I showed her a tiny plastic device that would go in my ear. "I'll use this and a thing that goes around my neck. They'll connect to my phone via Bluetooth. When the time's right, I'll call Tommy to establish the connection. Easy peasy."

"If you say so. At least the only thing dangerous about the pub is the damage eating there does to my waistline." Sloane gave Ursi a snuggle and got to her feet. "Let's do this. For Mrs. Napier."

A few minutes later, we arrived at my sister's restaurant. Since it was noon on a Friday, the place was packed. Exactly as I'd hoped. The greeter offered us our choice of two tables, one along a wall, the other in the middle of the room.

We chose the one in the middle.

Once we were seated, Sloane started fidgeting with her hair. The poor thing was getting nervous. Unless I calmed her down right away, she'd end up in a full-on anxiety attack. And my cover would be blown.

I went for the one thing guaranteed to make Sloane smile and forget about her troubles. I asked her how married life was treating her.

"OMG, Allie, it's amazing. To be honest, I was afraid that, after a few months, things might become routine, or, I don't know, the whole fairy-tale vibe would end. Instead, it keeps getting better. The other day, Luke told me he was going to put a garden in the backyard so I could have fresh vegetables. Can you believe that?"

"No way." Actually, I could totally believe it. A few weeks ago, Luke had asked for my thoughts about the idea. He'd been trying to figure out a way to help Sloane with her training and thought fresh vegetables might help her nutrition. I told him it was a fabulous idea.

What I didn't tell him was how much my heart melted as he talked to me about how much he wanted to help Sloane. He was my brother, after all. I didn't dare risk getting too mushy with him.

The transformation in Sloane was stunning. She stopped messing with her hair, eased back into her chair, and ordered fries with her club sandwich. She only ate fries when she was relaxed.

Now that she was calmed down, I was ready to move forward with the plan. I asked what she had planned for the evening. When she was finished answering, she asked me the same thing.

I let out an overly loud sigh to attract some attention. "I have more work at the library. I promised them I'd finish cleaning out Vicky's office tonight. I'm going in at closing time so I can work without distractions."

"Ugh. I wouldn't want to go back there." Sloane scrunched up her nose. "Not after what you found."

With some effort, I suppressed a smile. My friend was putting on an Oscar-worthy performance.

"I know. But it was only one package. Besides, the police did a search and didn't find anything else." I shrugged. If Sloane could act, I could do the same. We needed to be as convincing as possible, after all.

"Did they search the whole building?"

This was the key question and Sloane nailed it, even raising her voice just loud enough to appear unhappy with my answer.

"No. Just the office. Think about it. If she was really smoking pot, she would have been crazy to keep it where someone might come across it."

I glanced around while I took a sip of water. If people were eavesdropping on us, they were doing a good job of hiding it.

"You're right. It just blows my mind our sweet, old librarian was a pothead."

"Please don't use that term when talking about Vicky. I'm sure she had a good reason for doing it. My guess is it was to help her manage pain she didn't want anyone to know about."

"Sorry." Sloane stared at her plate for a moment. When she raised her head, her cheeks were pink. Now, that was convincing.

"It's okay. I know you didn't mean it. It just hurts having her memory tarnished. I wish I'd never found that package." I was laying it on a little thick but didn't want to risk being too subtle.

"If you hadn't found it, someone else would have." Sloane took a deep breath. "Let's be happy it was only one bag of pot and not anything worse."

"Agreed." I clinked my glass against hers. It was the signal we were finished.

Had we been loud enough without making our intent obvious? Had we provided enough information? Had anyone been paying attention? If so, did those who overheard us even care?

The only way to know for sure was to stick to the plan.

We chatted about a few other things while we finished our meals. When we were outside, I gave my bestie a high five. "Thanks. Mission accomplished. You totally rock."

She squeezed me back. "Go get 'em, K.C."

With part two of the plan complete, the next thing to do was go home and wait until it was time to go to the library. It was a good thing I had my interview with Goth Girl coming up. Preparing for and conducting the interview would make me focus on work. And keep me from obsessing about the plan.

I changed into a pair of khaki slacks and the forest green Cobb Literary Agency polo Mom had given me on the one-year anniversary of my time at the helm of the business. Something told me Goth Girl would be in black, so I wanted to counter the darkness, as it were.

"So far so good, Ursi. I'm gonna need some luck, though. If you have any to spare, I'd appreciate you sharing."

I gave my kitty a treat as a peace offering and scratched her along her spine until my hand ached. When I stopped, she gave my hand a gentle bite and followed that by rubbing the spot below her ear against my knuckles. Classic signs of Ursi affection.

Good luck, indeed.

A little while later, I went downstairs to Renee's. I was responding to a request from an editor for another week to decide on a manuscript when someone cleared their throat.

The young woman before me was a sight I hadn't experienced since I'd left New York. The Doc Marten boots were jet black. Her leggings were the color of a starless sky at midnight. Black nail polish. Heavy black eyeliner. Short, black hair combed to the side that fell over one eye.

The pièce de résistance was her top. It was a black T-shirt with "Daughters of Darkness" scrawled across it in white gothic-style lettering. It was, by a mile, the most unorthodox interview ensemble I'd ever experienced. At least her red and black plaid miniskirt gave the ensemble some color.

I got to my feet and offered to shake. "Allie Cobb. You must be Calypso."

"Call me Ishmael." She took my hand in a strong but not uncomfortable grip. The dozen or so bracelets on her arm rattled as we shook.

Caught off guard by the odd comment, I cocked my head to the side. Then an idea flared to life. Maybe Calypso was testing me.

"It was the devious-cruising Rachel, that in her retracing search after her missing children—"

"Only found another orphan." She released my grip and took the seat across from me.

"You're a fan of *Moby Dick*, I take it." My fingertips tingled as I sat. This young woman, if she wasn't bluffing, was someone I might be able to work with. It was one thing to know the opening line to the story. It was quite another to know the last one.

"It's okay. The theme of obsession leading to one's ultimate destruction resonates with me."

I gripped the arms of my chair like my fingers were a vice. Given what I had planned for later in the day, Calypso's words seemed prescient.

"Interesting." I looked at her resume to buy time while I got my thoughts in order. "Are you a fan of classic literature?"

She shrugged. "Some. I think Dumas is the greatest writer in history. Cervantes and Tolstoy don't work for me."

Given her offhand tone, it seemed like a waste of time to challenge her on the giants of world literature. Sometimes I couldn't help myself, though.

"If you don't mind me saying so, I haven't met many people barely a year out of high school who've read the authors you have."

"Yeah, well. I didn't see eye to eye with my parents very often. Reading was a good way to pass the time and avoid arguments."

Turning to books to escape the challenges of real life was something I could identify with. I'd done it more often than I cared to admit when my classmates had bullied me.

We talked about literature for a little while, then I turned the conversation back to her. "Have you been in town long? Other than the night at the pub, I haven't seen you before."

"I moved here a couple of weeks ago. I'm living with my aunt for now."

When I asked Calypso who her aunt was, she pointed toward the sales counter with her thumb.

"Renee's your aunt?"

"She texted me about your intern position. Said I could hang out with her for a while and if I got the position, I could stay as long as I wanted. If not, I could stay a few months and save some money while I plot my next move."

I swallowed my pride. So much for my powers of observation. Sure, I'd been out of town and then super occupied since I got back, but not even to notice a new person in the building? That was bad.

"Besides working at the restaurant, I'm cleaning the apartments on the third floor. That way—"

"It was you, then." I snapped my fingers. "A couple of nights ago, I noticed a light on in one of the apartments."

Calypso's cheeks pinked as she bit her lower lip. "I was cleaning the kitchen and forgot to turn it off. Please don't tell Aunt Renee. I don't want her to think I'm irresponsible. I've been keeping my fingers crossed nobody noticed."

Now it was my turn to be embarrassed. "Not at all. I was in the courtyard cleaning my bike. I just happened to see it. I've been meaning to ask Renee about it, but now I don't have to."

"Awesome. It's a cool apartment. Even though cleaning's hard work, I like hanging out up there."

I nodded. It was nice to have someone else who appreciated older buildings. New buildings, with their twenty-first-century wiring and the latest amenities, were nice and easy. They couldn't compare with the character that came with a living space that was almost a hundred years old, though.

"I know what you mean. I'm curious about something. Why didn't you mention your aunt when you sent me your résumé?"

"I want to get this job based on the merits. What I know. Not who I know." She straightened her spine and raised her chin a fraction, as if daring me to respond with anything other than a business-only follow-up.

"Tell me, then. What do you know that can help me? Other than words from dusty, old books."

Her eyes went wide then narrowed as she smiled. "Four years of English in high school, including two AP classes. One was English Language and Composition. The other was English Literature and Composition. Among other grammar subjects, I know the difference between a gerund and a split infinitive. Last calendar year, I read one hundred fifty books. You can check on Goodreads for confirmation. And I'm good at math, in case you need help with that."

I barked out a laugh. Despite my initial reservations, I was warming up to Calypso. Maybe, just maybe, I had my intern.

"Sounds like you've got what I'm looking for. Tell you what. I have a sample manuscript I'd like you to edit. I'll e-mail it to you. It's about fifty pages. Can you get it back to me by Monday?"

"Are you offering me the job?"

"I'd like to see your editing before I make a formal offer, but—"

"Because we haven't discussed salary or benefits or anything along that line."

She had a backbone. No doubt about that. I could play ball. "Do you have salary requirements?"

"I want to live on my own. To be independent. Like you." She leaned forward, placing her elbows on her knees and slid a piece of paper across the table toward me. Her gray eyes held me.

"I want that apartment. Between working at the pub and for you, I can do it. If you can meet this number."

I wanted to laugh. This wasn't some end-of-the-world negotiation, after all. On the other hand, her earnestness and clear interest in the position was irresistible. I flipped open the paper and did some quick mental calculations. This time I did laugh.

"Calypso, I believe we have a deal." We hammered out a few details, including her duties and a work schedule. Then we made our goodbyes with a plan to get together on Monday to have her sign her employment paperwork.

Having an intern was exciting. The things we could accomplish together would take the Cobb Literary Agency to a whole new level.

If I survived my night at the library.

Chapter Twenty-Two

My surprisingly productive conversation with Calypso freed my mind of a big worry. That let me focus on the final part of the plan with a clear mind. On the surface, it was simple enough.

At the time Matt and I agreed upon, I would ride my bike to the library in order to arrive right before closing. Once everybody else was gone, I'd establish contact with Tommy, who would be waiting in his car, a block away. Then, making sure the entrance doors were unlocked, I'd sit back and wait for the dealer to arrive. As soon as he did, I'd give Tommy the code word and he'd arrive within a minute.

As I'd reassured Sloane, easy peasy.

While the rain had moved out, the clouds had remained. The twilight conditions were going to make my attempt at being conspicuous on my ride more challenging. I crossed my fingers that between my green Day-Glo helmet the twins gave me for Christmas and my orange safety vest, I'd be impossible to miss riding up the Boulevard.

The library closed at eight. At half past seven, I scooped up Ursi and buried my face in her soft fur.

"I'll be home soon." Despite my confidence in the plan, my voice wavered. "Love you more than anything in the world."

This was serious business. I wasn't ignorant about the consequences of my actions like I'd been the first time I went after a criminal. Nor was I engaging in an adrenaline-fueled race to catch a killer, where it was all reaction and no thought.

I was older, but was I truly any wiser? As I descended the stairs with my trusty steed over my shoulder, I asked Dad for help in that area.

My route to the library initially took me south on Harrison Street until I reached the Rushing Creek Winery at the edge of town. Then I pedaled east for two blocks and arrived at the Boulevard.

The goal was to take my time, make eye contact whenever possible, and exchange greetings every chance I got. In short, make it look like a casual cruise through town. It was something I'd done so many times, I could do it in my sleep.

A group of diners was standing outside the pub having a smoke break as I pedaled by. A few returned my wave.

There was a line out the door at Marinara's. I spotted Lori and her daughter in the queue, so I shouted a greeting. They returned it, causing a few heads to turn in my direction. Good. Progress.

It was like that the rest of the way to the library. What would have normally taken five minutes instead took twenty. Five minutes of that was dedicated to a visit with Maybelle. She was hanging out in front of the pharmacy with two of her friends from breakfast. I couldn't pass up the opportunity to stop and let the ladies know where I was going.

Ashton greeted me with a shy smile when I entered the library. "I'm sorry I got you caught up in that nasty business yesterday. Are you okay?"

I gave her forearm a reassuring squeeze. "I'm fine. To be honest, if anyone was going to find that stuff, I'm glad it was me."

"I would have totally flipped out. I told my husband about it when I got home. He said the same thing. That with your track record, you'd know just what to do."

My cheeks got warm. It was reassuring people in town looked on my crime-fighting antics as a good thing, instead of some form of vigilantism. I'd earned that goodwill. Hopefully, I'd earn it again tonight.

"Happy I can help out." I jiggled a set of keys. "My goal is to finish up tonight. Brent gave me his key when he went home. I'll use it to lock up when I'm done."

Since Brent had done so much work at the library, Vicky had given him a key fob to the building. He'd been required to pass a criminal background check and pay a deposit for the fob before the library board approved giving it to him, but he'd proven Vicky's trust in him hadn't been misguided. I'd been meaning to return it but was glad I hadn't once I hatched the plan.

I was tossing twenty-year-old purchase orders into a box for recycling when Ashton knocked on the door. "Everyone else is gone. Do you want some company?"

My heart leapt into my throat. The last thing I wanted was to put someone in danger.

I put my arm around her and guided her toward the exit. "I'll be fine. It's cathartic for me. Even if I'm just getting rid of things at this point. Once I'm finished, I'll be ready to let her go."

Ashton's eyes got cloudy. Then she threw her arms around me. "You're a godsend, Allie. Text me when you're finished. Next time I see you at the soccer pitch, I'll buy you some popcorn."

"If it's not too late, I'll let you know I'm done. Promise."

Once her car drove out of the parking lot, I put the earpiece in place and called Tommy.

"Reading you loud and clear, Allie. I'll sit tight until you need me."

"Roger that, Officer Abbott." I chuckled. "Sorry, I always wanted to say that."

"And now you have. Remember, keep radio silence. If someone shows up, we don't want them to know we're in contact. Abbott out."

With my safety net in place, I went back to Vicky's office to finish my work.

And wait for a criminal.

After an hour on my own, I'd filled four boxes with paper for recycling and two more with junk for the dumpster. I plopped down in Vicky's chair for a breather and pulled out my phone. Brent and I had chatted earlier in the evening. I'd told him I was cleaning out Vicky's office, without divulging the reason behind it. He'd promised to check in.

There was nothing from him. Letting out a disappointed sigh, I tossed the phone on the desk and went to the break room for a drink. Granted, all he knew was that I was clearing out Vicky's office. While the coffee maker gurgled, I told myself it was one less thing for him to worry about. As I stirred sweetener into my cup of liquid gold, I felt a touch of self-recrimination. I'd lied to him about something important. That wasn't fair and wasn't conducive to a healthy relationship. I'd have to make amends next time I saw him.

Oh well, the best laid plans of mice and men, and all that.

With a cup of steaming coffee in hand, I took a swing through the building to confirm I was still alone.

I was.

With a few butterflies flapping their wings in my belly, I went to the entrance. I cupped my hands around my eyes and peered into the darkness. If a bad guy was out there, I couldn't see him.

There were a couple of empty boxes behind the checkout counter, so I grabbed them and plodded back to work. Even if I ended up making a fool of myself, at least I was getting Vicky's office cleared out.

A little while later, a squeak from the front entrance brought me to a standstill. I swallowed as a chill enveloped me.

"Allie? Are you here?"

The voice was one I wasn't expecting.

"I'm here, Freddie." I met her halfway between the office and entrance. While it was always good to see her, I needed to get her out of here ASAP. "What brings you by?"

"I heard you were working here tonight, so I thought I'd help. Finish faster that way." She went into Vicky's office.

"You don't have to do that." By the time I caught up with her, she was standing in the middle of the room, with her hands in her pockets.

"I'm almost done. See?" I waved my arm around the space, like a *Price Is Right* model. "Another hour and that'll be it."

"You've done more than your fair share for the library, Allie. It's the least I can do. I'm board president, after all." She unzipped her black Marinara's fleece. Remnants of flour clung to her work shirt.

"Stop. Please." For a second, I debated telling her what was really going on. She was the board president, after all. I decided against spilling the beans. Divulging the true situation could put her in jeopardy. I couldn't bear the thought of that.

"I need to do this. By myself. It's the only way I'll get through my grieving process. I hope you can understand that."

Over her protests, I took her by the arm and led her to the exit. "Go home. I'll be in touch as soon as I'm finished. Promise."

"If you insist. Vicky always said there was no changing your mind when it was made up." She gave me a hug and stepped outside. After a moment's hesitation, she turned and waved. Then she was gone.

I wiped a bead of sweat from my brow. *That was way too close.*

To be on the safe side, I did another stroll through the building, taking a look out the windows. It was too dark to see anyone.

A car's engine rumbled to life. Hopefully, that meant Freddie was on her way home, where she'd be safe and sound.

With her out of harm's way, my heart rate slowed from a gallop to a trot. Now I could get back to work. And get back to wondering when the dealer would show up.

And if the dealer was also Vicky's killer.

A little while later, the entrance door opened again with a squeak. I froze, my heart in my mouth. When the hairs on the back of my neck rose to attention, I backed up against a wall and held my breath.

It's time.

"Tommy, come in." I waited a few heartbeats for a response. When one didn't come, I made another attempt. Still nothing.

Pushing down the panic building, I reached for my phone. It wasn't in my back pocket. I checked the other one. No luck there, either.

Think, Allie. Think. I racked my freaked-out brain, desperate to remember where I'd left it. The desk! I'd left it there before I went to make coffee.

I dashed to the desk. It wasn't there, either. I picked up the desk phone to call the police. There was no dial tone, no busy signal. Only silence. The situation had gotten sticky.

"Work the problem, Allie. You can do this." The encouraging words brought back some focus. And an idea.

Maybe I'd left it in the break room. It was a desperate thought, but it was the only one I had. Without the phone close enough to make the Bluetooth connection, Tommy would never know if I was in trouble.

With no other ideas, the break room it was. I took a deep breath and made a run for it. Halfway there, I stopped. Freddie was back.

"What are you—" I stopped in mid-sentence as the truth finally dawned on me. It was a slap in the face and punch to the solar plexus at the same time.

"It was you all along." My breath had literally been taken away. I had to bend over and put my hands on my knees until I could breathe again.

"Well done." She withdrew my phone from her purse. "Though I'm afraid your silly little plan failed."

"So, you're the drug dealer. And you're probably mixed up in Vicky's murder, aren't you?"

She lifted her head toward the ceiling and laughed.

"I have to say, I'm disappointed in you, Allie. When I heard about your plan, I was impressed. Now? Not so much. I managed to pin everything on that pathetic Porter Rasmussen, but you couldn't leave well enough alone, could you?" She dropped the phone back into her purse.

"You won't get away with this." I cringed, fully aware of how lame that sounded. "The police know I'm here. They'll be here any minute." It was a weak lie, but it was the last card in my deck.

"I don't think so. Before my first visit, I surveilled the area. Imagine my surprise, *not*, when I came across Officer Abbott. Being a supportive citizen, I offered him a cup of coffee, which he readily accepted. The coffee was laced with Rohypnol. He won't be joining us anytime soon."

The panic I'd kept at bay overwhelmed me, and my flight instinct took over. I made a move for the entrance. I'd only traveled ten feet when, once again, I was brought to a sudden stop.

This time by a deadly weapon.

"That's enough, Allie." She pointed a nine-millimeter handgun at me. It had an eerie resemblance to the one Jeanette kept at home for her personal safety. "I'm sorry it had to come to this. You've done a lot for this town, but, like the saying goes, curiosity killed the cat.

"Or, in your case, the cat owner."

Chapter Twenty-Three

"On your knees." With the gun, Freddie gestured toward the floor. "It will be easier if you don't resist."

As I got down on one knee, she took a roll of duct tape from her purse. She bound my hands behind my back, making my eyes water when she wrapped the tape so tight my wrists couldn't move. I didn't yell out, though. Instead, I recited in my head one of my favorite lines from literature.

Where there's life, there's hope.

While it seemed obvious what Freddie had planned for me, I wasn't going down without a fight. What I needed most was time. Time to puzzle a way to get out of my predicament. Time to get help.

Time to stay alive. And avenge Vicky.

"I take it we're not going to the pub for a drink." The library's low pile carpeting was irritating my right knee, so I leaned to the side to give it a break. My movement was met by a boot to my lower back.

"Far from it. If you cooperate, you might see the light of day, though." She forced me to my feet, spun me around, and marched me into Vicky's office.

"So, you're a drug-dealing murderer. Why kill Vicky? I thought she was your friend."

"It was all an unfortunate mix-up." Freddie pushed me into a chair and bound my feet to the legs with the duct tape. I had to hand it to the woman. She was prepared.

"You need to understand something, Allie." She took a seat behind the desk. The gun rested on the desktop, but her finger was still on the trigger. "Running a business is hard. Running a restaurant, with its razor-thin profit margin, is even harder. Being a woman, keeping a restaurant afloat for over thirty years, is almost impossible."

"And you deserve all the credit in the world for that accomplishment." It wasn't false praise. Rachel and I had often talked about the challenges she had at the pub. Running a small business wasn't for the weak of heart.

"Thank you." With her free hand, she started rummaging through the desk drawers. "My bigger accomplishment is one virtually nobody knows about. You see, I've been involved in another business venture since I was in high school. My family didn't have a lot of money, so if I was going to college, it was up to me to pay my own way."

I had no idea where she was going with this, but the longer I kept her talking, the more my odds of escaping increased. For now, it seemed best to let her ramble.

"It was very different coming of age in the seventies. I had a job waiting tables at a restaurant, but it didn't pay much. What did pay was marijuana. Specifically, selling it. What started in high school as a way to supplement my savings turned into a steady job in college. Did you know Vicky smoked dope in college?"

"No. Tell me about it." I tried to move my wrists. It was like rubbing sandpaper against my skin, but my wrists were covered with stress-induced sweat, which allowed for a tiny bit of movement. Without access to a knife, it might be a fruitless exercise, but I wasn't going to give up.

"We met at a party. I was smoking a joint and offered her a toke. After inhaling, she practically coughed up a lung." Freddie laughed, like she was reliving one of her favorite memories. "She normally didn't indulge, but every now and then, when she was under a lot of stress, she made a small purchase."

"You dealt and she smoked dope in college. So, what? From what I've read, back then, practically everyone did that at one point or another." Visions of President Clinton testifying that he'd smoked, but not inhaled, came to mind. It was an absurd thought to conjure at such a stressful time, but it did serve to take the stress level down a notch.

She pointed her index finger toward the ceiling. "Ah, but therein was my dilemma. Selling dope paid most of my bills in college, so there was no way I was going to give it up when I graduated. I've been dealing from practically the day I arrived in Rushing Creek. And before you try some holier-than-thou attitude on me, that extra cash helped keep Marinara's afloat more times than I can count.

"Vicky knew what I was doing, though. She never said anything, but I could sense it. She held it over my head like the Sword of Damocles."

Freddie's description wasn't the Vicky Napier I knew. My hero was a kind, selfless person. She would never use a secret to wield power over someone.

Or had she?

Regardless, it was time for another delay tactic. "If Vicky knew, maybe she kept your secret because she was your friend. She was trying to help you. Did you ever think of that?"

"Oh, I thought about it. I thought about it almost every day." She slammed the final desk drawer closed and got to her feet. "That's why I stayed friends with her. Why I bought a house on the same street as hers. I even offered to keep an eye on her place and bring in the mail when she was out of town."

The puzzle pieces finally fell into place. My misgivings about Porter's guilt had been right. The satisfaction about that served to fuel my growing anger at Freddie.

"Let me guess. You went to see Vicky the morning she died. You knew she'd gotten her hands on the pot by accident. You wanted it back. When you couldn't reach an agreement, you poisoned her tea. You used something from the plants Porter grows to put suspicion on him."

"Well done. I used aconite. It comes from monkshood. He's grown it for years."

She looked behind the filing cabinets and tried to push the one closest to her away from the wall. "You see, when you're in my line of work, well, my off-the-books line of work, it's important to be prepared. If people wonder why I always have cash on hand, it's because I run a restaurant and deal with a lot of cash and tips. If people wonder why I've always supported the garden club, it's because I love flowers and plants. Those are great cover stories."

"You used Porter's crush on Vicky to your advantage. You knew how much he cared for her. You'd researched what plants he grew. Just in case." I let out a low whistle. "Credit where credit is due, I'm impressed with your planning. One thing I don't understand. Why now? She was all set to retire and move to Florida to live with her sister."

She sighed. It was long and sad and made me wonder what was truly going on in this mad woman's head.

"Like I said earlier, it was all due to a simple mix-up. Do you know why my deep-dish pizzas are only available Friday and Saturday?"

"I thought it had something to do with a secret family recipe. That you won't let anyone else make the deep-dish pizzas. And since you're the only one who makes them, they're only available on the weekend."

"It's amazing how an urban legend can take on a life of its own." She went from the filing cabinets to the credenza. "I use the deep-dish pizzas as one of my distribution methods. Certain customers know how to order something special in their pizzas, shall we say. I put that package you found into one of my special orders. Two weeks ago tonight, your friend was supposed to get a thin crust pizza with pepperoni and mushrooms, but someone screwed up the delivery. It's so hard to find good help these days."

"I know what you mean." While she burrowed through the credenza, I told her about my challenges in finding an intern. Anything to keep the dialogue going. Plus, the mention of only one told me what Freddie was looking for.

"Vicky, bless her heart, called me. She told me what she'd found. I suggested that she return what wasn't hers, I'd refund the cost of her pizza, and we could forget the whole thing. She said no. She had to go to the police."

"She didn't though. Why not?"

"I begged her to reconsider, to think of our decades of friendship. She began to waver, so I hit her in her soft spot. I reminded her of how much I'd helped her in my position as library board president."

"That was underhanded." I shrugged. "I mean, even within the realm of everything else that was going on."

To my amazement, she giggled like a schoolgirl. "It was, wasn't it. If there was ever any doubt about her one true love, her response ended it."

"Hanging the library over her head bought you time to get her to come around." It was the only possibility, given that she was killed four days after the pizza was delivered.

"I convinced her to wait until the weekend was over before making a decision. When we talked on Monday, she hadn't changed her mind." Freddie picked up the desk phone and threw it against a wall. It shattered into countless tiny fragments.

It was a fitting metaphor for the current state of my plan.

"She was going to ruin all I'd worked so hard for. All because of a stupid mix-up." She was shouting now. Her eyes were wild. A string of spit hung from the corner of her mouth.

"She thought it was over, but it was far from over. I told her if she went to the police, I'd implicate her in the whole mess. Claim she'd known about my illicit activities and been a willing co-conspirator. Then word would get out and my associates would pay her a visit."

I nodded. In a twisted way, it all made sense. "You scared her, so she offered to keep your secret and move away. You, in turn, agreed to keep your mouth shut about the whole affair."

"Close." She went behind me and tapped the gun on my head. "I agreed to keep my mouth shut if she returned my merchandise. The foolish woman said she needed to sleep on it. My patience had run out, so, a few days later, I showed up at her house before she went to work. Since she still hadn't gone to the police, I offered to come clean if she kept quiet. When she agreed, I offered to make her tea, as a peace offering. When she wasn't looking, I laced the tea with the aconite. With the dosage I used, I knew it wouldn't take effect until she got to work. You know the rest."

"You had all your bases covered."

"I did, didn't I."

"Except for me." While she rifled through a filing cabinet, I worked on loosening the tape. The discomfort helped me focus on the task at hand. Keep her talking until I could make a move.

"You've always been too much of a busybody for your own good, Allie. I would have thought you learned your lesson last fall." She slammed the cabinet drawer closed and pointed the gun at me.

"Now that you know the story, it's time to pay the storyteller. There were four packages in that pizza. You only turned in one. Where are the others?"

"They're not here." My refusal to give Freddie a straight answer amounted to attempting a tightrope walk across the Grand Canyon without a net. It didn't matter. My wrists ached, my legs were numb, and I was angry this criminal had killed my hero.

I wasn't going to give her the satisfaction of an easy victory.

"Then where are they?" She pressed the barrel of the gun to my temple. "Out with it. I haven't got all day."

The moment of truth had arrived. She wouldn't shoot me here. Not here. There would be too much mess for her to clean up. The woman might be unhinged, but she wasn't stupid. The game needed to continue.

"First, take that stupid gun away from my head." I licked my lips and swallowed. My blood pounded against my temples as I waited for her response. I thought some of my negotiation sessions over books had been serious. They were nothing compared to this.

After what seemed like decades, the pressure of the barrel against my head eased. It took all the control in my body to refrain from closing my eyes in relief. I wouldn't show weakness.

"Well? Spill it. I need those packages." She put her hands on the arms of the chair and leaned close. Our noses were centimeters from touching. Her breath was sour, as if she'd been drinking cheap whiskey. "Where are they?"

"I don't know."

"Liar." Her shout bounced off the walls and left my ears ringing. She stomped to the far wall and back again, running her free hand through her hair.

She came to a stop in front of me, standing erect so I had to look up at her. Classic power move. She wanted me to feel weak and intimidated.

It wasn't going to happen.

Somehow, some way, I was going to get out of this mess. The longer I dragged this out, the more likely it became that Freddie would make a mistake. And when she did, I'd be ready.

"Let me put it this way. I have an unhappy customer who hasn't received an order. I also have an unhappy supplier who doesn't want their product ending up as police evidence. That leaves you between a rock and a hard place. So, I'll give you one more chance. Where are those packages?"

I waited a moment before I smiled. A warm sensation of resolve, strong as tempered steel, filled me. Despite what Freddie seemed to think, she was the one who had lost. Not me. The game was over. It was simply a matter of playing it out and making my move at the right time.

"Well?"

"I don't know where they are." I shook my head. "I mean, the police have them. I know that. You'd have to ask them if you want specifics."

The color drained from Freddie's face. Her expression was almost comical as her eyes grew as wide as saucers and her jaw practically fell to the floor.

"That's it. It's time to take a ride." She took a pocketknife from her purse, cut my duct tape bindings, and yanked me to my feet.

"Where are we going?" I clamped shut a scream as the pain of a million pinpricks went through my legs.

"To your final resting place." She covered my mouth with duct tape. "You might want to say your prayers."

Chapter Twenty-Four

With the gun to my back and her hand clamped onto my shoulder like a vice, Freddie directed me out of the library. My bike was missing from the bike rack by the entrance. The chain securing it to the rack lay on the concrete surface. Someone had cut it.

"Keep moving." She poked me in the back with the gun. "If you try to run, I'll shoot you right here."

A black sedan was the lone occupant of the parking lot. I scanned the area. There was nowhere to run. Despite my demonstration of bravado while we were inside, I was in no mood to test Freddie's marksmanship by making a break for it.

As we came alongside the car, the bike's handlebars came into view. It was in the back seat. A massive set of bolt cutters lay draped over the top tube. Again, I had to give her credit. She'd thought of everything.

Check that. Almost everything. Her first mistake was her failure to count on my involvement. Strike one. Her second mistake was assuming there was marijuana left to be found in the library. Strike two.

One more mistake, one more strike, and Freddie would be out.

That was the hope I clung to as my captor popped open the trunk. The space was a dark, foreboding cavern.

"I guess it's good you're so small. It would have been harder to squeeze your boyfriend in here." She gestured with the gun toward the opening. "In you go."

She pushed me until I cracked my knees against the back bumper. I held my ground while I scanned the interior to buy more time. My gaze darted back and forth, up and down. Freddie hit me in the back of my knees. I staggered but kept searching. Something. Anything.

Then it came to me!

The trunk was spacious. At least, for me, it was. That would give me the wiggle room I needed. I wanted to end up in the trunk with my back to the panel. That would give me the element of surprise I'd need later.

To create space to make my move, I called on my kickboxing skills and struck backward at Freddie with my foot. As I did so, I leaned forward with my left shoulder. The goal was to look like I'd lost my balance in an attempt to get away. Then, when she reacted, I could go into a controlled roll and land in the trunk the way I wanted.

"I'm going to enjoy getting rid of you." Freddie practically spat the words at me, then shoved me into the trunk.

While I'd never recommend allowing oneself to be forced into a car's trunk at gunpoint, I was pleased with how I landed. My arm took the brunt of the fall, allowing me to avoid any trauma to my shoulder, and more importantly, my head.

There was no point in wasting energy by fighting Freddie, so I pretended to resist her and maneuvered myself into the position I wanted while she forced my legs into the compartment.

"Say goodbye to Rushing Creek, Allie. I hope your cat doesn't starve to death waiting for your return." She let out a laugh that was like a witch's cackle and slammed the trunk shut.

The *whump* of the metal enclosing me might have been disconcerting. The absence of light could have been terrifying. The dearth of information about where I was being taken should have been petrifying.

They weren't.

Because Freddie had made another mistake. Mentioning my beloved Ursi was a stark reminder that there were people, both two-legged and four-legged, who depended on me. I couldn't let them down. I wouldn't let them down.

With a jerk, the car moved forward. The movement was disorienting and reminded me of being on an indoor thrill ride at Disney World. God, I hated those things. I'd survived those rides by closing my eyes and taking slow, deep breaths.

As the lurching in my stomach calmed, I let my mind drift back to the night that would get me out of my tight spot. I'd been editing a client's thriller manuscript and came to a point in the story that seemed implausible.

The hero had been taken captive by terrorists, who used zip strips to bind his hands and feet. The bad guys left him unsupervised for a minute. He used that time to free his hands by lifting them above his head and bringing them down as hard as possible against his abdomen while trying to pull his wrists apart.

The force of the maneuver caused the strips to snap. With his hands free, the hero unbound his legs. He then went on to knock out his captors and escape.

While the sequence had me on the edge of my seat, I found myself wondering if the hero's escape method had any basis in fact. One of the things I'd learned early in my career was that readers of fiction would usually let a writer get a little loose with facts in exchange for an enjoyable story. However, the author couldn't abuse that allowance. If something was too outlandish, the reader wouldn't buy it.

If the reader wouldn't buy it, as an editor, I couldn't allow it. Thus began one of my more unusual nights going down the rabbit hole of online research.

It didn't take long to confirm that, yes, one could escape the hold of zip-strip bindings by bringing them down from above the head with as much force as possible. It was totally not what I'd expected, so I couldn't resist watching other escape videos. Before I knew it, I'd lost three hours to the internet.

And gained knowledge I thought I'd never use. Until now.

A couple of the clips I watched that fateful night included demonstrations of escaping from duct tape bindings. With nothing to do but focus on the memory, I was able to visualize the post with high-definition clarity. My task was simple. All I needed to do was rub my wrists back and forth until the tape loosened enough for me to slip one hand, then the other, free.

Like everything in life, actually doing the trick was much more difficult than it seemed. To the best of my ability, I ignored the bumps in the road that caused me to bang against my metal surroundings.

I worked up a heavy sweat as I performed the task. To my pleasant surprise, the perspiration helped because it made the tape expand. Even though the perspiration-caused expansion wasn't much, combined with my other labors, it loosened the tape enough that, within a few minutes, I worked my way free.

"Thank you, Lord." I massaged my raw and bloodied wrists as tears ran down my cheeks. Now I had a fighting chance.

A sharp turn jostled me and rammed my head against the trunk's ceiling. The pain reminded me of my tenuous situation and the next question to be answered. How much time did I have to come up with a plan?

I closed my eyes and let the vibrations of the vehicle flow through me as I ran through potential scenarios. Freddie was bigger than me. Given how hard she worked at Marinara's, I had no doubt she was stronger, too. I was quicker than she was, though.

Surprise and speed. That's what I had in my favor. I was also free. And angry.

It was payback time.

Controlled, deep breathing centered me as I visualized my escape plan. Freddie intended to kill me and dump my body. No doubt about that. But, as frightening as that thought was, it let me narrow the potential scenarios down to one.

Bargaining and pleading for my life would be fruitless. Instead, I needed to take the offensive and use the element of surprise to my advantage.

The car turned onto a tooth-rattling road that knocked me around so much I could practically feel bruises forming on my limbs. The constant dips and lurches indicated we were probably on a gravel service road. Byways like this wound through the abundant forests and public lands of southern Indiana. That meant isolation, so shouting wouldn't help.

That was fine. I'd gotten myself into this situation. I'd get myself out of it.

After untold minutes, the car came to a stop. I'd had time to catch my breath and come up with a plan. It was time to execute it. For Vicky. For Ursi. For me.

After a few silent moments that left my nerves in shambles, the driver's door opened. It closed with a *thump* that rocked me side to side. The motion actually helped me scoot into position, though. Thank goodness for lucky breaks.

I pulled my knees to my chest and placed my hands against the floor. And waited.

"Yoo-hoo, Allie. Wakey, wakey." She knocked on the trunk and laughed.

She didn't see me as a threat. That was another mistake. She was wrong.

There was a rattle of keys. I tensed. Literally ready to spring into action.

The trunk lid lifted. Freddie stared at me with her gun pointing at my chest.

I screamed at the top of my lungs as my legs shot out, crushing her in the abdomen. She stumbled backward and fell, shouting a string of obscenities at me, as I scrambled out of the trunk.

Clean, invigorating air filled my lungs as I made contact with the ground. I chanced a quick look around. Mature trees surrounded us on three sides. At first, the fourth side appeared to be clear. Then my gaze fell upon a rusted sign tacked to a tree.

private property. quarry is not open to the public.

trespassers will be prosecuted.

Abandoned limestone quarries were scattered throughout southern Indiana. A dozen were within an hour's drive of Rushing Creek. They were basically humongous holes in the ground partly filled with water; young people loved to visit them during the summer months to go swimming. The problem was, between their steep drop-offs and sharp rocks and other debris beneath the water's surface, the quarries were as dangerous as a rattlesnake. Every year someone got hurt or even killed due to screwing around near an abandoned quarry.

Freddie had parked alongside one of those abandoned quarries.

The implication of where we were sent a shiver down my spine. And redoubled my resolve to escape.

"There's no getting away, Allie." Freddie got to one knee and fired a shot.

I dove behind the car for cover as the bullet embedded itself in a nearby tree. Thanking my lucky stars for Freddie's lousy aim, I grabbed a handful of rocks and threw them at her in rapid succession.

Since she lacked cover, three hit the target, including one that glanced off her arm, causing the gun to drop to the ground. She reached for it, but I hit her with a flying tackle that would have made my football-loving brother Luke proud. As we tumbled along the gravel and leaf-covered ground, the firearm skittered away.

"I told you before. You're not getting away with this." I got my arm around Freddie's neck to subdue her with a choke hold.

My grip didn't last, though. She drove her fingernails into my raw wrists, shooting tear-inducing pain up both arms that left me defenseless for a few precious seconds. Just enough for Freddie, gasping for air, to crawl away from me.

Fatigue was setting in. My knees nearly gave out as I got to my feet. My work wasn't done, though. I made another lunge for Freddie.

With only a few stars and a quarter moon piercing the cloud cover, we struggled in virtual darkness. Each of us fought to gain an upper hand, while also trying to find the gun. Freddie tried to get her hands around my neck, but I blocked her with a mud-caked arm and landed a blow to her ear.

At that moment, I caught a gleam of the gun's barrel. It was inches from the cliff's edge. We went for it at the same time. I slipped and fell to my hands and knees.

Freddie let out a victory whoop as she launched herself at the deadly weapon. Her momentum was too much. As she slowed to scoop up the gun, her foot slipped on some loose rocks. Her forward motion carried her to the edge.

"Freddie!" I lunged for her but came up with nothing but air.

She tried to find a handhold, but there was nothing to grab. Time slowed as she reached out to me. Then she fell, crashing into the water fifty feet below me.

I shouted her name. Once, twice, but there was no answer. Just like that, I was alone. The only thing to break the silence was a frog croaking in the distance. Suddenly shivering, I wrapped my arms around myself and staggered to the car.

Freddie's purse lay on the passenger seat. My phone was still in it.

"Please, God, let there be service out here." Wherever here was. My fingers were shaking so badly, it took three attempts to dial Matt.

"Allie, what's going on? Where are you?" His tone carried a sense of urgency I'd rarely heard before. He must have already found out my plan didn't turn out like we hoped it would.

"It was Freddie. The murder, the drugs, it was all her." I gave him the highlights. When I finished, I squeezed my eyes shut to hold back a flood of tears. "God, I'm tired. I want to go home and hug my cat."

"I understand, but I need you to sit tight. Keep this line open. We'll use it to come to you." A keyboard rattled as if Matt was typing something. Hopefully, it was a way to get a fix on my location. "Stay inside the car and lock the doors if that makes you feel safer, but don't go anywhere."

"Copy that, Chief."

Staying in the car owned by my attempted murderer made my skin crawl, so I perched myself on the hood. I leaned against the windshield and stared at the clearing sky. The bright stars among the infinite blackness comforted me.

Once again, I was battered and bruised. Once again, I'd confronted a murderer. Once again, I'd emerged victorious.

A hoot owl's call was a reminder it wasn't about me, though. It was about Vicky. And having justice served in her name.

I pointed at the brightest star in the sky. "I tried, Vicky. I hope I did okay."

Chapter Twenty-Five

Normally, my Saturday mornings consisted of household chores and going for a walk with Ursi. This Saturday morning was the furthest thing from normal.

I was awakened by the delightful aroma of dark-roast coffee and the mouthwatering sizzle of bacon in the frying pan. Since Brent wasn't in town, curiosity as to the chef's identity, and my growling stomach, urged me to get out of bed.

The second I attempted to lift the covers, the muscles and joints throughout my body screamed in protest. At the same time, the events of last night cascaded over me, like floodwater from a burst levee.

Oh yeah. I'd solved Vicky's murder.

And had watched in complete helplessness as the murderer fell to her death.

When Matt found me, I'd been curled up in the fetal position and sobbing so long, my eyes burned almost as much as my wrists ached. Without a word, he'd picked me up and carried me to his car. Once I was in the back seat, wrapped up in a police-issued blanket, he turned on the car's heater.

I clutched onto his hand, desperate for physical connection with an ally.

"I'm sorry. I didn't mean for her to fall." I choked back another sob. "It was her or me."

"I know." He gave my hand a reassuring squeeze. "I'm sorry, too."

The next thing I could recall was him escorting me into my apartment and into Mom's waiting arms. The rest of my family enveloped me in a group hug. After that, my memory went blank.

With a grunt, I got myself into a seated position. My back joined the chorus of complaints coming from my arms and legs.

"Sloane? Is that you?" My little gray cells were firing like a nineteenth-century pistol left out in the rain for a month, but I was pretty sure my bestie had insisted on staying with me last night.

"Last I checked it was."

A moment later, the bedroom door swung open and she entered the room, cradling my Wonder Woman coffee mug. Ursi trotted in alongside her.

"Breakfast is almost ready." She put the mug on the nightstand and stared at me for the longest time. Then she hugged me.

"OMG, you are the bravest, most amazing, fearless woman on Earth. When you told us what happened, I couldn't believe it. Can I have your autograph?"

I laughed, but the laughter turned into a cough, thanks to my head-to-toe bruising. "You're killing me, Smalls." I grimaced. "Sorry, too soon for a joke like that. Instead, you can feed me."

"Aye, aye, K.C." Sloane helped me up and escorted me to the kitchen.

The spread she'd prepared took my breath away. In addition to the coffee and bacon, there were English muffins with blueberry jam, scrambled eggs, and strawberries coated with a light dusting of powdered sugar.

"Wow." I took a drink of my coffee, partly to hide the tears leaking from the corners of my eyes, as I took a seat. "I don't deserve having you as my bestie."

"That's true." Sloane munched on a slice of bacon. "Man, this is good stuff. I need to raid your fridge more often."

"You can thank Brent for that. Brings it when he visits." I bit into a strip and let out a sigh as the savory morsel melted in my mouth. Sloane was right. It was amazing.

Growing up, I hadn't been much of a bacon eater, but as I got older, I became a fan. The delicacy became a permanent fixture in my kitchen when Brent and I got serious. The man was an absolute bacon fanatic. And I couldn't deny the endless supply of it was one of the unintended benefits of dating him.

"I'll give him a high five next time I see him." Sloane took my plate and filled it until the white surface was invisible. "Eat up. Your mom wouldn't go home last night until I promised I'd make you eat a full breakfast. I'm supposed to make sure your wrists are okay."

I stopped spreading jam on my muffin and studied my arms. A smattering of mottled brown bruises were ugly reminders of my wrestling match with Freddie.

While the bruises didn't look good, I'd suffered worse. Besides, I could wear pants and long-sleeve shirts until the discoloration faded away.

It was the angry, red, swollen areas where the tape had been that gave me pause. The abrasions went all the way around both wrists and called to mind an awful second-degree sunburn I'd gotten one summer while in college. My injuries didn't look like they'd end up blistering like that sunburn did, but I envisioned using gallons of lotion over the next couple of weeks.

In a show of self-assurance, I held out my arms for Sloane to see. "This stuff? It's no big deal. I've had worse."

Sloane put down her fork and gave me a long look. "Sure, but it's different this time. You had to watch someone lose their life. A bad someone, but still."

And there it was. My family knew my physical injuries would heal. They were more concerned with my emotional ones.

God love 'em.

"I'll probably end up taking an express elevator straight to the lowest of Dante's seven levels of Hell for saying this, but Freddie got what she deserved. She was a drug dealer and a murderer. And a kidnapper and attempted murderer. This town will be better off with her gone."

Sloane's mouth drooped downward. It was a rare display of unhappiness from my eternally optimistic friend. "You know how harsh that sounds, right? You were closer to Mrs. Napier than I was, but I don't think she'd approve of you saying that. Do you?"

My bestie's gentle admonishment was more effective at making me stop and think than if she'd slapped me across the face. Sloane loved friendly trash talk and wasn't above a practical joke. What she didn't like to do was what she'd just done with me. She'd put me in my place. Sloane lived for positivity. It hurt her heart to tell someone they were wrong.

If Sloane thought I was in the wrong, then I was.

"You're saying I should forgive her?"

"Well, to be honest, I can't help wondering if this was really about justice or if it turned into something else."

"Like what?" I took another drink of my coffee.

"Vengeance." She chewed on a forkful of eggs. "I'm not wrong, am I?"

In all my life, I'd never lied to Sloane. I wasn't going to start now.

"No, you're not wrong." At the admission, a weight that had been hanging around my neck slipped away.

"At first, all I wanted was to find Vicky's killer. Then, Freddie told me what she'd done and why she did it. When you combined that with what she did to me, something inside changed. I wanted more than justice. I wanted payback. Does that make sense?"

Sloane let out one of her laughs that was full of mirth. "Honey, I grew up in a house with an alcoholic father and an ice queen mother. I know all about letting negative emotions eat you up. It's like having a cancer grow inside you. The only way to get rid of it is to practice forgiveness. You have to let those negative emotions, that darkness go. If you don't, it will eat you from the inside out until there's nothing left."

Let the darkness go. I'd collected a lot of it over the past couple of years. It hadn't been intentional. It seemed that choosing to delve into the netherworlds of societal behavior meant there was no way to avoid it.

Could the act of forgiveness really be that liberating for my heart and soul?

"You need to forgive the other murderers, too. Believe me, it wasn't easy learning to forgive my dad's killer, but doing it helped me move on. Don't get me wrong. I'm not saying you should forget about what happened. You do need to forgive, though."

"I'll try."

"Good." Sloane gave me a fist bump. "With that settled, finish your breakfast. Matt will be here soon. He needs to go over last night with you. I don't want my Kickboxing Crusader talking to the police chief on an empty stomach."

As I was finishing my last bite of English muffin, there was a knock on the door.

"Sit. I'll get it." Sloane was out of her seat and halfway across the room before I could even move. She opened the door and was greeted with squeals of delight from the twins.

"Auntie Sloane." Tristan wrapped his little arms around her.

"Grandma didn't say you were going to be here." Not to be outdone, Theresa hugged my bestie, turning her into a Sloane sandwich.

"You guys know me. I'm always full of surprises." With a twin glued to each of her hips, she reached her arms out toward Mom. "All's well, Mrs. Cobb."

"With you in charge, I have no doubt." She gave Sloane a hug. "Come on, kiddos. Let's go say hi to Aunt Allie."

The twins released their lock on Sloane and raced to me, shouting greetings along the way.

Ursi, who'd been sitting quietly at my feet, made a dash for the bedroom. She tolerated my niece and nephew, but they tended to be louder than she preferred, so she often hid under my bed when they were around.

"Come here, you monsters." I got up, opened my arms wide, and let them take me to the floor in a laughter-filled tackle. My joints shouted their objections to the full-contact greeting, but it was what the three of us did when the twins came to visit.

I hugged them a little tighter and held onto them a little longer than usual as we rolled on the floor, but they didn't mind. It wasn't until Tristan asked why I was crying that I let them go.

"I'm happy to see you guys, and I love you so much." I squeezed them both with all my might as I struggled to my feet. "Who wants bacon?"

In the blink of an eye, they abandoned me and were seated at the table, a strip of bacon in each of their hands.

"I think you're going to need some more." Mom winked at me as she took the final slice.

"On it." Sloane skipped to the stove and, in no time, the comforting sound of sizzling bacon filled the kitchen.

I wiped away another tear with the palm of my hand as the twins started telling me about their upcoming soccer game.

Mom came alongside me. "Are you all right?" She kept her voice low, no doubt to avoid getting the twins' attention.

"Yeah." I nodded and put my arms around her. I was among family, some of the most important people in my life.

My visitors reminded me there were forces way more powerful than greed and lust for power. There was kindness, trust, and forgiveness, and one more thing above them all.

Love.

In the way a student loved her favorite teacher, I had loved Vicky. Her absence had created a hole in my heart that wouldn't be filled in a long time. If ever.

Because of that, I vowed to keep Sloane's wise words close to my heart, right next to my memories of Vicky. I wouldn't let that hole be filled with the darkness of vengeance and anger. I'd let it be filled with laughter, light, and hope.

I couldn't bring my hero back, but I could use her life, one spent serving others, as a reminder of the right way to live.

"I'm definitely all right. More than all right." It was true. I was going to be okay

A little while later, there was a knock on the door.

"I'll get it," the twins shouted and scrambled toward the door, each more determined than the other to serve as greeter.

Their efforts were rewarded when the person on the other side of the door turned out to be their father.

"Hey, kids." Matt scooped up one in each arm and gave them loud, wet kisses on their cheeks. "You look great in your soccer uniforms. What time's your game today?"

He grinned when they told him four. "Excellent. Aunt Allie's going to help me with some police work for a few hours and then we'll see you at the game, okay?"

Once their feet were back on the hardwood floor, the kids exchanged high fives with their father and returned to the couch, where Sloane began reading *The Lion, the Witch, and the Wardrobe* to them.

I grabbed my jacket and took a deep breath. "Let's do this, Chief."

Chapter Twenty-Six

"My memory from last night is fuzzy. What's this trip for, exactly?" As I climbed into the passenger seat of Matt's police cruiser, I was ready to help with what was left of the investigation in any way I could. If that meant spending the next few hours in an interview room or revisiting last night's crime scenes, so be it.

"First, a quick update." He started the engine and eased the car into traffic. "Given the case's potential magnitude with the drugs involved, and with Tommy down for the count, I called the county sheriff for help. We simply couldn't handle three crime scenes at once."

We turned north onto the Boulevard. As we passed the Brown County Diner, he slipped into an open parking spot.

"Been up all night. I could use some java. Be right back."

While I didn't like being left hanging, the dark circles under Matt's eyes and facial stubble made it clear he'd been hard at work. It was after eleven. Some serious developments must have occurred while I slept.

A few minutes later, he returned with two cups of coffee and gave one to me. Once we were moving again, he resumed his report.

"The sheriff's office took the lead at the quarry scene, so I got Jeanette out of bed and sent her to the library. Then I went to Freddie's house with Gabe Sandoval." He took a sip of his coffee and turned into the library parking lot.

"I take it you found weed stashed somewhere?" I cringed as I recalled my exchange with Freddie about the marijuana.

"That, and a lot more. She was also dealing opioids and other narcotics. There was a sizeable chunk of cash and even a cache of weapons." He shook his head as he put the cruiser in park. "I've got the state police going over every inch of her house right now, including two laptops."

"Whoa." My blood went cold when I considered how much more danger I'd been in than I'd realized. "Does that mean there was a lot?"

"Enough to put a major dent in the distribution of illegal drugs in this part of the state. It's a huge victory. We're planning on holding a press conference once we have all of the contraband catalogued."

I shook my head as I got out of the cruiser. "All because of a crazy, mysterious mix-up."

"Yeah. Tell me again what happened last night." He took his notebook out of his pocket as we approached the library's entrance.

When we entered the building, it looked like business as usual. An employee was checking patrons out, a volunteer was leading a small group of children in a read-along, and adults were wandering around, their arms filled with their selections.

One glance at Vicky's office door confirmed things were far from business as usual.

Once again, a strip of bright yellow police tape was strung from one side of the frame to the other. The door was open a crack. Matt pushed it all the way open with his foot.

Jeanette was on her hands and knees, collecting scraps of duct tape from around the chair Freddie had strapped me into. Yellow evidence markers were scattered throughout the room. A small stack of paper evidence bags sat on a corner of the desk.

"Almost finished, Chief." She nodded to Matt then to me. "Allie, when I first met you, I never thought you'd be so good at getting into trouble."

"She wasn't this way when we were growing up." Matt patted me on the shoulder. "I think her time in the big city corrupted her. So, what have we got?"

My friend gave her boss a summary of her findings. So far, there wasn't a lot of physical evidence to connect Freddie to this crime scene, but some footprints and scuff marks would likely yield some results.

When she was finished, Matt asked me to take them through everything that happened in the library from the time Freddie first arrived. It wasn't a pleasant exercise, but when I finished, I felt like another weight had been taken off my shoulders.

"Good job." Matt patted me on the shoulder again, then turned his attention to Jeanette. "When you're done here, I want you to pay Marinara's a visit. Tommy's there now. When you get there, see what you can find to help us fill in the timeline."

With our business at the library complete, the next stop was the quarry. I was dreading going back there, so I decided to keep the anxiety at arm's length by talking.

"You mentioned Tommy. How is he?"

Matt cracked a half-smile. "Physically, he's fine. He has no recollection of last night's events. Fortunately, he still had the cup Freddie gave him, so we'll get it analyzed for traces of Rohypnol. Emotionally, not so much."

"I'm so sorry. I shouldn't have put him in that position."

"You didn't put him in that position. He put himself there by accepting that coffee. That was a dumb mistake."

"But it was just a cup of coffee. There's no way he could have known she'd put something in it."

"Exactly." He pointed his finger at me. "He didn't know where it came from or what was in it. As a cop, you simply can't be too careful. Don't worry, though. He'll get over it."

I considered the results of my suggestion to set the trap. A long-term member of the community was dead. A cop was in trouble with his boss. One of the most popular restaurants in the area was facing an uncertain future.

What had I done?

"I'm sorry, Matt. I never meant for everything to go so horribly wrong. I should have done what you told me from the start and kept my nose out of it."

His only reaction was a slight nod. With his eyes hidden behind his dark sunglasses, he was impossible to read. After a few moments, he cleared his throat. "Maybe so. On the other hand, Freddie did a masterful job of framing Porter. An argument can be made that, if not for your doggedness, an innocent man would have gone to prison."

"Do you really believe that?" It was a stunning admission.

And one that left my emotions all over the place. On one hand, guilt from the train wreck I'd caused wanted to consume me. On the other, relief that I'd caught the killer, if not brought her to justice, spread through me. The fact that I'd helped keep an innocent man out of jail lifted my spirits.

"I do. While I'd prefer you stick to your day job, I can't deny I read this one wrong. You kept after it, and, because of that, you figured out who killed Vicky Napier and brought a drug ring to an end at the same time. That's not a bad result."

I didn't know what to say to that, so I looked out the window. The backdrop of Brown County was becoming greener every day. Nature's annual rebirth served as a timely reminder of Sloane's lesson.

I'd stared into the void and almost allowed it to consume me. Instead, my best friend had thrown me a lifeline and pulled me from the brink. Like the trees and plants around me, I had a chance to begin again.

I'd been given an opportunity to live my life with my focus on things like forgiveness and grace instead of vengeance and payback. I promised myself I'd take full advantage of this new opening. To do anything less would be an insult to Vicky, Sloane, and everyone I cared about.

And who cared about me.

A few minutes later, we turned from the highway onto a service road so choked with weeds it was barely visible. A chill went down my spine. Only twelve hours earlier, I'd been brought down this exact road, which was little more than a walking path, in the trunk of a car.

We came to a stop a behind a sheriff's department SUV. A deputy, in a familiar brown uniform, was busy collecting evidence as we approached.

While he conferred with Matt, I wandered toward the cliff. Little yellow flags were stuck in the ground, like flowers, to mark where pieces of evidence had been found. Freddie and I had been engaged in quite the row.

At the edge of the cliff, I let out a long breath and looked down. The water was dark, foreboding, and unforgiving. The county coroner's van was parked on the other side of the quarry. Two deputies, one in diver's gear, were at the water's edge.

Matt came up next to me. He put a piece of nicotine gum in his mouth and chewed while we stared downward.

"What are they doing?" I pointed at the diver.

"They recovered the body a little bit ago. Next, they'll search for the gun. If they can find it, we'll be able to match the bullets to it."

I nodded. While Freddie had worn gloves when we were in the library, she'd removed them by the time she opened the trunk.

"Her hands probably were getting sweaty, so she took the gloves off. Didn't count on me fighting back."

"I was thinking the same thing. We found the gloves on the floorboard in the back seat." He adjusted his Rushing Creek Police Department baseball cap. "You ready to get to it?"

"Yep." Matt wanted me to reconstruct last night's events here, just like I had at the library. Once again, I thought of Sloane and chose to use the exercise as a cathartic event, to get past what had happened instead of allowing it to fuel more thoughts of vengeance.

After an hour of me going through what happened, answering questions, and identifying pieces of evidence to the best of my ability, Matt declared our work finished. I shook hands with the deputy and made my way to the car.

"If I never see that place again, it'll be too soon." I buckled my seat belt and took my cell phone out of my pocket. It was easier to look at the screen than the disturbing surroundings.

"You did great, Allie. Everything you told me today will help us tie up any loose ends. You did great last night, too. You're a real hero."

"I don't know about that. I was trying to do the right thing. Nothing more."

"That's what heroes do." He started the car and turned it around. As we bounced down the road, he checked his watch. "Plenty of time to get to the soccer game."

"Good. I'm ready for some harmless fun. It'll be fun to cheer for the kids."

"They idolize you. I hope you know that. The last twenty-four hours are why I hope that never changes. I hope they grow up to be just like you, Allie."

A lump formed in my throat. I'd known Matt for years. He wasn't one to express his feelings very often. The fact he'd chosen to share this one with me made me feel ten feet tall. Which gave me an idea.

"It would be great if they grow up to be like me. Promise me you'll do what you can to make sure they end up taller, though. Having to use a step stool to reach the cabinets in my kitchen is a real hassle."

He laughed a long, hearty laugh that just kept going. It was so full of mirth that after a few seconds, I joined him. When the laughter ended, he gave me a soft punch on my shoulder.

"Copy that, Allie. Let's go watch some heroes in the making."

Chapter Twenty-Seven

I scratched my head and stared at the contract in front of me. My palms were sweaty. My heart was galloping away as if it was a horse racing to the finish line at the Kentucky Derby. The pen to the right of the page mocked me.

"For God's sake, Allie. We've been through this a dozen times." Rachel put the pen in my hand. "It'll be okay. I know what I'm doing."

"It's not that. I've looked at the financials and everything checks out. I just never planned on becoming a partner in the restaurant business."

My sister snorted. "A partner? An investor. Nothing more. Nothing less. A silent one, at that."

It had been a month since my showdown with Freddie. Since then, there had been a lot of changes in Rushing Creek. The library board had appointed a new member to fill Freddie's vacancy. I was the new member. It had also completed its search for a new library director.

Porter Rasmussen had chosen to make the best of a trying few weeks. Since his notoriety as a florist had grown, he'd started selling his flowers out of a kiosk on the Boulevard. He also had an eye on an empty storefront across the street from Creekside Chocolates, in case things went well.

And Rachel had rescued Marinara's, first by stepping in as a temporary manager, then by offering to buy the business.

All that remained was for me to sign the contract. It would make me a partner, along with Luke and Mom, in Rachel's expanding business portfolio. She needed additional capital to close on the Marinara purchase. The cash we were kicking in gave her what she needed. In return for our investment, we were official minority partners in Cobb Dining Services, Inc.

"Partner." I flipped to the last page and signed my name with a flourish. "Where's the champagne?"

"That'll have to wait, Boss. I need to talk to you about the mystery manuscript you assigned me to edit." Calypso took the contract from me and went to the copier in the corner of the room, her Doc Martens clunking against the hardwood floor with each step.

"Then we need to discuss my proposed website upgrades. And you need to be at the library at two for your board meeting. Since you're announcing the new director today, you should wear something professional that fits with the occasion."

With wide eyes, Rachel's gaze went from me to Calypso and back to me. "I've overheard her telling some of the staff at the pub that she tells you what to do. I like it."

"What can I say? She keeps me on task." I leaned back so I could make eye contact with my intern. "Even though you scare me a little, right, Calypso?"

With a smile, the young woman clunked back across the room. She handed one copy of the contract to Rachel and the other to me.

"I don't scare you, Boss. I keep you on your toes."

We shared a laugh while Rachel gathered her things. On her way out the door, she thanked me for having confidence in her and gave me a hug. As she descended the stairs, she brushed something from her eye.

While Rachel would never admit it to me, something told me it was a tear of joy.

For the next hour, Calypso and I discussed the edits she'd made to the manuscript. It was a good conversation, as I took on the role of teacher and my intern the willing and eager student. While she had plenty of self-confidence and had an excellent base in grammar, she also absorbed my feedback like a sponge.

Time spent like this was an investment in the future of the agency. It was also a joy to talk about things like the most effective use of Track Changes with someone who shared the interest. Lord knew Sloane had always been, and would always be, my BFF, but the details of my job bored her.

Calypso had a passion for good storytelling that couldn't be faked. She was as raw as d'Artagnan had been when he met the Three Musketeers, but, with my help, she had a future in publishing if she wanted it.

She was tech-savvy, too, and gave me confidence that, in a few months, I'd be able to turn things like the agency's social media accounts and website over to her. It meant we could take on more clients. Which meant bringing more books to the world.

The future looked bright for the Cobb Literary Agency.

But first, I had a task to complete as the newest member of the Rushing Creek Public Library Board of Directors. It was one I couldn't wait to fulfill.

A little bit later, I emerged from my bedroom in a new outfit I'd bought specifically for the meeting. And the celebration dinner to follow.

"What do you think?" I executed a pirouette, which wasn't easy in the three-inch heels I was wearing.

Calypso tilted her head to the side and furrowed her eyebrows. It was a sign I'd learned that meant she wasn't sure what to think. Or say.

"I love the suede boots, but I thought you didn't like heels. You're not making compromises just to make a man happy, are you?"

"No. Well, maybe." The boots were the final piece to an ensemble that was much flashier than I was known for. I'd matched a formfitting black blouse with a pair of oh-so-comfortable black leggings. To complete the ensemble, I was wearing a thigh-length blazer in the same shade of blue as the boots. As a bonus, I was wearing a funky, woven belt that featured the seven colors of the rainbow.

"I'll give the heels a pass this time, Boss, given the circumstances." She crossed her arms and smiled. "You look pretty amazing. Good job."

"Thanks. Your fashion style is rubbing off on me."

It was true. I would never be seen in public wearing a Ramones T-shirt with rips at the shoulders, like Calypso was sporting today. And black jeans with tears at the knees wasn't my style. I liked her black-and-white checked slip-on sneakers, though.

"Whatever." She rolled her eyes and rattled her keys. "Let's go. I'll drive."

A little while later, I took my seat at the table with my four fellow library board members. As the meeting was gaveled to order, my eyes got watery. It was going to be an emotional event.

There were four items on the agenda. The first was a vote to formally appoint me to the board. It passed unanimously. I dug a tissue out of my purse and wiped away a tear. I sensed Vicky was smiling down on me. I felt it.

The second was to name new board officers. In short order, a new president, vice president, and secretary were approved. As a board newbie, I breathed a sigh of relief nobody wanted me to take on an officer position. Someday, maybe, but not today.

Today wasn't about me. It was about honoring the library's past and embracing its future.

When it came time for agenda item three, I cleared my throat. "In honor of the longest-serving librarian in Rushing Creek's history, I move that the name of this building be changed from the Rushing Creek Public Library to the Victoria Napier Memorial Library of Rushing Creek."

Before I had time to take a breath, the motion was seconded and approved. The members of the public in attendance applauded. I had to wipe away more tears.

The last agenda item was the most newsworthy. It was to name the new library director. I looked up from my agenda to Brent, who was sitting among friends and family in the crowd. He was alternating between wringing his hands and running his fingers through his hair.

I winked at him. He returned the wink with a nervous smile.

The new board president said a few words about the search for a director. Five candidates had been interviewed. One of them had checked all of the board's boxes—a background in library science, supervisory experience, and a dedication to the Rushing Creek community.

"It's my pleasure to make a motion to name, as the new director of the Victoria Napier Memorial Library of Rushing Creek, Mr. Brent Richardson."

Since it was common knowledge Brent and I were an item, I had recused myself from the search for a new director. It was an excruciating few seconds while we waited for the motion to be seconded, even though the ceremony was a formality. Brent had been offered the job three days ago and accepted immediately.

The moment the motion passed, I got to my feet and led those in attendance in a standing ovation.

Brent shook hands with Sloane and Calypso then came forward to shake hands with each board member. He saved me for last.

Had decorum prevailed, I would have shaken his hand like the others and told him congratulations. Instead, I hugged him and planted a kiss on his lips.

When the meeting ended, Brent was surrounded by well-wishers offering pats on the back and words of welcome. After that, he sat for an interview with Kim Frye, the reporter from the *Brown County Beacon*. It was his moment in the sun, and I was thrilled to sit back and let him revel in it.

When things wound down, Brent and I made our way to the Rushing Creek Public House for a celebration. I held it together until we walked into the banquet room. The moment we stepped across the threshold, the gathering gave Brent his second standing ovation of the afternoon.

And the dam broke.

I leaned against my boyfriend and struggled to wipe away the tears as we took our seats. The last time I'd cried this hard had been the night I fought with Freddie. Those were tears of despair. Tonight, they were tears of pure elation.

I looked around the table. My entire family was with me, from Mom the matriarch with her new friend Terrance, to my siblings Luke and Rachel, to the twins, who embodied the promise of the next generation. My friends Sloane, Diane, Lori, and Jeanette were there, too. Matt had gotten away from work to join us, taking a seat between Tristan and Theresa.

Once everyone was seated, Calypso bumped my arm and handed me a notecard. Since Brent was my boyfriend, the official words of welcome fell to me.

"Brent, you and I have been through some interesting adventures together. Today, it's my distinct pleasure to welcome you to Rushing Creek, where we can now share our adventures with everyone in this room. Cheers!"

As everyone lifted their glasses and drank, the tears began anew. Here, in this room, Rushing Creek's past and future had come together in celebration of good times.

I had more than my share of joy. My agency was growing. My family was together. My boyfriend was moving to town. With a job that was perfect for him.

I'd been through the darkness caused by Vicky's murder but come out the other side. Bruised, yes. But not broken. I'd made it into the light, thanks to the guidance and warmth of family and friends. It was a wonderful place to be. A place Dad and Vicky would approve of.

I was ready to enjoy it.

Printed in the United States
by Baker & Taylor Publisher Services